“THIS IS
IN A CA

For a while he just looked at Marcy. The waves in his short, dark hair caught the golden light from the table lamp; his hazel eyes glowed gold and silver. His lips moved slightly to form a tempting smile.

Marcy glanced at her cordial glass as she turned it in her fingers. “You seem to be in a perfect mood.”

“This seems to be a perfect time, a perfect place,” he told her, his eyes languidly roaming over her face and body.

She felt the insistent tugging at her heartstrings that she always did whenever Dan was attentive, seductively pleasant. A part of her seemed to be awakening, a part that had lain dormant for too long.

Why couldn't circumstances be different?

ABOUT THE AUTHOR

Kelly Walsh has lived in Washington, New York, Chicago, Virginia and Texas, and now resides in beautiful Clearwater, Florida, where *Cherished Harbor* is set. This promising new Superromance author has had a rich and varied employment history, too, having worked as a cryptographer, a television producer-director and a teacher. Indeed, Kelly has reams of material to draw on and will no doubt be writing fascinating, action-packed stories for years to come!

Kelly Walsh

CHERISHED HARBOR

Harlequin Books

TORONTO • NEW YORK • LONDON
AMSTERDAM • PARIS • SYDNEY • HAMBURG
STOCKHOLM • ATHENS • TOKYO • MILAN

Published February 1987

First printing December 1986

ISBN 0-373-70248-5

Printed in Canada

For Mary V.,
a fan and friend.

CHAPTER ONE

THERE HAD BEEN A TIME when Marcy loved to shop. A smile of remembrance eased her taut facial muscles as her eyes swept across the items under the glass display case. She recalled the exquisitely tooled leather handbags at Hermès in Paris and the silk print scarves at Roberta's in Naples. Her lips tightened again, and she pointed to an object in the display case. Without looking up at the clerk, she said, "That one."

He unlocked the glass case and took out the Beretta nine-millimeter parabellum she'd pointed to. He laid it on top of the smudged glass and watched her tense features as her nervous fingers touched the cool steel of the handgun.

She was repulsed by it, hated the sight of it; yet, sne was also a frightened woman. She stared down at the gun and was oblivious to the clerk's impatient tapping of his finger on the glass case. But the sound itself seeped into her brain and became louder until it turned into the judge's gavel in the L.A. courtroom two years ago. Snatches of recollections swam before her mind's eye, glimpses of faces: her dead husband's, Ed Moray's and his angry son's. She'd never forget the hatred in *his* eyes.

Dirk Moray. He couldn't have been more than seventeen years old when he'd sat in that courtroom listening to her testimony from the witness stand, Marcy mused. A shiver of fear rippled down her spine as she again saw the icy darkness of the boy's eyes boring venomously into hers, as she recalled the prosecuting attorney's questions to his key witness.

"MRS. KEPPLER, do you know the defendant, Edward Moray?"

"Yes," she answered quietly as she looked over at the dark-haired man sitting at the table on the left-hand side of the courtroom with his eyes lowered. Her fingers were cold, and she hadn't yet gotten used to the dull ache in her head that had recently become her constant companion.

"How well do you know him?"

"He is... he was my husband's partner. We knew him socially."

"How long have you known him?"

Marcy tried to clear her thoughts. There had been so many questions for weeks now. All she wanted to do was find some quiet place to rest. Everything was so repetitive: the questions the night of Robert's death, the numerous depositions in the days that followed, the pretrial preparations. But she knew she had to answer whatever questions were asked of her, no matter how they tore her apart. Her lashes blinked nervously over her blue-gray eyes as she said, "Excuse me?"

He repeated his question. "I asked how long you've known the defendant?"

"For approximately two years now."

"Was he a frequent guest in your home?"

She nodded. "Yes, particularly since his wife died last year. Ed...Mr. Moray was having a difficult time. My husband and I tried to be supportive."

"And was he at your home the night your husband was killed?"

Marcy cast a quick glance at Ed Moray. His head was still lowered. Then she braved a furtive look at his son Dirk. On his young face was a mask of hatred. She felt a stab of anxiety rush through her as she replied, "Yes."

"Tell the jury, Mrs. Keppler, what happened that night."

Marcy squeezed her fingers until they ached and were white from the pressure. After taking a deep breath, she began softly. "I was upstairs in my bedroom. It was late. Robert, my husband, was still downstairs in the library, going over some papers he'd brought home from the office. I had fallen asleep, but then I heard something that sounded like a light bulb had burst." Her low chuckle was painful as her fingers moved over her left temple. "I remember thinking how odd that was because I had never even heard a bulb explode. But I was concerned. When I came out of my room and looked down over the railing, I saw Ed rushing through the entryway toward the front door. I assumed that he and Robert had been arguing again."

"*Again*, Mrs. Keppler?"

"It was only recently that they had been. Robert told me it was a business matter." She paused, swallowed with difficulty, and then continued, her eyes widening as she relived the scene. "I went downstairs into the library. I didn't see Robert. I called him and was just about to go out onto the terrace when I—I saw his leg sticking out from behind one of the sofas." Her hand covered her mouth as she felt her stomach jolt. Then, with moisture welling up on her eyelids, she forced out the words "The side of his head was . . . was all—"

THE GUN CLERK told her again, "I said there'll be a three-day waiting period before you can pick it up. County rules."

With her middle finger, Marcy wiped away the perspiration over her upper lip. "Yes," she said, "that will be fine."

"You know how to use this thing, lady?"

She looked up at him with eyes that seemed confused. "Use it? I don't intend to use it."

"Oh," he said. "Just to scare prowlers, huh?"

"Something like that."

"Well, if you don't know how to use it, I wouldn't keep it loaded, if I were you."

She began filling out the form he'd given her and told him, "I don't want any bullets for the gun."

In Washington later that day, a computer in the FBI Building spewed out the information that a Marcy Keaton in Clearwater, Florida, had purchased a handgun and was waiting the required period for the receipt of same. The printout was flagged "Cross-check file," and minutes later the information was transmitted to the office of the U.S. Marshal Service in Clearwater, Florida, marked, "Attention: Witness Protection Program."

Dan Elliott looked up at his boss, who was tapping his finger on the paper he'd just tossed on Dan's desk. "Read it and weep," the older man said. "It came down to us as 'priority,' and that means you drop everything else and get on it."

Dan's less than polite four-letter-word response did little more than bring a wry smile to his boss's face, and a straightforward comment. "With Addison transferred, witness protection is how you earn your bread now, Dan."

Dan tugged the tie under the collar of his blue oxford shirt again and loosened the top button. He read the transmission, took a swallow of cold black coffee and looked up. "What's her problem?"

The older man tapped the thick file he'd also put on the desk. "It's all in here. Two years ago she was Mrs. Robert Keppler. Keppler's partner, Ed Moray, was charged with his murder. At first Moray maintained that Keppler started an argument with him over Mrs. Keppler. Said Keppler pulled a gun. There was a struggle, and Keppler got it. Moray panicked and ran."

Dan leaned back in his chair. "It was Keppler's gun?"

"Yeah, and the defense just about had the jury convinced until the state brought the Feds in on it. Seems they had the firm Moray and Keppler owned under investigation for dealing with the syndicate... selling microchips or something."

"So it wasn't over Keppler's wife?"

Sitting on the edge of Dan's desk, his boss made an uncertain, wavy gesture with his hand. "That's kinda iffy. Depends on whom you believe. Moray changed his story. Said he found out that Keppler did have a sideline venture going with the syndicate. They argued and bang. Moray got sent up for manslaughter. It's all in the transcript here." Again he tapped the file.

Dan picked it up and held it as though he were weighing it. "Thanks," he said dryly. "How'd we get the wife under the Witness Protection Program?"

"Story gets better. Right after the murder trial, the Feds cracked the microchips case. Turns out it was Keppler who was dealing with the syndicate. A swarm of indictments followed. Mrs. Keppler... our Marcy Keaton... was able to identify several of the syndicate boys who'd been to their home. Hubby had told her they were business associates. She'd also found some of Keppler's papers, which she turned over to the Feds. Her testifying helped them put away some of the biggest West Coast baddies."

Dan asked, "You think she did it to save herself? To cover up her relationship with Moray, or her knowledge of Keppler's involvement with the syndicate?"

Getting up, his boss suggested, "Only she can tell you that." Then he left Dan alone with the file.

An hour later Dan was still reading. Leaning back in his swivel chair, he chewed on the soggy egg-salad sandwich he'd ordered from the cafeteria on the first floor before they'd closed for the day—he'd known supper would be late again tonight—and reached for the description sheet he'd scanned earlier.

Marcy Keaton. Thirty-one years old. Five feet seven. One hundred and fifteen pounds. Light brown hair. Blue-gray eyes. Born Patricia Dodd. Widow of Robert Keppler.

He tossed the sheet down on top of the papers strewn over his desk, and then he dialed his boss's extension. "Should we let her have the gun?"

Over the phone he heard, "No law says she can't have it, and she may need it. You find out why."

THE THREE-DAY waiting period had gone by slowly for Marcy. Again, her attention was drawn to the dark green Cutlass that was circling her block. She'd noticed it several times in the past two days. She pushed back the drapes at her front window so she could peer out. She wasn't sure, but she thought the dark-haired man at the wheel was the same man who had followed her the day before into the building where the Oceanview Villas, Inc., office was located. She also thought it was the same car that had followed her to the shop when she'd picked up the gun this morning.

"So I'm becoming paranoid," she whispered into the silky panel as she let it slowly close into place. *If it were only that simple,* she told herself as she returned to her desk to recheck the master schedule for Mark Godette of Oceanview Villas. She had to keep her mind on the public relations campaign she was organizing.

She sat down and reread the release dates on her proposed radio and TV spots announcing the company's plans to begin a multimillion-dollar land-development project on an island off the coast of Clearwater. After marking another firm check on her campaign schedule, she began tapping the desk with the eraser on the tip of her pencil.

Her eyes closed, and again the nightmare of two years ago forced itself into her thoughts. She could still see the cool look on the faces of the jury when the foreman had said "Guilty."

With her testimony it had been an open-and-shut case. The FBI had told her it would be, and they'd guaranteed her safety when the phone threats had started just before the trial. The threats had continued during the trial, even when she'd been under protective custody. But all that had taken place two years ago! Why was it all starting again now? she asked herself.

For a time it had ended. After the trial, Mrs. Robert Keppler had been given a new identity as Marcy

Keaton and had been relocated to Florida and placed under the Witness Protection Program operated by the U.S. Marshal Service. Slowly and painfully, she'd obtained some peace of mind, despite the radical change in life-style. After a year of Marshal Ron Addison's periodic checkups, she'd felt secure enough to tell him she wanted to withdraw from the program, that each of his visits only renewed the ugly past events in her mind.

The passage of time had almost made her forget. She'd begun a new life with a new name, a new background, and she'd made new friends—not many, though. She was leery of people, of the questions they would ask, the seemingly innocent queries about her past. She'd never quite gotten used to the necessary lies, the phony history behind the woman called Marcy Keaton.

Yes, she had coped well, but she had not forgotten. And now it was all starting again—the phone calls, the threats. *Why?* she asked herself again. It had been two weeks since the first call, and for two weeks she hadn't had a peaceful night's sleep. She would lie awake ruminating about the newspaper stories: the photographers, the faces in the courtroom—particularly that of Ed Moray's defense attorney as he had cross-examined her on the stand...

"MRS. KEPPLER, you've stated that the defendant was often a guest in your home."

"Yes," she said softly, trying not to be affected by the coldness in his eyes.

"Was your husband always present when Mr. Moray visited?"

"Of course." Her blood turned to ice. She knew what was coming. The attorneys for the prosecution had warned her that the defense would try to discredit her and her testimony. Ed Moray, under advice, was maintaining that his argument with Robert Keppler had been over Keppler's wife.

"Did you ever meet Mr. Moray outside of your home, for...cocktails, *without* your husband being present?"

Marcy's nervous eyes swept across the faces of the jurors. Her lips were dry and her throat was parched.

"Please answer the question, Mrs. Keppler."

Looking down, she quietly said, "Yes."

"I don't think the jury can hear you, Mrs. Keppler. Did you ever meet Mr. Moray...alone...for cocktails?"

She raised her eyes and her chin slightly. In a firmer voice she told him, "Yes. We were friends. Why would—"

"Just yes or no, Mrs. Keppler."

She paused and then answered, "Yes."

The defense attorney swaggered over to the jury box and rested his hands on it as he scanned the faces of the men and women sitting there. Without glancing back at the witness, he smiled and asked, "How often did you and Mr. Moray meet for some cozy little rendezvous?"

"Objection, your honor! The defense is implying that the witness—"

The judge interrupted with "Objection sustained." He warned the defense attorney, "Confine yourself to questions without the benefit of colorful innuendos."

Marcy sat immobile on the witness stand, appreciating the judge's intervention, but knowing full well that the damage had been done already.

Again the defense attorney directed his question to the jury. "Mrs. Keppler, how often did you and Mr. Moray have dinner together... just the two of you... *without* your husband being present?"

He turned to face her, and she looked into his watery and lifeless eyes. For a moment there was a silent exchange between them, and then she said, "Several times."

"Several?" He walked in front of the jurors, his right hand trailing casually along the top of the railing. "Three times? Five times?" He turned suddenly to face the witness. "A dozen!"

Her hands were like ice again, and yet her face was hot with the flush that had risen there. Prying her dry lips apart, she answered, "Perhaps five times."

"Did you ever meet him in his home?"

"No. Never."

"Mrs. Keppler... were you in love with Ed Moray?"

MARCY THREW down her pencil and rushed to the kitchen. She turned on the cold water faucet and splashed water on her aching forehead. For a moment she leaned forward, holding on to the sink. She sighed softly.

Quickly she returned to her desk and checked the top left drawer. The gun she'd placed there earlier shone up at her, the empty clip intact in the handle. She slammed the drawer shut and again went to the front window.

A feeling of panic grabbed her chest as she saw the dark green Cutlass parked across the street. Her panic turned to terror as she watched the man get out of the car and start toward her house.

Yes, there was no doubt in her mind now. It *was* the same man who had been following her. She'd seen him up close in the office building yesterday, had taken note of the dark brown hair—short but slightly waved—and the sullen, dark eyes that had insolently stared at her and pierced right through her just before the elevator doors had closed. It was him all right, and now he was heading up her walkway.

The pounding in her chest echoed at her temples. The sudden sound of the door buzzer made her jump. There was a short silence, and then the jarring buzz again.

Back she went, all the way to her desk. Without looking down—her eyes were riveted to the door—her right hand eased the top drawer open and took hold of the gun.

Silence again. *Damn!* she thought, knowing her car was parked in the driveway. Her eyes widened as she saw the man peering into the front window and then resume his relentless buzzing.

With the gun held in her trembling right hand behind her back, she slowly moved to the door. After fastening the safety chain, she opened the door a crack. Her knees weakened when her eyes were confronted with his hard, cold stare. His nose looked as though it could have been broken once; his ruddy complexion already showed the telltale signs of a beard. He was younger than she had suspected at first.

Her mouth was dry, but she tried to sound casual. "Yes?"

CHAPTER TWO

"MARCY KEATON?" he asked, his voice low and curt.

Her casualness deserted her. "Why are you asking?"

He became more insistent. "You *are* Marcy Keaton?"

"Yes." The mailbox would have told him that much. Suddenly she regretted answering the door. "I'm very busy right now, though." She started to shut the door, but he made a hard fist and quickly jammed it between the door and the framework.

With his other hand, he reached inside his suit coat pocket and withdrew a piece of folded brown leather, which he flicked open and shoved at her to see through the crack in the door. "Daniel Elliott, United States marshal. I need to talk to you."

The only marshal she had even known was Ron Addison. She glanced at his identification suspiciously. "So it says."

With his index finger he tapped the badge opposite the identification card. "My badge, Miss Keaton," he said condescendingly.

"It's pretty, but how do I know it's real?"

He slipped his identification back into his pocket and made a second fist to keep the other company. "Marcy Keaton," he began. "Née Patricia Dodd. Ex-Mrs. Robert Keppler. Thirty-one—"

"Twenty-nine."

"Thirty-one," he repeated, still gazing straight at her with brooding hazel eyes. "Birthmark on your—" He interrupted himself this time and smiled brightly. "Want more?"

She felt the blush warm her face. "No."

The chain came off the door, and she opened it to let him walk inside. The gun was still behind her back; she could feel the moisture from her palm oozing all over the handle. If he was who he said he was, there'd be no trouble. But she was no longer a participant in the Witness Protection Program. What was he doing here? In fact, she'd moved from the last address they had on record for her.

She closed the door behind her and planted her feet solidly on the carpet, watching him as he looked around the spacious living room. No, he wasn't just looking. He seemed to be assessing her living habits and her taste in furnishings. He was intruding on her personal life, and she didn't like it.

Without turning toward her, he said, "You seem surprised that I tracked you down."

She jerked the gun up in front of her and aimed the barrel directly at him.

He turned, saw the gun, and his eyes rose slowly to meet her determined glare.

Was it her imagination, or did she see a sudden twinkling of gold and silver in his eyes? There was no mistaking the equally surprising transformation of his mouth as his lips turned up in an amused smile.

He said, "You are the cautious one, aren't you?"

"I make it a habit to be cautious."

Despite the gun pointed at him, he strode nonchalantly over to her desk and began to rifle through her papers. He glanced over at her. "Why do I think it's your nature?" Then he started across the room toward her.

"Stay right where you are," she ordered. "Just tell me why you're here."

He pushed back his suit jacket and set his hands firmly on his hips. "How'd you like to be booked for assault with a deadly weapon?"

"One more step, and you can make it homicide." She thought she sounded brave, but the queasy feeling in her stomach was getting stronger.

He tilted his head slightly as though to get a better look at the gun she was holding. She backed away as he moved toward her with sure, slow steps, and her back smashed against the front door.

He grabbed the gun from her hand. "Why don't you just shoot yourself in the foot and get it over with?" Holding the gun up in front of her, he continued. "Of course, you'd have to learn how to use this first. See this little crossbolt safety above the trigger. You push it to Off, slide the top back and forward again—" she jumped at the snapping noise "—and now it's ready to go." His eyes twinkled again. "Which foot?"

Marcy began to feel a little foolish, and the smile that broadened on his face wasn't helping any. "What's so funny?" she asked, her palms flat against the door behind her.

He moved closer. "Funny? I'm told that I have an infectious smile."

She tossed her head and eased her way past his looming form. When she decided he couldn't see her, she closed her eyes and took a deep breath. Then she turned to face him. "What's this great need you have to talk to me, Mr. Elliott?"

Now he leaned against the door. He crossed his ankles and casually held up the gun. "Why'd you buy this?"

"My dates are becoming insistent." *If he wants to be flip,* she resolved, *I can be just as flip.*

"Why do I have this gut feeling that that's a bunch of crap?"

"Indigestion, maybe," she suggested.

His face lost its smile. *This I get,* he told himself, *when I could be taking care of serious business.* "Listen, Miss Keaton, I don't want to be here any more than you want me here. The taxpayers don't want me here. But here I stay until you satisfy me with an adult answer. Why'd you buy the gun?"

Marcy leaned back against her desk, deciding she'd had enough of his curtness. "Politeness isn't one of your virtues, is it, Mr. Elliott?"

Sullenly he asked, "What's with virtues now?"

She forced a weak smile. "You must have some."

"Very few. Easier to keep track of them. Why'd you buy the gun, Marcy?"

Standing erect, she crossed her arms in front of her, looked away from him briefly and then returned her eyes to the man standing so casually against her front door. Her timing seemed to her to be ridiculous, but she couldn't help but notice the curves beneath his blue shirt, nor could she help but perceive the power in his legs. His body was lean, but he was definitely in excellent shape. She blinked away her sudden musings and told him, "You seem to know everything about me. Why do you think I bought it?"

His eyes started at her white high heels and eased up over her well-formed legs and the attractive curves that filled out her tasteful beige dress. He stopped his brazen inspection momentarily, and his gaze lingered on her sleek light brown shoulder-length hair. Then his eyes peered directly into hers. "I almost believe the boyfriend bit. You're an eye-stopper, all right. I can understand a healthy man's attraction to your type."

"My type?"

"Attractive, dangerous," he told her, almost as though he meant his words to be an insult. He saw her face pale and watched as she moved to the sofa to slowly let her body sink onto it. He noted the slight trembling in her slender fingers as one hand grasped the other. Sitting there on the sofa, she didn't look at all dangerous to him. She looked confused and scared to death.

He placed the gun on top of the desk and quietly sat down next to her. "Look, Marcy," he began hesitatingly, "I didn't mean to give you a hard time, but I've got a job to do, and you're not making it any easier for me to do it." He leaned back and spread his arm along the back of the sofa. She'd crossed her arms again and had begun stroking one of them with her cupped fingers. He smiled slightly and said, "We have to stop not liking each other like this."

Her blue-gray eyes shot toward his. "You mean be *friends*?" Her tone was mocking.

Dan didn't at all like the look she gave him. "Not exactly. If I want a friend, I'll get a dog or a drinking buddy."

"Get a dog!" she pronounced, jumping up. She put the gun back in the desk drawer and started to straighten the papers he had moved out of place. Suddenly she stopped and faced him. "Just what makes you think I'm dangerous, Mr. Elliott?"

"I've read your file. I know all about the trial and about your life-style in California. You lived pretty well. Rivers of alcohol, tons of caviar."

Her fingers clenched at her sides. "I never knew what was really going on. I didn't know our money was dirty."

"Oh?" he said questioningly, one eyebrow lifted. "You didn't know that your husband's firm received federal research and development funds for the testing of new integrated circuit chips?"

"That I knew," she eased out from between compressed lips.

"And that he was selling copies of the circuit chips to organized crime sweatshops?"

Her deep sigh of despair sounded genuine to him, and when she said, "That I never knew... until the trial," something in him wanted to believe her. Yet the job of protecting people with new identities had made him cynical. He'd seen too many creeps who had given evidence to shake off federal charges and then walked away scot-free in exchange for their cooperation. Yeah, he told himself, he had a lot to be cynical about lately. But there was no sense in unloading it all on her.

"Okay," he said finally, "you didn't know."

"You believe me?"

"Until you give me reason not to."

Marcy felt the tightness in her chest let up a little, and she suddenly realized how important it was to her that he did believe her. The past two years had been lonely years, lonely not out of choice, but out of fear, and if the very people who said she'd be safe and protected didn't believe she'd been a victim, well then— But he'd said he believed her. Out of gratitude she wanted to like him. She looked at his face and felt she was seeing it for the first time. It was a nice face. His dark lashes lifted and he looked directly at her. Yes, Marcy decided, his eyes were definitely hazel, hazel with little golden flecks; and even when he wasn't smiling, the come-hither line of his mouth was fascinating. In spite of his brusqueness, Marcy decided she needed a friend right now. She said, "Mr. Elliott, I'm going to have some coffee. Would you like some?"

Over coffee, which she served at the table in her well-ordered kitchen, Dan decided not to press so hard, to give her a little space, so he put aside the matter of the gun for the time being. He asked, "Why'd you want out of the Witness Protection Program, Marcy?"

Aimlessly stirring her black coffee, she told him, "The first year went so well...no trouble...I decided I just didn't need the reminder of what happened in California."

"You should've at least kept us advised periodically. Naturally, if citizens don't want us bothering them, we don't do it, manpower being what it is. But that's neither here nor there now. How are you getting along?"

Appreciating his friendlier attitude, she was able to smile, and then she said, "Fine... just fine. I worked as a reporter for a while in California...but I guess you know that. Anyway, now I work out of my home here doing free-lance writing. I have several accounts. The biggest one right now is for an out-of-state land developing firm that's planning a multimillion-dollar project. It's to be called Oceanview Villas. I'm writing news releases and radio and TV spots that they'll be using when the project receives final approval." She looked at his cup. "More coffee?"

"Half, please."

As she poured, she continued. "Once Oceanview gets the go-ahead, I'll be doing the releases for local business editors, and I've already begun research for a major background article for a national magazine."

Dan thanked her for the refill and then said, "Well, you seem to have adjusted with little problem. How's the social life of Marcy Keaton?"

She leaned back in her chair and her pleasant expression faded somewhat. "That's the difficult part. It's like living a lie, having to negate the fact that Patricia Dodd Keppler ever existed. It's hard, Mr. Elliott—"

"Dan," he told her.

"Dan...extremely hard. Oh, I have friends, go out for dinner occasionally, but I have to watch everything I say, it seems. That's not a pleasant way to live." She let out a sigh. Though the subject depressed her, it felt good talking to someone about it. "Sometimes I think I should just move somewhere else and start all over again as Patricia Dodd."

Dan studied her face carefully, noted the distress in her eyes, and he began to believe for the first time that the woman sitting there so quietly, so still, had truly been a victim of circumstances not of her own making. Cheerfully he said, "But you've got a good thing going right here, and you seem to be enjoying it."

Marcy's eyes brightened mischievously. "Yes...my work keeps this *dangerous* woman off the streets."

He reacted with a smile that she found a little disconcerting, and the casual pat of his warm fingers on her hand definitely fazed her as he said, "Forget I ever said that, okay?"

"I'll try," she told him, quickly breaking eye contact. Yet she couldn't ignore the feel of his fingers. The sensation shot up her arm and sent adrenaline rushing into her heart. She glanced down at his fingers on her hand and then looked back up at him.

"Marcy," he said softly, "you're going to have to tell me why you bought the gun."

"The gun," she said absently, slipping her hand out from under his touch and raising it to her throat to toy with the gold chain she wore. Funny, she had almost—but not quite—forgotten the reason for his visit. She got up from the table, took their coffee mugs to the sink and began to rinse them. "You must have read about the threats I received before and during the trial in Los Angeles. That if I agreed to testify, I'd never—"

"Yes," he interrupted, knowing how the recollection must be terrifying her. "And you testified, anyway."

She nodded while drying her hands. "And when I testified as a government witness in the trial that followed, the threats continued. I was so frightened."

Dan watched her walk away from the sink and into the living room and found himself wondering if it were possible that she had been having an affair with Ed Moray. She didn't seem the type to him. But was there a type? Personal experience had told him there wasn't. He recalled reading the transcript. It had all seemed so simple: a beautiful woman, two men, one killing the other. It was a classic scenario.

He got up and walked to the door between the kitchen and the living room. Leaning against the doorjamb, he studied her. She was standing at the desk with her back to him. Starting at her calves, his glance rose slowly up over the curves that were in all the right places. He felt a sudden pulsation, but it wasn't in his heart. Then he asked, "Why are you so frightened now?"

Turning, she told him, "It's the phone calls. They've started again. Why now? I was just beginning to believe I'd awakened from a bad dream. Why again?"

"When did they start?"

"About two weeks ago."

"Two weeks ago! Why didn't you notify us?"

She sighed and said, "To tell you what? That I'm getting crank calls from some kook who could just have singled out my number by chance?"

He suggested, "Have the number changed."

"Mr. Elliott—"

"Dan," he reminded her.

"I run a business from my home. I can't be changing my phone number every time a weirdo calls."

He asked, "You think that's all it is?"

Marcy looked away and slowly shook her head.

"Well, it is possible," he suggested. Then he added, "These phone calls. How often do you get them?"

Marcy pulled a tissue from the box on top of her desk, blew her nose in as ladylike a manner as possible and tossed the tissue into the small brown wastebasket beside the desk. "I'm sorry. My nerves aren't quite what they should be."

"Should be, hell. I'd be a wreck if someone were doing a number on me." He watched her sit down in the easy chair across from the sofa and studied the way she gracefully slid onto it and crossed her legs. Unobtrusively she adjusted the hem of her dress. To himself he repeated, *She's an eye-stopper, all right.* "Marcy," he said as he sat on the sofa to face her, "tell me about the phone calls."

"Three, maybe four times a week—at anytime, day or night. That's what's so nerve-racking.... I never know if it's going to be a business call or the... voice. Except late at night. Then I'm pretty sure it'll be him."

"'The voice'?"

"That's how I think of it... of him."

Dan was making mental notes of everything she told him. "Exactly what does he say?"

She leaned her head back in the chair. "It's usually the same. He says, 'Your time's running out.'"

"That's it?"

"That's all he says," she replied tiredly.

"Marcy, this is important. Is there anything about his voice that you recognize as having heard before?"

She sat upright. "Not really, but it's so frightening. I mean, he speaks in a strange way. I guess to mask it."

Dan leaned forward, placed his elbows on his thighs and clasped his hands together. He looked as though he were deep in thought. Looking over at him, Marcy began to feel an inner calm that had eluded her in recent days. But that calm was accompanied by something else—a sudden interest in Daniel Elliott, the man.

There was an aura of strength and a vibrant masculinity about him. It was crazy, but she could almost feel it reaching out to her, moving around her, circling her body. The feeling was comforting and very special. And basic. Perhaps this was what a woman experienced when she was truly attracted to a very special man, she mused.

Unfortunately she'd never really known that feeling. Her early years hadn't prepared her for a knowledge of true affection and attraction between a man and a woman. She'd been born just outside of Paris. Her father, a general in the Air Force Systems Command, had been a stern man who had treated her more like one of the troops than a girl who was gradually becoming a young woman. Her soft-spoken mother had been treated in much the same way. The general had even come down on her when she'd taken to drink out of boredom and neglect. Eventually she'd divorced him. No, Marcy had never seen much affection between her parents.

After the divorce she'd been shifted from school to school in Europe, and then, at eighteen, the general had packed her off to his sister in California, Marcy's maiden aunt, a strict woman who had taken care of her out of duty rather than love.

Then there was her disastrous marriage to Robert Keppler. What had started out as a fairy-tale romance had turned into a nightmare during the second year of their marriage. Just the thought of him sent a shock wave of revulsion charging through her. She'd found out things that she'd never dreamed were possible, and then, when she had thought she'd discovered the worst, she'd found out that he had become involved with dangerous criminals.

Marcy looked back over at Dan, and again a soothing sensation washed away her brief, troubled reminiscences. She found her lips forming a soft smile as she studied his face.

Dan's dark lashes were raised, and his hazel eyes seemed intrigued by her apparent interest. Then he touched the tips of his fingers together and said, "If...only if there is a connection between the calls and the trial, and if it's the same person trying to scare you, I just can't understand why now."

"The same person? You mean the syndicate," she said. "They were trying to frighten me into not testifying at the trial. If I hadn't seen Ed leaving the house, there might not have been a trial; it would have been thought a suicide. The attorneys told me that the syndicate was afraid Robert's involvement with organized crime would come out . . . and it did. You know what happened then."

Dan nodded. "A slew of indictments that the Feds made stick . . . thanks to your help."

Marcy's arms went out, her palms up. "But what would be their motive for harassment now?"

"Revenge. Spite. A warning to other witnesses," he suggested. "That is if it is the syndicate." After a few quiet moments he asked, "What about Moray's family? Didn't he have a son?"

"He has two. I saw Dirk several times at the trial, but James, his older brother, was away at college. I barely knew him, but I know he's the fair-haired one. Dirk is dark, like his father."

"They'd be pretty bitter, wouldn't they?" The minute he said that, he wished he hadn't, but it was too late. He saw it in her eyes. Quickly he went on. "But how would they locate you? We do a pretty good job in covering up tracks when we relocate someone like you."

Someone like me, she thought, his remark ringing in her ears, sending a cold chill down her spine. *Never mind,* she told herself. If that's what he wanted to think, it didn't matter to her. He was only doing his job. He'd already told her that. Casually she said, "I guess the files in the Witness Protection Program aren't as complete as you'd like to think."

"They're pretty complete."

"Anything in them about my debut on national TV a month ago?"

A gush of air slipped through his lips; he leaned back and slowly shook his head.

"Well, a senator from Washington was here in Clearwater to dedicate a new bridge. I was just returning from Oceanview Villas' office, and someone rammed my car from behind, sending me plowing into the senator's. In seconds, security was all over me and so were the news cameras that were following the senator for coverage. That night Patricia Dodd, or I should say Marcy Keaton, made the six o'clock news."

He added, "And it was picked up by the networks." He slapped the arm of the sofa and exclaimed, "For crissake! Anyone in the country could have seen you."

"Two weeks later the phone calls started," she told him quietly.

"The voice, Marcy, could it be the same one you heard during the trial? Does it sound at all similar? Is it an older man's or a younger man's?"

Her eyes told him she was desperately trying to remember, but then she admitted, "All I know is that I think there's something familiar about it. It could be the same, but I'm just not sure." She leaned her elbow on the arm of the easy chair and rested her chin pertly on her curved hand. Then an unexpected smile softened her worried look.

Dan tilted his head. "Nice that you're beginning to see the humor in all of this."

Her blue-gray eyes brightened also. "Earlier, I thought you were my nemesis."

His low chuckle was followed by "Me?"

"Yes. I'd noticed your car cruising around here, and I spotted you in the office building yesterday. When you came to the door, I thought 'This is it!'"

Dryly he said, "Tell me about fear. When I saw your shaking hand aiming that gun at me, all my thirty-six years zoomed by."

She leaned forward. "You mean you were actually nervous? It's not loaded."

"I realized that after I took it from you. It was too light. But I wouldn't have been nervous if I'd thought you knew what you were doing. It's the flakes with the jitters I worry about."

"So I'm a dangerous flake now?" she said teasingly.

"You told me you'd forget what I said before."

Was it the way he said that, or was it the golden gleam in his hazel eyes that made her feel suddenly uncomfortable? Or was she feeling too comfortable? He was nice, and he was trying to be considerate. She examined him momentarily, thinking he looked like a lawyer, a businessman, even a kindly doctor; he looked very *nice*. And she liked his voice, liked the music in it. There was something else, too: just the slightest hint of a Brooklyn accent. She asked, "Is your home in New York?"

"It used to be."

"Brooklyn?"

His eyes lit up. "You know, you'd make a pretty good marshal yourself."

She laughed, and it felt good to laugh again. "That's all they'd need. I've got so many names, they wouldn't know how to make out my paycheck." She thought for a moment, and then, wanting to know more about him, she asked, "Do you like working for the Marshal Service?"

"Sure. It's a powerful organization."

"And you get a great deal of satisfaction from working for a powerful organization," she suggested.

"The world we live in needs powerful organizations. Real life is not a bowl of cherries."

"And you believe I think it is?" She was sorry she said that. He was just making conversation—a conversation she'd started—and now she'd brought back the reason for his visit. He was just doing a job, and he obviously wasn't too thrilled about doing this particular one.

"No," he said, interrupting her private thoughts. "I know what you're going through. I know it hasn't been easy for you." He looked over at her, and impulsively he felt an unreasonable desire to see that no one, but no one, hurt her—and not just because it was his job. She didn't have it coming to her. At least he wasn't sure she did. "You've been handed a raw deal, Marcy, but you seem to be handling it with style."

She smiled at the compliment. "Maybe you've changed your opinion of me just a little, then?"

"Want the truth?" he asked.

"The truth."

"When I scanned your file, I had you pegged for a spoiled rich lady who'd come out of the whole mess smelling like roses. But when I saw you in person, I put you in the nice-girl-gone-tough class."

"Not very flattering," Marcy told him, but her eyes twinkled at his assessment.

"That smile looks good on you. You should wear it more often."

She felt warm inside again. "I haven't had that much to smile about in the past few years." After a pause, her smile faded. "I did my duty as a wife and citizen, and it cost me."

Abruptly, Dan's face darkened and his jaw tightened. The change was so abrupt that it startled Marcy. He noticed her reaction. "Yeah, I know what you mean," he said casually. "Doing what we think is our duty can cost us, can't it? And it can cost those we love." He got up from the sofa. "I've got to check back in at the office," he told her as he walked over to the desk. He took a piece of paper and wrote something down on it. "Here's my home phone number and my work number in case you need me. I'll be checking on you for a while, until we figure out what's going on with these calls." He handed her the paper with the numbers on it, and as he did he noticed the slenderness of her smooth fingers and their well-manicured look. His thumb casually brushed across them as she took the paper from him and thanked him.

It was then that he caught the whiff of some light fragrance that she wore, a nice aroma that reminded him of the flower cart where he used to occasionally pick up a bouquet for—

He forced that thought out of his mind quickly, but the fragrance lingered; he liked it a lot. Looking into the silvery glow of Marcy's blue-gray eyes, he decided he liked them, too. A brief silence passed between them, and then he asked, "Mind if I use your phone?"

"No, go right ahead." She went into the kitchen with the pretense of having something to do.

When she returned, Dan was winding up his conversation. Then she saw him to the door.

Marcy was surprised at the emptiness she suddenly felt now that she was alone once again. Yet, much of the fear she had experienced over the past two weeks had subsided. In fact, her spirits had lifted so much, she decided to phone her friend, Gloria, and reschedule the lunch Marcy had canceled the previous week. But just as she lifted the receiver, the door buzzer sounded again.

She found herself smiling at the thought that Dan had forgotten something and had returned. She was wrong.

Standing there when she opened the door was Mark Godette, her contact at Oceanview Villas. He was tall, slender and immaculately dressed, as always. Marcy assumed that he was in his late forties. His perfectly groomed dark hair was streaked with gray; his mustache, almost totally gray. His pale blue eyes were cold.

"Mark?" Her tone registered her surprise.

"Miss Keaton," he greeted her with his usual formality. "May I speak with you? It will only take a few minutes."

"Certainly." She opened the door wider, and he sauntered in.

After scanning the room, he turned. "I want you to know how much I appreciate the efforts you've put forth for the Oceanview project, but we no longer need your services. I've come by to collect the information folders and material I gave you and to give you—" he reached inside his coat pocket "—this check. I'm certain you'll find it satisfactory."

Marcy was taken aback for a moment, and then she asked, "Have the county commissioners turned the project down?"

Momentarily he hesitated, arched his eyebrows, and then told her, "No, not at all."

Marcy waited for some further explanation for her dismissal, but none came. She asked, "Are you unhappy with the work I've done so far?"

"Quite the contrary. It's been exemplary."

There was another strained moment. "Well, Mark, I am curious. Have you hired someone else to do the PR work we talked about?"

"Really, Miss Keaton, I am quite pressed for time. May I have the information folders and any material you have regarding Oceanview Villas?'' He extended the check.

Marcy moved toward him and accepted the check. One look at it and she commented, ''It's quite generous. I'll get the material for you.'' Then she went to her desk.

''Good,'' he said. ''I'd hoped there wouldn't be a problem.''

She glanced over at him as he stood there in the middle of the living room. ''Problem? Why should there be a problem? They're your papers, and you've already paid me for the radio and the TV spots. Are you going to use them?''

''Possibly,'' he said, looking as though he'd sniffed something sour.

Marcy continued to gather some folders from her desk drawer, but purposefully left behind the one folder that had the information for the long background story that she'd begun to research. What she'd been having a hard time finding out was who the parent company or companies were and their status in the corporate world.

She handed him the folders. ''Here you are. Everything you gave me on Oceanview and the work I've completed recently.''

He took them and almost greedily glanced through the folders. But he didn't find what he was looking for. He said, ''The background story isn't here, Miss Keaton.''

"That work is mine, Mark. All the papers you gave me, you're holding in your hands."

His face reddened. "You're going ahead with the article?"

"Yes, I am. We discussed it last week. When you said the article wouldn't be required, I told you I would submit it as a free-lance writer."

"You can't do that, Miss Keaton."

"Oh, yes I can, Mark, and I will. I don't need your permission to do it. A project that size concerns the public, and they have a right to know where the money is coming from, what securities are being sold to finance it and what guarantees prospective buyers have."

His eyes were like ice cubes. "You're asking for trouble, Miss Keaton. We were afraid you would."

Marcy leaned back on the edge of her desk and crossed her arms. After shaking her head slightly, she said, "I don't understand you, Mark. Why don't you want me to use the story? I've done half the research, which, by the way, you haven't made any easier for me. If the county commissioners do their job, they're going to dig much further than I will before your firm gets final approval to go ahead with your project. They're going to have to know more about your organization."

She saw him wince. "Of course, I may now have to change the slant on the story. I was prepared to laud your company's efforts, but I'll probably treat it as more of an investigative reporting job now."

"You are an extremely stubborn young woman," he said rather slowly as he set the folders he was holding on the end table next to the sofa. Then he asked, "May I have the remainder of the box of stationery with the Oceanview letterhead on it, please? And the envelopes?"

"Sorry, Mark. I forgot about them. They're in my file cabinet. I'll get them." Marcy turned and went to the cabinet and retrieved the stationery from the bottom drawer, where she had stored it.

At the front door he asked her one more time not to submit any story unless cleared by him. She refused to listen. "Goodbye, Mark, and have a nice day."

Closing the door behind him, she locked it. "Of all the—" Again she shook her head, not understanding the man's motivation. After a quick check to make sure her own Oceanview file was still there, Marcy straightened up her desk for the day. And what a day it had been, she mused. One man had come into her life—Daniel Elliott—and one had just departed—good ol' Mark. *Good riddance,* she decided as she checked the freezer for dinner possibilities.

THE UNITED STATES marshal did stop by the following day, and Marcy was able to report that there had been no phone calls from "the voice." Dan came by the day after that, also. Still there had been no more upsetting threats. Marcy almost wished there had been—but not really. She was beginning to get used to seeing Dan, and she realized that without the phone calls there'd be no reason for him to ever visit again.

Except for looking forward to his stopping by, Marcy's days again began to take on a humdrum sameness. Her PR work had kept her busy, but the life she'd been living for the past two years had been restricted, generally. She'd purposefully chosen to work out of her home in order to maintain a low profile. She would accept invitations occasionally and would entertain once in a while, but not with the enjoyment and spontaneity she had had in the past. There was too much to hide, too much to try to forget.

Her closest friend was Murphy, the housekeeper, who came in three times a week, even though twice would have sufficed. Although Marcy had the time for it, housework was not her forte; it never had been. She'd known Murphy for almost a year now, but in spite of their friendship, not even she knew anything about Patricia Dodd Keppler.

This day began like all the others: the usual morning ritual, the quick breakfast, and then to work. The only thing that made these days different was Dan's daily visit. But the morning passed, and the afternoon went on its way with no Dan. She felt a disturbing sense of loss, and chided herself for even imagining that a friendship had been developing between her and the man who had lately occupied much of her thinking. He had simply been doing his job. *So much for vague fantasies,* she thought irritably. Unfortunately, today wasn't one of Murphy's working days, either.

It was a little after six o'clock. Marcy closed up shop and wandered about the downstairs rooms of her home. She tried sitting and reading a magazine, but she couldn't really concentrate; her eyes kept drifting toward the clock on the mantel over the fireplace.

Then she heard it—the slamming of a car door in the driveway. A few moments later, two buzzes were followed by three. Dan's buzz. She hurried to the door, opened it and looked into his smiling face as he stood there with one arm propped against the doorjamb.

She didn't want to admit her excitement even to herself, so she tried to explain the butterflies in her stomach as indigestion from the leftover meat loaf sandwich she'd eaten too quickly while working earlier. But she couldn't control the dancing light in her eyes that had begun the second she had opened the door.

"Hello again," she said, trying to sound casual. "I wasn't sure you'd be by today." For a few moments she stood quite still, just gazing into his piercing eyes.

Taking note of her intense expression, he asked, "Gonna invite me in?"

"Oh...uh, I'm sorry. Of course." She moved back, watched him stride easily across the entry hall, and then closed the door.

In the living room, he sank onto one of the easy chairs across from the sofa. "How'd it go today?"

She knew what he was asking. "Quiet," she told him, wondering if his next words would be *Farewell, Marcy Keaton. Your problems seem to be over.*

But he didn't say that. He said, "Good. Maybe the creep's tired of bugging you." He glanced up at her as she stood there attentively. "Today has been something else...didn't even have time for lunch. How about you? Had dinner yet?"

"Dinner?" She looked at him as though he'd asked if she'd had a hair transplant, but the surprise she felt quickly changed to an excitement she wasn't fully prepared for.

Noticing her hesitation, he suggested, "You usually eat dinner, don't you?" He rose from the chair.

"Uh...yes," she stammered, staring at the attractive man standing there patiently waiting for her answer. *Why not?* she asked herself.

"It'd be a good idea for us to go grab a bite, Marcy," he said, trying to convince her. "If someone is watching you, I want him to know you're not alone anymore."

"But that's not neces—"

"Listen, do you have any idea what it cost Uncle Sam to pay for my specialized training?"

She shook her head, determined to control the happy smile that was preparing to burst all over her face.

Dan smiled for her. "Then let me do the thinking, okay?"

Marcy let her smile blossom and said, "Okay."

CHAPTER THREE

EATING AT TACO BELL was not exactly Marcy's idea of a dinner date, the thought of which had put a shimmering light in her eyes, which departed promptly when Dan drove up to the fast-food restaurant. Once inside, her eyes glazed over as she watched Dan load his disposable tray with tacos, burritos, tostadas and a salad.

"Soft drink?" he asked. She nodded, and he ordered two.

Marcy put her drink on her tray next to the one taco she'd requested and then followed Dan to the outdoor patio where they unloaded their "dinner" onto the concrete table inlaid with small colored tiles.

The air around her was warm, and the sun was making its final colorful display before dipping down beyond the waters of the Gulf of Mexico. A gentle breeze rustled through the fringe dangling from the umbrella over their table.

Looking over at her lone taco, Dan said, "You don't have much of an appetite, do you?" Then he picked up one of his tacos with both hands, opened his mouth wide and chomped down on it.

Marcy heard the crispy crunch and was amazed at the neatness of the entire operation. As she watched him chew away and saw that he was savoring each morsel, she remembered the disaster her one previous bout with tacos had brought on: at the first bite the thing had wound up all over the table and her lap. Delaying the inevitable, she sipped her cola.

"Eat," he told her as he started on a burrito, "or you'll waste away to nothing."

Gingerly she reached for her taco, and after a silent prayer, she held the crispy wedge and sank her teeth into it. Oh, the sweet taste of success! Now, all that was left to do was to casually ingest the shredded lettuce dangling from the corner of her mouth and somehow chew gracefully. *Why is he smiling?* she wondered as the tip of her tongue curled out and did its job.

"Fun, isn't it?" he suggested and reached for a tostada.

"Um-hmm," she mumbled and swallowed. Before she could breathe adequately, he lifted a plastic forkful of his salad to her lips.

"Open," he ordered, and she complied.

When she could talk, she said, "Feeding me is not part of your job, Dan."

"Keeping you alive is," he reminded her, "and you have to eat to stay alive."

She glanced down at the generous portion still in front of him. "I hope your culinary inquisitiveness goes beyond Mexican food."

"If the job demands it."

"This job will," she told him as she attacked her own taco again. Then, enjoying her newfound expertise with the thing in her hands, she asked, "Why'd you become a U.S. marshal?" She paused to sip her drink. "The money?"

Dan groaned. "Please... give me some credit."

"Why, then?"

He thought as he attacked another taco, and then he told her, "I don't know. The excitement, maybe. You become addicted to it. Like needing a fix. Doesn't leave much room for a normal life, though... or for love." He stopped chewing momentarily as if to ponder his own remark.

Marcy didn't miss his subtle change of mood, nor had she missed the word "love," which he'd said with a certain sadness. Her own encounters with love had only brought her sadness, and she wondered if Dan, too, had been hurt somehow. She hoped not. She knew, almost as if it were an absolute fact, that she would never hurt him—not that way, not if they were to—

She ordered herself to stop thinking such silly thoughts, and she grasped the plastic container of cola tightly, feeling the icy coldness surge into her palm. Wanting to change the subject, she asked, "It's dangerous work, isn't it?"

His casual air returned. "Depends on how well you know your job." He took another forkful of salad into his mouth.

"Something tells me you know yours exceptionally well," she said, thinking that the sound of his voice was becoming very pleasant to her ears. "You must meet a lot of interesting people...in your job, I mean."

He asked, "Interesting women?"

"No! I meant people in general," she clarified quickly, and then, feeling the warmth on her cheeks, she apologized. "I'm sorry. I didn't intend to pry, Mr. Elliott."

"Dan," he told her again and added, "You weren't prying, just making conversation."

Relieved, she said, "Exactly."

He took a sip of his drink and told her, "Yeah, I meet lots of people, mostly people in trouble, but the women are more interesting than the men."

Her curiosity was piqued by that. "How so?"

Smiling hazel eyes bore into lovely blue-grays, and then he said, "Women will do the damnedest things when they're on the spot. You wouldn't believe. There was this one broa . . . lady . . . who offered to—"

Marcy wasn't sure she wanted to hear the rest of that story, so she cut him off by saying, "And all the men are victims. Right?"

"I didn't say that. It's just that women have such marvelous imaginations when they're caught."

She wondered if that were the category Dan Elliott had placed her in. Seeing that he'd finished his last burrito, Marcy thanked him for "dinner" and asked him to take her home, telling him she had work to do, deadlines to meet. But she admitted to herself that something about Dan Elliott had disturbed her. His curtness, maybe. His piercing hazel eyes? Definitely!

Outside her house, he parked and then walked her to the door. She was about to thank him again when he said, "You know what I'd love right now?"

Lightly she suggested, "Another taco."

He shook his head. "A cup of that coffee of yours."

Unlocking the door, she informed him, "That coffee of mine is going to have to be instant until I get to the store tomorrow."

"No problem," he told her, then entered, removed his jacket and made himself completely at home. He singled out one of the easy chairs, sank onto it and said, "Nice place you've got here, Marcy. Kinda big for one person, though."

As she set her handbag on the desk, she said, "When you've been shuttled back and forth to as many girls' schools as I've been, you crave space of your very own." She headed to the kitchen.

"That's right," he called to her, recalling her file, "you were raised in Europe."

"Until I was eighteen," she called back. "Then I became a citizen of Southern California."

"That's where you met Keppler."

Silence filled the house, and then Marcy appeared at the kitchen door. Dan angled a glance toward her and saw the rigid look on her face as she responded, "Not when I was eighteen." Then she went back into the kitchen.

Dan abruptly changed the line of conversation, asking, "They say travel enriches a person. Is that true?"

She replied, "It can tire a person, too. I'm ready to settle down in one spot."

"Here?"

Carrying in his mug of coffee, she said, "Right now I'm functioning on a day-to-day basis. Here's your coffee."

He took the mug. "Thanks. You know, a woman like you should—" The ringing of the phone on her desk stopped him midsentence. His narrowed eyes shot up at Marcy as she jumped. "Answer it," he told her quickly.

Hesitantly she went to the desk and lifted the receiver to her ear. A second later her eyes closed. Grabbing the receiver from her hand, Dan listened.

". . . running out." That was all he heard and then a firm click. He could almost feel the vibrations of Marcy's trembling. "Bastard!" he said as he took her in his arms. It was a hell of a time to think about it, he told himself, but there was that nice fragrance again. Not at all like the cloying sweet fragrance some women wore. No, the smell of her filled his nostrils with that warm, sensual odor that made him want to kiss wherever she'd put the stuff on.

He held her a little tighter, and Marcy's arms reached up over his broad shoulders for support. She gasped and then slipped deeper into the curve of his neck and shoulder. "I'm sorry, Dan. I'm not usually so clinging, but that man is getting to me."

"You cling as much as you want," he told her as he began a soothing massage up and down her back. Under his palm, the material of her dress was silky smooth. As he stroked her comfortingly, he found himself rubbing his cheek against the cushion of hair under his face. He felt the muscles in his arms and legs tense and his Adam's apple bob suddenly. His warm tongue slipped slowly over his lower lip.

Similar reactions swirled through Marcy's body. For a moment she was immobilized, torn between welcoming the wondrous feeling and the icy realization that she had no right to be in this man's arms, no right to feel as safe as she did. Her brain sent her a picture of a wife and two beautiful children, and she knew instantly what he must be thinking of her. She eased herself from the arms that had been so comforting, so understanding, so wonderfully masculine.

"I don't imagine this is part of your job description," she said, trying to sound carefree.

Dan swallowed hard. "Comes under fringe benefits." Why couldn't he take his eyes off her face? He was glad she stood there looking down; he didn't want her seeing what he knew she'd find in his own eyes. Then, an idea occurred to him. He wasn't sure if it had originated in his brain or his heart, but the more he thought about it, the more he liked it. Taking hold of her shoulders, he asked, "Marcy, will you be all right for just a little while if I leave?"

"Do you have to... right now?"

"I'll only be gone about a half hour, and then we'll have that coffee and talk. Okay?"

"All right," she said reluctantly, not wanting him to go—not just now, after that telephone call.

She locked the door after him, but a long hour passed before she heard his buzz again. Even if she had wanted to, she couldn't have erased the thankful smile from her face. Again she opened the door to greet him, and again there was that pleasant glow in his eyes that she'd gotten used to. But then her smile evaporated as she glanced down. There, next to him on her doorstep, was a suitcase, and he was holding a small cardboard box.

He reached for the suitcase and walked past her, all but pushing her aside. Then he set the suitcase down at the bottom of the stairway and placed the box on her desk. He turned and gave her a boyish grin. "Aren't you going to close the door?"

Automatically she did.

"You didn't lock it," he told her.

She looked at him, then down at the suitcase, and raised her eyes to his again. "Are you going somewhere?" she asked innocently, assuming he was leaving for parts unknown.

"Me? No." He walked over to the suitcase. "I'm moving in with you."

Marcy froze at the door. She repeated his words to herself mentally and let them sink in. Then she said, "That's funny, Elliott."

He smiled brightly and said, "No, it's practical."

"But impossible," she said firmly. "If you think you're actually—"

"I don't *think* it. That's the way it's going to be. Your caller's threat that your time is running out isn't just the usual obscene phone call. Uncle Sam said you'd be protected, and like it or not, you're going to be protected, not just checked on occasionally." His arms went out to his sides. "I'd invite you to my place, but it'd by a little crowded."

The suitcase seemed to be getting bigger and bigger to Marcy, and she sallied forth. "If you think that you and I are going to—"

"We'll discuss it over coffee," he informed her, and then he glanced up at the stairway. "A house this size has gotta have at least two bedrooms." His eyes went back to her. "You do live alone, don't you?"

Before he knew it, she was up a few steps, glaring down at him with fire in her eyes. "Yes, and I plan to keep it that way."

In a flash, strong, large hands were encircling her waist, lifting her and setting her down on the carpet. "I'm the trained marshal, Marcy Keaton. I know what's best for you right now."

He started to pick up his suitcase by the handle, but her high-heeled shoe struck the top of it. With one foot on the suitcase, she informed him, "Listen, Elliott, I grew up with my father telling me what to do. At least he was a general. And then my husband told me what to do. And now you're telling me what to do! When do I get to do what *I* want to do?"

His eyes sparkled playfully, and as though talking to a child, he twitched her nose, asking, "What is it you want to do so badly, Marcy? Just tell me. I'm a pussycat when it comes to beautiful women."

Energetically she brushed his hand away. "I'm not beautiful, and don't change the subject."

"Looked in the mirror lately?" he asked. Then he took off his jacket, laid it on back of one of the easy chairs and sat down on the other.

Marcy paced in front of him, stating all the sane reasons why he was not going to move in with her. Dan listened politely. She continued to assert herself vigorously, telling him how old-fashioned she really was, regardless of whatever he may have read in her file. And Murphy, her part-time housekeeper, would be in tomorrow morning. What would she think? Dan listened assiduously.

With hands on her hips, she looked down at him, her eyes wide. "And the neighbors? My friends? What am I supposed to tell them?"

"You picked me up in a singles' bar." Then he got up and joined his suitcase. "Give me a hint. Where do I crash?"

Marcy groaned. "Upstairs...to the right...the last room."

Up he went—whistling.

She let her body fall back onto the sofa and began tapping her fingers on the soft rounded arm. She tried to convince herself that this was not happening. Neither Patricia Dodd nor Mrs. Robert Keppler would permit a man they barely knew to move in with them, she thought to herself grimly. It was all Marcy Keaton's fault. What was Marcy Keaton really like, and just what was she getting into?

The melodic whistling got louder again as Dan ran jauntily down the carpeted steps. "Nice room," he complimented, grinning broadly. "Is the coffee ready?"

Marcy stared at him in disbelief. She'd always been the perfect hostess, caring and considerate of her guests' every possible desire, but this man standing in front of her, rolling up the sleeves of his white dress shirt, was no guest. He was forcing himself on her, and the preposterous thing about it all was that he had the weight of the United States government to back him up.

Dan immediately became preoccupied with the box he'd placed on the desk. Then he started to do something to her phone.

She asked, "What are you doing?"

"I'm connecting a tape recorder to your telephone...and a tap detector." He connected a wire between the phone and the wall jack. The detector itself was a small sleek box with a red light and a green light on top. As he laid it on the desk next to the phone, he told her, "When the light is green, we'll know the line is free of eavesdroppers."

"And when it's red?"

"We'll know we have company."

She didn't like the sound of that at all. "Who would want to hear any of my phone conversations?"

"Just a precaution. I've set the recorder so it will automatically tape all phone calls. When your friend does his thing, we'll at least have something definite, get a voice pattern on him." Dan brushed the palms of his hands. "How about that coffee now? I always have coffee in the evening."

"There's no need to give me a list of your personal likes and dislikes," she said in a brittle tone. "You won't be here long enough for me to remember anything about you."

Dan sat down on his preferred chair, leaned forward and let his clasped fingers dangle between his spread thighs. "Marcy, on a case like this, you never know. Could go on for months."

"Months! Can't you catch this nut sooner than that?"

"Catching him is not my job. Mine is to protect you, not run after your nut. I make my reports, and the FBI guys follow up. You—" he pointed directly at her "—are the only person I'm concerned about right now."

Forcing her eyes from him, she quietly said, "Months? I've known people who were married for less time than that." Her leery eyes darted over to him. "This is normal procedure in the Witness Protection Program?"

With the fingers of one hand stroking his chin and the fingers of his other crossed under his armpit, he said, "Perfectly normal. Happens all the time." Then he gave her a smile that could have melted the snow on Mount Everest.

Marcy's heart started to bang against her chest, but too much was happening too fast. It was confusing her. Yes, she'd become attracted to Dan. She had even begun to miss him. But to have him so close, day and night, well, that was another matter entirely. Of course, she did feel safer. Or did she?

"Being roomies will be fun," Dan suggested with a twinkle in his eye. "We can do each other's toenails."

Marcy only glared at him and stalked into the kitchen to fix the coffee.

Dan laughed to himself as he listened to the thrashing going on in the other room. "Could be worse," he muttered as he searched the room for an ashtray. Finding a small, presently unused crystal candy dish, he lit a cigarette, stretched out his legs and crossed his ankles. He was worried about her, and it definitely wasn't all a matter of job dedication. He'd had his share of women—he'd even married one—but none of them had ever affected him the way Marcy did, hadn't excited him as much.

He took another puff, shaped his lips and let a smooth stream of smoke shoot out while he thought about one of the passages out of the transcripts of the trial: the defense had claimed that Mrs. Robert Kepler and Ed Moray were having an affair. He wondered how much of the fatal argument had been over microchips and just how much had been over Marcy.

It wouldn't have been the first time he'd heard that reason for someone blowing a man's brains out. And he could see a man doing just that because of Marcy. She had class along with her good looks. The way she walked, that way she had of jutting her chin up just a bit and using those long brown lashes of hers . . . sure, she could drive a man to murder. But she didn't seem to know it, and that made her all the more dangerous. *Look what she's doing to you!* he warned himself.

"Sorry," she said as she handed him his coffee, "but I'm fresh out of tacos to go with this."

"No cake or ice cream?"

"Not even a cookie. Here, take your coffee. Since you're on guard duty, I hope it keeps you awake all night."

"I'm a light sleeper." He took the cup and saucer she offered and watched her take the now-used candy dish into the kitchen and return with a legitimate ashtray. She plunked it down on the table next to him. "Aren't you having any coffee?"

Without waiting for an answer, she strode back into the kitchen, returned with her coffee and sat down on the sofa.

"Where's that smile of yours, Marcy? I miss it."

"What's to smile about? I feel like a prisoner in my own home." She took a sip of the steaming coffee and put the cup and saucer down on the cocktail table in front of her. "Look, Dan, you're not serious about this business lasting for months, are you?"

"Naw," he said, his Brooklyn heritage showing a bit in the way he shaped the vowel. "I don't think you're in serious trouble. If anyone wanted to kill you, they'd have done so already."

Marcy's pupils dilated. "Kill me? I thought we were just talking about someone trying to scare me."

He saw the fear in her eyes, could almost smell it. "Sure, that's all we're probably dealing with. Some sicko who gets his jollies frightening pretty ladies. The world's full of them."

Why doesn't that help? Marcy thought. She took another sip of black coffee, and glanced at the man across from her. She wondered about that tough exterior of his. She'd seen his sensitive side, but obviously he wasn't comfortable in revealing it a lot of the time. Suddenly she wanted to see that side of him again, wanted to see him being kind and sensitive. At the same time, she knew that if he *was* nice to her, it would mean trouble.

Out of the blue, she asked, "Dan, have you ever really killed anyone?"

When in doubt, Dan usually opted for the truth. With her, though, he'd have to treat it lightly. "You mean recently?"

"I mean *ever*."

"Well, the last guy was a real dirt bag. He had an ugly operation going, selling angel dust to kids in three states. I caught up with him in a fish house near Biloxi. Real nice view overlooking the Gulf of Mexico, but it was a god-awful night. You wouldn't think it'd ever get cold in Biloxi, but it was cold that night. We were sitting at this table, and he was giving me all this gobbledygook about being straight as an arrow, and all the time I knew he had a small-caliber pistol in his lap pointed straight at my gut." Dan stopped and took a sip from his cup.

Marcy hadn't blinked since he began. "What happened?"

"I spilled his hot soup on his groin. He took off like a scalded rat. Got as far as the parking lot."

"You shot him?"

"Identified myself. Told him to stop."

"Aren't you supposed to read people their rights before you shoot them?"

He just looked at her, baffled by her naïveté. "What am I? A walking troubadour?" Seeing that she was still nervous, he tried to sound nonchalant. "So, you see, you're in good hands, nothing to worry about."

"Dan, it's just that . . . that I've never roomed with a trained killer." She thought a moment and then added, "I'm sorry. I didn't mean that the way it came out."

"Marcy, you have to stop that."

"Stop what?"

"This 'I'm sorry' business. You go around apologizing for breathing."

"I do not!"

"Sure you do."

"Dan, you're sounding like my father, the general, again. Don't give me orders. I don't like it."

"You're right," he acquiesced, "I tend to do that, don't I? Well, no more. You're looking at a new man. Anything you want to do is all right . . . as long as you do it with me. Friends. Okay?"

"Friends," she returned, again feeling that odd sensation rush through her at the smile he flashed her. Quickly she finished her coffee, but he still hadn't. She asked, "Doesn't your wife worry about you roaming around the country . . . moving in with women?" *Marcy!* she screamed silently, *where did that come from?*

He answered simply, "No more."

"Oh." Then, Marcy died a little inside. There again was the mental image of a woman and two beautiful children. "What's her name?" she asked as though she were requesting the time of day.

His eyes narrowed. "Hope."

Marcy lifted her empty cup and sipped nothing. "That's a sweet name . . . Hope."

"She's a sweetheart, all right."

Suddenly her throat felt like it held a golf ball in it. "And your children?"

"Only one. A boy. His name is Daniel junior. Not very imaginative, is it?"

Why couldn't she be in France right now? Marcy asked herself. She swallowed the golf ball. "A boy. That's nice. How old is he?"

"Almost two."

"That's nice, too... almost two." She laughed—a low, nervous laugh. "I didn't mean to repeat everything you said. I'm sorry."

He angled his head. "Marcy..."

She jumped up. "I'm tired. I think we should go to bed now." She turned with their cups in her hands, stopped dead in her tracks and spun around. "No! I didn't mean *we* should go to bed. I meant I should and you should—"

"Go to bed," he continued for her, enjoying her embarrassment.

"You lock the doors!" she sputtered and made a beeline for the kitchen. She was up the stairs to her bedroom in record time.

Once there, she locked the door and checked the locks on the windows. With the drapes closed, she sat in the easy chair across from her vanity and stared at her own reflected image. "Patricia Dodd," she mumbled, "what have you gotten yourself into now?" For a while she debated whether to sleep in the chair or try the bed fully clothed. *Don't be ridiculous,* she told herself. *He's a United States marshal.*

After a few more minutes of mental balancing, she began undressing for bed. As she did, her thoughts tumbled on. *Dan's a happily married man with a sweet wife and an adorable baby boy. How do I know he's adorable? He'd have to be. Look at his father. Adorable? That's a laugh. How could a man who eats tacos and goes around shooting people be adorable?*

Marcy scrubbed her face a little harder than usual and finally slipped under her pink flowered sheets. A smile of uneasy satisfaction curved her lips as she remembered that he'd be sleeping on yellow flowers. She was certain he'd prefer stripes.

Yet, she was happy that the bedroom had been in readiness. She'd kept it that way, although no one ever used it. Somehow it made her lonely life seem more normal. And what did it hurt to pretend a little, to make believe she was expecting company, old friends who would stay awhile?

At the tap on her bedroom door, she jerked her body to a sitting position.

"Marcy, are you awake?" His voice was gentle, even tender.

"No!" she hollered across the room as she gathered the top sheet up around her nightgown.

"Good. Just wanted to assure you I've never walked in my sleep... as far as I know."

"You woke me to tell me that? Go to bed, Elliott!"

She heard his low laughter through the closed door and then, "Now you're the one sounding like your father... the general."

"In this house I *am* the general, and don't you forget it. Now, please... go to bed."

"I'm not sleepy. I feel like talking."

"Fix yourself some warm milk," she told him. Then she let her head fall back onto her pillow and covered her face with the sheet.

He tapped the door lightly. "Want some?"

Up she sat again. "Get this straight, Elliott. There's no way we're ever going to have midnight rendezvous. You happen to be a married man. Now act like one."

"Oh, that. Didn't I mention that Hope is my ex-wife? She divorced me a year ago. Now, how about that warm milk? It'll make you sleep securely."

Securely! Marcy repeated to herself. Why was it she thought she'd never be secure again? Not with him in the house, anyway. "No, you *didn't* mention that. A gentleman would have."

There was his soft laughter again, and he said, "I'm no gentleman. I'm a U.S. marshal." He listened for her response. None came. "'Night, Marcy. Sleep well."

CHAPTER FOUR

"WELL, LOOK WHAT the cat dragged in!"

Dan was bounding down the stairs in his pajamas when the grainy voice greeted him. Halfway down he stopped and peered over the railing. Looking up at him with a cigarette dangling from her lips was a woman who looked about fiftyish, with pulled-back auburn hair just this side of being natural. Her print dress would have made Edith Bunker proud. Dan watched in amusement as her cat-green eyes all but undressed him.

She nodded her head in approval. "Not bad for seven in the morning," she told him. "Want some coffee?"

"Murphy, isn't it?" he asked, flashing her one of his charming smiles.

"He's bright, too," she said in a complimentary tone as she caught the pile of ash that dropped off her cigarette in the palm of her hand. A clatter of pans came from the kitchen, and Murphy turned her head toward the noise. "He's up, Marcy!" she shouted. "Sit," she told Dan. "I'll bring you some wake-up brew." After dumping the ashes from her palm into the ashtray on the table next to the easy chair, she went into the kitchen to join Marcy. Dan sat as ordered.

Marcy was busy breaking eggs into a bowl when she felt Murphy's gentle nudge. "You didn't tell me he was a lady-killer."

"You don't know the half of it." She smiled and began mixing the eggs.

"Worth holding on to, I'd say. But listen, gain a few pounds. A man wants something he can grab hold of, doesn't wanna mistake your arm for a broom handle in the dark."

"It's all strictly business, Murphy. Don't start talking marriage to me."

"So? Marriage is a business. A partnership kinda thing."

Marcy turned over the sausage she'd been frying. "You should know. You've gone through three husbands already. I should think that'd be enough partnership for one lifetime."

"Next time I'm gonna pick a healthier partner," she announced over her shoulder as she carried Dan's coffee into the living room.

"Here," she told him, handing it to him, "wash your tonsils with this."

Dan thanked her and watched her place her right hand on her hip. For a moment, Murphy just stood there giving him the once-over again. Then she said, "This business of protecting Marcy. Does it have to be done inside the house all the time? That girl's almost been living like a hermit. It's not natural. She's too young to be cooped up in here day after day, working all the time. She needs to get out more, have some fun.''

Dan asked, ''No boyfriends?''

''You'll have to ask her about that, but I doubt it. And this jerk who's been phoning her. When you nail him, give me two minutes alone with him. I wanna play accordion with his vocal cords.''

Dan sipped his coffee and said, ''Seems like Marcy tells you everything.''

''No, she doesn't, but I can tell she's in some kind of trouble. I don't pry. I'm not the type. And she's one very nice lady.''

''Breakfast!'' Marcy called as she carried two dishes into the dining room adjacent to the kitchen. ''Have some coffee with us, Murphy?''

''No,'' she called back, ''I've got my thermos with me.'' She picked up Dan's half-filled cup and carried it into the dining room.

Marcy lowered her voice. ''Well, if you run out, there's a new bottle of gin in the kitchen cabinet.''

''Good morning, Marcy,'' Dan said as he seated himself. ''Did you sleep well?''

''Yes, very well,'' she answered cheerfully. ''And you?''

''Thanks to you, I slept better than I have in the past year.''

Marcy spilled most of the coffee she was pouring onto his saucer. Murphy eyed both of them and picked up Dan's cup and saucer. ''I'll take care of this while you two finish saying good-morning." She watched Marcy sit down slowly, and then Murphy turned to Dan, winked and gave him an impish Irish smile again.

Toying with her scrambled eggs, Marcy asked, "Don't you usually sleep well, Mr. Elliott?"

"It's Dan," he reminded her. "And no, I haven't been sleeping all that well. I'd gotten used to walking into a home after work, and it's not quite the same entering a lonely apartment."

"Maybe you should reconsider that dog," she suggested.

He looked across the table at her and began to say something.

Just then, Murphy brought him a fresh cup and saucer and poured his coffee. She left the room silently this time.

"Toast?" Marcy asked, holding a plateful.

He took a slice along with some strawberry preserve. "Yes sirree, this is nice and homey." He began to chew slowly and darted a pleased look in her direction. "Good night's sleep, good food, good company. What more could a man want?"

"You ought not talk with your mouth full," she said. Then she became preoccupied watching the way his lips slowly moved, became entranced as his strong jaw gyrated rhythmically. Her eyes raised, and she found herself looking directly into those beautiful hazel orbs of his, into those dancing golden flecks that made her feel all mushy inside. Lowering her eyes, she attacked a piece of sausage. "You should have told me you weren't a married man before you half moved in."

"You got a thing about married men?" He started on his eggs.

Now she stared at him. "I'd certainly feel much better about this arrangement if you were married."

"Better?"

"Safer."

He asked, "How do you feel about divorced men?"

"They're not going to practice on me until they get it right." She started on her own eggs.

"Aren't you being a tad harsh? Not all divorced men are cads, you know."

"Oh? And just what is your great philosophy on divorce?"

"It's the pits." He smeared more strawberry preserve on another piece of toast.

Suddenly she felt sorry for him. "I take it the divorce was not all your idea."

"None of it was."

That surprised her. "Oh," was all she said and began on her scrambled eggs.

"Hope couldn't take my constant periods away from home. Worried too much about the bullet I took in my shoulder."

Marcy's fork stopped, poised just outside her opened mouth. "Bullet?"

"Just a graze. Looks like a botched-up vaccination."

Her forkful of eggs went back on her plate. "That'd be enough to unnerve any wife."

"Hope wasn't just any wife. She lived in her own fantasy world, wanted everything in life to be perfect, including me." He looked over at her and arched his eyebrows. "You're not going to believe this, but I'm *not* perfect."

She had to smile. "That would be fantasy, wouldn't it?"

Dan wiped a smidgen of preserve from his lips with his napkin and leaned his elbows on the table. "Is it true most women prefer fantasy to fact?"

"Fantasy?" She thought for a second. "Maybe it's more of an ideal we're thinking of."

"Ideal. Meaning what?"

"The kind of man we want to love us." She sipped her coffee and glanced at him over the rim of the cup. "The kind of man we want to love."

He remembered the transcript of the trial. A hint of unkindness colored his tone. "Was Robert Keppler your ideal man? Or was Ed Moray?"

She felt as though he had just slapped her in the face; she reddened as though he had. Slowly she stood up and held on to the edge of the table. "That's none of your business, Dan."

He leaned back in his chair. "Just my boyish curiosity surfacing," he said apologetically. *For crissake,* he thought, *I'm testing her again.*

"Curiosity," she repeated. "The word sounds rather cold, doesn't it?" Then she went to her desk to begin working, feeling very much alone again.

Murphy came into the dining room and took the dishes Dan had started to carry to the kitchen from his hands. "I thought you were one of the good guys," she whispered brusquely.

"You've got big ears, Murphy."

"And you've got a big mouth. Get in there and be nice."

"Yes, ma'am." He went over to Marcy's desk, leaned down and said, "Thanks for the breakfast. You're a good—"

The jarring ring of the phone on the desk make Marcy jump. She looked up at Dan with pleading eyes. Incoming calls always set her nerves on edge now.

"Go ahead," he told her, sliding his body next to hers so he could listen in. An anxious Murphy stood in the doorway.

Marcy picked up the receiver. "Yes," she said, her voice much weaker than it had been a moment before.

"Your time's running out." *Click!*

Marcy paled. Dan took the receiver from her clenched hand and placed it on its cradle, and then he put a strong hand on her shoulder. "Hear anything in the voice this time?" he asked softly.

"Dan, I can't even think anymore when I hear him."

He felt her begin to tremble. Turning to Murphy, he asked, "Got any brandy around here?"

"Something better." She went into the kitchen and quickly returned with three small juice glasses and her thermos. She poured a little white fluid into each and handed Marcy and Dan a glass each. "May the bastard get a goiter," she toasted, and the three of them emptied their glasses.

Marcy gagged. Dan did little better. Murphy beamed.

Running his hand across his mouth, Dan asked, "What the hell was that?"

Murphy smacked her lips. "I call it a White Fantasy. Gin, vodka and tequila."

Dan noticed the tears in Marcy's eyes, but then he realized his own had moistened, so he chalked it up to Murphy's White Fantasy instead of the phone call.

"Listen, you two," Murphy said, "why don't you both clear out of here for a while so I can get some work done. Go to the beach or something. Get your mind off of that guy."

"How about it, Marcy?"

She would have liked nothing better, but she asked, "How are we going to find out who the voice is at the beach?"

Leaning back against the edge of the desk, he crossed his arms. "That's not your job, and right now it's not my job."

She looked up at him. "Just what *is* your job?"

He touched the tip of her nose with his index finger. "I've already told you. To keep you safe and happy."

"I'll settle for safe."

"We'll be safe at the beach. Go get ready." He saw her stiffen at his command. "Please," he added quickly.

Marcy's smile was more of a gloat. "When did you start being so polite?"

"Today," he told her, starting for the stairs. He turned. "You've got five minutes to get ready." Up he went at his usual fast pace.

Murphy saw Marcy's mouth open in defiance. "You heard the man. Get ready, or I'll go with him."

"Listen, Murphy, you're supposed to be on my side."

"I am. Get going. He's not a man to keep waiting."

Marcy got up from behind the desk. "And I'm not a woman who goes running when a man curls his index finger at me."

"That's a good-looking finger, Marcy," she told her as she screwed on the top of her thermos.

"You know, Murphy, that White Fantasy of yours is affecting your judgment."

"It's affecting your sense of time. You've got four minutes to go."

"All right, all right, I'm going, but it's because I want to go."

She started toward the staircase. Murphy whispered after her. "Wear a bikini."

Marcy turned, pursed her lips and then tried to smile pleasantly. "I don't have one."

CLEARWATER BEACH was unusually quiet. It was still early. Marcy told Dan it was probably because the tourists hadn't quite gotten over the previous night's revelries. The morning sun was already hot; the sand was warm under her touch, but not as warm as the feeling inside her as she felt Dan's smooth hands glide over her back as he applied lotion to filter out April's strong rays. She felt him ease her head forward gently. Arching her back a little more, she felt him lift her shoulder-length hair and begin a soothing massaging at her neck and across her shoulders.

"Your skin's like satin," he said softly, beginning to cover the back of her thigh with lotion.

Marcy felt her flesh quiver under his touch and quickly took the plastic bottle from him. "I can do that."

"Sure." He watched her pour the thick fluid into her palm and rub it across her outer thighs; his eyes followed her movements as her slender fingers gracefully eased over the soft skin of her inner thighs.

She was about to cap the bottle when he said, "Me next," and rolled over onto his stomach, angling his arms and resting the side of his head on his folded hands. Marcy saw his eyes close and dared a quick scan of the man lying next to her on the beach blanket. He looked better than any of the men she'd seen in advertisements lauding the beauty of the white sand and emerald-green waters of Florida's coastline. His body looked incredibly powerful, his firm thighs, his solid curvature and his brief, white swimsuit all tantalized her.

Hesitantly, she poured lotion into her palm and began a tentative stroking along his taut back muscles . . . upward and then back down to the edge of his suit. Another dab of lotion and her encouraged fingers slid across the rounded firmness of his shoulders. Then she noticed it: the small, round scar tissue on his left shoulder. She gentled her touch as she applied lotion to the now-healed wound, wondering how he got it and thinking how much it must hurt to be shot. Not at all liking the thought, she dismissed it and moved her fingers down across his powerful biceps. So preoccupied was she that she didn't hear his soft sigh of contentment as her fingers caressed his strong neck, as her thumb strayed up into the soft, dark hair at his nape.

It had been a long while—too long—since Marcy had felt the power of a man's body beneath her touch, too long since a man had held her in his arms and passionately told her she was loved. As her fingertips deftly moved over Dan's body, she felt her own awaken to sensations that were but a memory, felt her throat tighten with the expectation of what it would be like to make love to Dan, to have him make love to her. She hated his gruffness at times, but it was that very harshness that intrigued her, made her believe that underneath that veneer of complete control there lurked a tenderness that he hid for some reason known only to himself.

"Oh, that feels good," he murmured. "Be a sweetheart and put some on the back of my legs."

Her hand jerked up from the lengthy caress she'd been giving his neck and shoulders. "You look tanned enough," she suggested weakly.

"Can't be too careful. Sick leave for sunburn is frowned upon." His eyes opened a slit. "Just a little. Please?" He closed his eyes again.

Marcy squeezed more lotion onto her palm. Why were her fingers trembling? Why was her heart racing? She brushed at the moisture above her upper lip—the sun, no doubt. Then she turned her hand over and lowered it slowly until she felt the heat of his thigh spread across her palm like wildfire. His flesh tensed under her touch. This time she heard his deep moan. She hurriedly applied the lotion and recapped the plastic bottle.

After rubbing what lotion remained on her hands onto her arms, she put her sunglasses on and lay back on the blanket, trying to control her erratic breathing.

Dan edged his elbow nearer toward her until it just touched her shoulder. "You'd make a helluva masseuse," he whispered.

With closed eyes, she asked, "Does that automatically go into my file?"

He raised himself up on his elbows and glanced down at her. His jaw tightened. "You're getting paranoid, Marcy."

"Uh-uh. Paranoid people only *think* they can't trust people."

"Are you saying you don't trust me?" He looked at her and saw that her eyes were still closed.

"You put me off balance, Elliott. One minute you're nice to me and the next you do or say something to make me crazy."

He looked confused. "What did I do?"

Marcy sat upright with her knees raised and looked straight ahead across the still Gulf water. "That remark you made at breakfast. About Ed Moray being my ideal man."

Dan rolled onto his side, bent his arm and rested his jaw in the palm of his hand. "You're very sensitive, Marcy."

Her head jerked toward him, and she pulled off her sunglasses. Her blue-gray eyes glared at him. "Wouldn't you be if the press had given you the going-over it gave me during the trial?"

Looking and listening, Dan decided that her eyes had the right amount of indignation in them and even her tone of voice backed up the premise that she'd been unjustly dealt with. Had she been? Watching for her reaction, he said, "You admitted on the stand that you'd been seeing Moray before he killed your husband."

Now it was her turn to assess his eyes; they were accusing. She turned back to face the water again, feeling the same hopelessness that had burdened her two years ago. Quietly she told him, "A drink with a friend, a dinner."

"The defense said there was more to it. You did, too."

"All right, a few drinks, a few dinners. What difference does it make?" She leaned back on her elbows, happy that there was only silence between them now. She'd been through all this too many times during the trial. She was sick of trying to explain, but she didn't want Dan thinking she'd been involved with Ed—not in that way. Controlling her voice, she said, "Dan, the defense thought the jury would buy a crime of passion more than it would an argument over the fact that Ed had found out that Robert was dealing with the syndicate. Ed's attorneys were just trying for a lesser sentence."

"All those meetings between you and Moray were friendly chitchat?"

She looked over at him. "Why would I lie?"

"Why would any woman caught in a situation like that lie?" He looked skyward and studied the wispy cloud formations far out over the Gulf. "I saw Keppler's photograph in your file. Handsome guy, wasn't he? Blond, blue-eyed. Should've been in the movies instead of into microchips. Would have been healthier."

A sadness filled her eyes when she said, "Yes, Robert was good-looking." Tilting her head toward Dan, she added, "He was referred to as the golden-haired boy of Silicon Valley," and then just the thought of him sent a shiver of loathing rushing across her chest.

Dan said, "Life with the golden-haired boy must not have been all that great."

"It became unbearable. I had filed for a divorce two weeks before he died."

Dan started to say something, but Marc[illegible] didn't give him the chance. "No more, Dan. Please." She put her sunglasses back on and lay down again.

"Sure," he said quietly, but he wanted to know more: wanted to know how she ever got involved with a man like Robert Keppler, wanted to know more about this general father of hers, wanted to know everything there was to know about her, wanted—hell, yes, he wanted her. His eyes ran the full length of her lying there. Why couldn't she have been the kind of woman he'd thought she was at first? They could have had a good time. But now that he was getting to know her better, he knew she wasn't just a good-time lady. He liked believing that. He wanted to believe it.

Yet, he had this nagging mistrust. *Why?* he wondered. Residue from the one lady he'd put his trust in—Hope? Possibly. Probably. Hope had run his emotions over the hot coals. Finding out she'd been seeing another man had made him lose faith.

But the woman lying next to him was different, he was sure. He wanted to reach over and touch her face, tell her that, but instead he asked, "Swim?"

"No, you go on," she said rather too quietly.

Dan stood up, adjusted his swimsuit and took another look at her prone figure lying there. Yes, he decided, he needed a cold swim. "Don't go 'way," he told her.

She lifted her glasses and peered up at him. "Without my keeper? I wouldn't dare."

His grin broadened, and then his entire face lit up into a smile that said more than either of them had been prepared for.

Marcy's breath caught, and in that instant she knew she would forever remember the face of the man looming over her; that even when she would reach old age, there would be a special place tucked away in her heart for this very special moment.

Then she watched him turn, jog down the beach, plod into the surf and dive headlong into an oncoming wave. He surfaced and then began powerful strokes that moved his body with speed and grace.

Dan's flesh tingled from the cold water. He needed the coldness, needed the exertion to get his mind off the woman on the beach, the woman who moments ago had looked so tempting that he'd wanted to make love to her right there and then. With the grace of a dolphin he dove under, resurfaced and continued his purposeful exercise until he was near exhaustion. Finally he lifted his head out of the water and shook his head violently to one side to move the wet strands of hair that veiled his eyes.

Glancing toward the beach, he saw Marcy talking to a young man with blond hair. A twinge of jealousy grabbed at him. With forceful strokes he headed for the beach and Marcy. As he ran out of the water, he saw her point toward the parking lot, and the man took off in that direction.

Marcy was okay, so Dan slowed his pace, and when he got to the blanket, he took the towel she held up to him. "Who was that?"

She answered matter-of-factly, "I don't know. He wanted to know where the nearest phone was."

"Oh," he said and then suggested they go back to the house. He wanted to get the tape of the caller to the Service.

They were near his car when she felt him take hold of her arm abruptly. She looked at him and saw that his attention was focused on the automobile. He had a serious expression on his face.

"Wait here," he told her in his no-nonsense voice.

Marcy watched him go over to the Cutlass, take a handkerchief from his beach robe pocket and remove a folded piece of paper from under the windshield wiper. He read it.

"What is it?" she asked, not liking the look on his face.

He held the paper between the handkerchief so as not to get his prints on it and held it up for her to read. The words had been typed.

Enjoy yourself while
you still have time.

"Dan?" She couldn't think of anything else to say, but her stomach did a flip-flop. Now someone was actually following her.

"That guy on the beach, Marcy. Had you ever seen him before?"

"No, not that I remember, but I wasn't even thinking about this business. Why would he want to—" Her brain worked furiously, trying to match up the face with those of countless young men she'd met in California.

"The man, Marcy," Dan repeated. "He was about five-nine, slender, blond hair. I'd say about twenty-four, twenty-five. Could it have been Dirk Moray?"

"No," she answered quickly. "Dirk was dark-haired, and he'd be younger. No, not Dirk . . . but—" her fingertips touched her lips "—Ed's other son was blond, like his mother was. His name is James."

"Well?" Dan waited a few seconds. "Was it James Moray there on the beach?"

Marcy felt the pulse at her temples grow stronger and knew it was the beginning of another headache, the same kind she'd experienced all through the trial two years ago, the same kind that had begun again in recent weeks. "I can't be sure. James was away at college when I was in California and during the trial. It was Dirk who had been hostile. He even blamed me for his mother's death."

Dan asked. "What happened to her?"

Leaning back against the car fender, Marcy sighed deeply and she said, "Ellen had suffered from chronic depression for years. One night she took an overdose of pills. Ed was devastated. He blamed himself, and then at the trial Dirk was blaming me. I guess he imagined that Ed and I had been seeing each other even before his wife died." She raised her eyes to meet Dan's. "We weren't. Honestly, we weren't."

Dan wrapped the note carefully in the handkerchief. "So," he said in a low voice, "now we've got two Morays to worry about."

The expression on Marcy's face turned quizzical. "Dan, you don't really believe that Ed's sons would actually do this to me, do you?"

When he answered, she didn't like the look in his eyes. "Imagine what they think you did to their parents." Dan unlocked the car door. "Come on, Marcy. We've got things to do."

CHAPTER FIVE

"MURPHY," DAN SAID back at the house, "make sure she stays put till I get back."

Still holding the handle of the vacuum cleaner she'd been using when they arrived, she asked, "Whaddya want from me, Dick Tracy? I'm only the cleaning lady."

Marcy stood quietly with her arms folded and listened to the two of them discuss her as though she weren't even there. Finally, Dan acknowledged her existence by turning to face her.

"I'm going to the office to put a tracer on Moray's sons, find out just where they are, or where they're supposed to be. When I leave, I want you to lock the doors. I'll be right back."

"When?" she asked.

Casually he told her, "I'll be back."

"And I'm supposed to sit here and twiddle my thumbs while you're out playing sleuth?"

There was that determined look on his face again, the one she hated. "Let's get it understood, Marcy. I am the watcher. You are the watchee. That's the only way we're going to get along."

Dryly, she replied, ‘‘Anything you say, Dan. After all, you’re the expert.’’

He beamed. ‘‘That’s my good girl,’’ he complimented, then on second thought he corrected himself, ‘‘good *woman*.’’ He left.

Murphy finished wrapping the cord around the vacuum. A smile curled her lips. ‘‘So, now you’re his good girl. The beach wasn’t such a bad idea after all, huh?’’

‘‘*He* enjoyed himself,’’ Marcy muttered as she started to gather some papers from her desk. Then she mumbled to herself, ‘‘Lock the doors and sit here.’’

Murphy didn’t like the sound of that. ‘‘You are gonna be good, aren’t you? And do like he says?’’

‘‘Like who says? Emperor Elliott?’’ She shoved the papers into a manila envelope. ‘‘I’m not his two-year-old son. I don’t have to take orders from him.’’

‘‘A son? He’s married?’’

‘‘Divorced.’’

‘‘Whew! You had me worried for a minute, Marcy.’’

‘‘Well, he’s had me worried ever since he showed up on my doorstep,’’ she said as she started up the stairs to shower and change.

Soon she was back in the living room, carrying her handbag. Murphy watched as she reached for the manila envelope and a legal-size pad.

‘‘He said to stay put, Marcy. What do I tell him when he finds you gone?’’

"Tell him to go stuff himself on tacos," she said over her shoulder as she went out the door and headed over to her blue Thunderbird.

On her way to the library, Marcy reflected that she'd gotten to know the reference librarians pretty well during the past two years; she was on a first-name basis with all of them. Knowing that she was a writer, they'd been jewels in saving her time by tracking down information she'd needed for various projects. Maybe they could help her now, she thought.

Once at her destination, she waved to Anna, her main stand-by as she crossed the reference room and made her way to the cubbyhole that housed the four microfilm machines and the steel drawers that kept in chronological order microfilms of the local newspapers and the *New York Times*. If Dan hadn't been so dictatorial, she would have told him she had thought there might be a way of confirming whether or not the stranger on the beach was Ed Moray's son.

She set her handbag and pad down next to the machine closest to the door. Then she ran her finger down the index labels on the drawers of the metal cabinet where the *New York Times* microfilms were kept and finally located the one she wanted. She pulled the drawer open and removed one of the hundred little boxes therein.

Remembering the exact day the trial had begun on was no problem; it was forever burned in her memory. Robert's murder hadn't originally warranted national coverage, but when the prosecuting attorney had introduced evidence that Robert was involved in selling top secret testing information of new integrated circuit chips to organized crime—well, that had gotten the attention of every newspaper in the country. She remembered the pictures in the *Los Angeles Times*—front-page pictures—of Ed and his sons coming out of the courthouse. A wire service had undoubtedly picked it up. It was worth a try, anyway.

Quickly Marcy threaded the microfilm in the machine and ran it forward. Damn! She looked away for a bit because the blurred pictures always made her dizzy. Soon, she slowed down the forward movement, checked the date, turned her eyes away again and advanced it some more. She stopped again, and there it was: March the tenth. She rolled it backward to the front page and scanned the various headlines. Nothing. She checked the first few pages. Still there was no mention of the trial. Again she ran the film forward to the eleventh of March and stopped at the front page. There was no mention of the trial on any of the first pages.

Marcy reached into her handbag and took out a handkerchief. The viewing room was always warm. She wiped her forehead and stuck the handkerchief back into the bag. She was just about to run the film forward again when her eyes landed on a headline:

FBI PROBES INTERSTATE LAND FRAUD
N.Y. BUSINESSMAN INVOLVED

She scanned the article quickly. It told of the suspected executive's dealings with bogus firms in southeastern states that were ripping off prospective home buyers, selling them homes that were never built and also selling unregistered securities. Allegations connecting the executive, Victor Lasky, were not proven.

Marcy sat up straight in the chair. "Land fraud," she said quietly, her reporter's nose itching. Why was she suddenly thinking of Oceanview Villas and Mark Godette? *No,* she told herself. Everything was so out in the open regarding Oceanview. Certainly the county commissioners would have had the firm thoroughly checked out. Yet, Mark had been so secretive about the upper echelon of his organization. He'd been happy enough with local publicity, but had shied away from national coverage. She recalled a story she'd done in California. An FBI spokesman had told her that far more was stolen every year by pen and computer than by gun. Marcy scribbled a few notes regarding things to check and people to see about Oceanview, and then she turned her attention back to the more pressing problem at hand—trying to identify James Moray.

She moved the microfilm forward again to March the twelfth. "Bingo!" she whispered excitedly. There it was, right on the front page. The picture she'd remembered of Ed and his sons coming out of the courthouse. But it was grainy. She adjusted the focus knob and then tried lowering the photo on the screen. She could make out Ed and Dirk, but not the features of the young blond man walking behind them. She squinted as she tried to see a resemblance between the young man behind Ed and the man she and Dan had seen on the beach this morning.

It could be him, she thought, but it was impossible to say for sure. The picture was just not clear enough. She tried to remember how the man on the beach sounded. Could it have been the same voice that was phoning her, trying to scare her half to death? She didn't know.

Disappointed, Marcy flicked off the light on the machine. She was just about to rewind the microfilm when Anna stuck her head in the door.

"Got a phone call, Marcy. . . on Fred's desk." And then she was gone.

"Anna—" Too late. *Who'd be calling me here?* she wondered. She didn't remember having told Murphy where she was going. But maybe she had. She'd been so infuriated by Dan that she might have said anything. Hurriedly she unthreaded the microfilm and placed it on top of the cabinet. Then she gathered her things and went to one of the desks in the reference room.

"Marcy Keaton," she said into the receiver.

"Who's the boyfriend, Mrs. Keppler? He's not going to be able to help you." *Click!*

She felt her stomach jerk, felt the blood rush to her head. Quickly she laid the receiver down on the desk and grabbed her handkerchief from her purse. She held it to her mouth, and seconds later she was in the parking lot, leaning on her car, trembling.

A BLANCHED-FACED Marcy opened the door to her house. No sooner had she done so when she was greeted with Dan's "Where the hell have you been?"

"Not now. Please," she said and closed the door behind her.

Dan took one look at her face and knew something was wrong. "What happened?"

Murphy asked, "Want the thermos?"

Marcy looked at her and shook her head. "Just let me sit down a minute."

"Fix us some coffee, will you, Murphy?" Dan said and watched Marcy walk over to the sofa and let her body sink onto it. He sat down on the chair across from her and studied her face. He knew it had happened again, but not where or how. "You got another phone call, didn't you?"

She nodded.

He banged the arm of the easy chair with his fist. He was about to read her the riot act, but out of concern for her, he checked his tongue. Instead he said, "They're going to throw the key away on that sucker when I get hold of him."

Murphy stuck her head out from the kitchen. "After I give him a jowl-lift with no anesthetic."

"Coffee, Murphy," Dan repeated. "Today."

"Humph!" Her head disappeared into the kitchen.

"Marcy, why didn't you listen to me? I told you—"

"I know, I know. But I don't like orders. I told you that."

"Okay. We'll do it your way...the hard way. I'm going to turn in my company car and take the keys to your car. It you want to go anywhere, you'll go with me, and if I have to, I'll tie you up whenever I have to go somewhere."

She just looked at him through slitted eyes.

Murphy came in with the coffee. "Hate to be a party pooper, but here's your coffee." She handed Marcy a cup. "It's instant." When she gave Dan his, she added, "You said you wanted it today."

"Thanks, Murphy," Marcy said, putting the untouched coffee on the cocktail table.

"I'm gonna take off now, Marcy. See you Monday." She picked up her purse from the table in the entry hall and turned to them. "The knives are all sharpened and the Band-Aids are in the downstairs bathroom. Have fun, you two." The door closed after her.

"Where'd you meet her?" Dan asked. "At a flea market?"

Marcy smiled, but her cheeks hurt when she did. She chalked it up to tense muscles. "She came recommended."

"By whom? AA?"

Picking up her coffee, she said, "By a very respectable agency."

Dan lit a cigarette and took a puff. "Tell me what happened."

She did, but somehow it didn't seem so frightening as she spoke about it—with Dan being so near. She told him about the photograph on microfilm, and said that she really couldn't be sure if the man at the beach had been James Moray, and then she told him about the phone call.

"Boyfriend? I'm complimented." He took another puff. "He must have followed you. Probably called from a public phone inside the library."

Marcy cringed, thinking of how close to her "the voice" had been. Then she told him, "Dan, we're not dealing with a weirdo or crank calls. Now he's calling me 'Mrs. Keppler.' Whoever it is knows me from California."

"I know, Marcy," he said, realizing he'd never really thought they'd been crank calls, though he had been hoping they were. Trash from the underworld didn't go around taunting people like her, following them, scaring them half to death. She didn't, as far as he knew, have anything else to spill out that would be damaging to the syndicate, and if they'd been out for revenge, she'd have been history for some time now.

He watched her take a sip of coffee, saw that her fingers shook a little—not much, but enough to tell him she was hurting inside. *Another woman,* he thought, *would probably have gone to pieces by now, but not my Marcy. My Marcy?* No, she wasn't his, and from all indications, he decided, chances were she would laugh in his face at the idea.

But he wasn't laughing as he looked over at her sitting there. *Damn it!* He was yearning; yearning to be close to her. He wanted to take hold of her, comfort her and protect her. He wanted to do something, say something that would please her, make her take note of him as a man. But that was a pipe dream, he told himself. His macho style had been driving her up the wall ever since they'd set eyes on each other. Like it or not, though, he was going to stick with her until this thing was settled. No one was gonna mess with his Marcy.

Without looking up from her coffee cup, she said, "Do you think they hate me that much?"

"Who?"

"Ed's sons."

"No sense dwelling on that until we know more about who's doing what. I talked to the Marshal Service in Los Angeles. They're going to track down Moray's boys, check on their whereabouts the past few weeks. Unfortunately, there were no prints on the note left on the car."

She smiled wanly, looked up and said, "I guess you people are pretty efficient."

"We like to think so." He watched as her fingers slid through her hair. The light from the wide front windows made the light brown sun-streaked strands shine, and he remembered the way her hair had smelled when he first held her in his arms, recalled the softness under his jaw.

"Dan," she said, "you were kidding about taking my car keys, weren't you?"

"No, I wasn't. I've got you all figured out, Marcy Keaton. The only way I'll get you to do the right thing is to make your life a living hell."

She straightened up in the chair. "What kind of psychology is that?"

"Behavior modification."

"Don't talk behavior to me, Dan Elliott, not after you—"

Both of his palms went up to stop her. "There you go again...trying to pick a fight. What's with you? You can't stand peace and quiet? Besides, we don't need two cars. Think of all the money we're going to save the taxpayers."

"But what about my business contacts? I may need to pick something up, and what do I do if you have my car? What if my computer breaks down?"

"What's the computer for?"

She explained that it was tied in to a client's main terminal and that she pulled updated information she needed for periodic stories she did for a trade magazine. And then she went on to give him multitudinous reasons for needing her car at her disposal.

He listened patiently and then told her, "You won't have business contacts for a while. Not until we find out more about the Moray boys, where they've been and if they're clean."

"You mean I can't even do my job?"

"What's so pressing that can't be put off for a few days?" He leaned forward. "Are you covering a summit meeting or something?"

She leaned forward, too, and placed both palms down on the coffee table. "Dan, my work may not be important to you, but it's all I have right now, and yes, some of it is important."

"More important than your peace of mind?"

She told him, "I haven't had that for some time now." Then she got up and went over to the fireplace. With arms crossed, she said, "The work helps. It helps a lot." Facing him, she told him, "And, Dan, I think I may be on to something very important. I was doing some work for a firm called Oceanview Villas."

"I remember your telling me."

"Well, there's something not quite right about them, particularly Mark Godette, and while I was at the library today, I came across an article about land fraud."

"Land fraud?"

"Yes, and I want to do some checking around. I mean serious checking."

He asked, "Isn't this Godette guy being cooperative?"

"Cooperative? He fired me."

"For what reason?"

"I suspect I was doing my job too well and was making him nervous. Dan, he's hiding something, and I mean to find out what."

Jokingly Dan said, "We'll get the FBI on him." More seriously he added, "Right now, we've got problems enough."

Marcy felt a twinge of resentment at Dan's disinterest in her job, but she decided not to pursue the matter further with him. She'd take care of it on her own. And perhaps he was right. She did have enough problems for the time being.

"Now that that's settled," Dan said, "what's for dinner?"

The last thing Marcy wanted to do was cook, but she knew if she suggested going out they'd wind up back at Taco Bell. "I'll have to go to the store." She reached for her handbag.

"Correction," he said, standing up. "*We* have to go to the store."

"Dan, I'm perfectly capable of shopping all by myself."

"Marcy, Marcy...that's not the point. It's my job to watch over you. Let me explain."

Here it comes, Marcy thought. *The big lecture.*

"You see, if anything happens to you, it doesn't look good on my record. If you chip a fingernail, there are reports to be filed in quadruplicate. If you so much as sneeze without me hearing it, I could be brought up on charges of incompetency. If you—"

"Enough, Dan. I get the picture."

"Good. From now on, think we, we, we."

"Oui," she said in French. Her eyes lit up suddenly. "And, Dan—" her face was grace itself; her

voice flowed like the softest of music *"—Quand il s'agit de baratiner, il n'est pas ton égal."*

"That was lovely," he remarked sincerely. "What does it mean?"

Her hand was on the doorknob. She turned and asked, "You don't speak French?"

"No. Spanish. I tried French, but it gave me a sinus headache." He smiled. "C'mon, what'd you just say?"

The smile she sent back to him was all sweetness and innocence. "Loosely translated, you're full of . . . hot air." She went out the door and strode defiantly toward her car.

"How about that?" Dan murmured loudly enough so that she could hear. "She speaks French, too."

Although it was dinnertime, the supermarket was jammed. Dan's eyes moved around the lines at the checkout counters and down the aisles looking for . . . he wasn't sure what—anyone suspicious, particularly the young man he'd seen on the beach talking to Marcy. If he were the caller, he'd have to be following her: how else would he have known she was at the beach and at the library?

Dan pulled a shopping cart from its row. He asked, "Want to push or pick?"

"You push and I'll pick. I'm not going the taco route again."

"No tacos. I promise."

Marcy started down the first aisle. He followed, obediently pushing his cart, watching paper napkins, coffee and sundry other items go into it. She stopped by the bread counter to pick up her favorite stone-ground whole wheat, and Dan pushed his cart to the side to let a woman with a baby in her cart pass. Dan looked at the baby, and the baby looked at him and reached over to grab hold of Dan's finger.

"You're a cute one," he told the infant. The mother apologized, but Dan said, "No problem. We've got two ourselves." He nodded toward Marcy. The woman smiled at her and continued on down the aisle.

Without taking her eyes off Dan, Marcy tossed the bread into the cart. "What are you doing? Living out some secret fantasy? Why did you tell her that?"

"I don't know. Supermarkets do strange things to me. Make me feel all warm inside . . . homey."

"Humph," was all she said in response.

She promptly turned and headed for the frozen-food section. After selecting several entrées, she told him to pick something else out if he wasn't satisfied with her selections, and then she headed toward the frozen vegetables. It wasn't until they were at the checkout counter that she saw the frozen enchiladas moving down the black conveyor belt.

In the parking lot, Dan was loading the trunk of Marcy's blue Thunderbird when he heard a woman's voice call "Marcy!" His head snapped up, and he saw an attractive blonde walking toward the car.

"Gloria," Marcy said, "I was going to phone you and ask for another rain check on our luncheon."

Gloria gave Dan the once-over. An approving glimmer shone in her eyes as she nodded to Marcy and said, "I don't blame you. Is this someone from that past of yours that you're so hesitant to talk about?"

Marcy again felt that uneasiness that always accompanied any questions from her friends regarding her "past." She'd been well-schooled by the Witness Protection Program; she had learned what to say about this new woman, Marcy Keaton, but she had never come to be comfortable suppressing her real self.

"Uh...yes," she said. "Gloria, I'd like you to meet...Charles Winters. Charles, Gloria Beckworth."

Dan's brows lifted slightly toward Marcy, and then he took Gloria's extended hand. He smiled warmly and said nothing. He wasn't sure what Charles Winters should say, but he was sure that Gloria squeezed his hand a little too firmly, held it a little longer than she should have.

Gloria asked, "Are you from New York, too, Charles?"

Sensing Dan's momentary confusion, Marcy decided to give him a taste of what it was like to live a lie. "No," she said, "Charles is from Colorado. He's a ski instructor at Aspen. We're old friends, known each other since college days...haven't we, Charles?"

"How fascinating!" Gloria broke in. "I adore skiing. We were at Aspen just last year. Were you—"

"That's not all," Marcy interjected. "Charles is also a balloonist...into hot air."

Dan's eyebrows went up a little more.

"A balloonist!" Gloria repeated with a certain animation. "Aren't you terrified drifting over all those isolated mountain peaks?"

Marcy asked, "Are you, Charles?"

Dan's nose wrinkled a bit. "Not really. Once you've seen one, you've seen them all." To Marcy, he said, "We'd better get going, sweetheart. Don't want the ice cream to melt, do we?"

Now it was Gloria's eyebrows that lifted at Dan's "sweetheart." "Marcy," she said, "*call* me and we'll talk."

Inside the car, Dan said, "Cute... very cute. Why didn't you tell her that I was a concert pianist?"

"I didn't think of it, but I knew you'd be able to handle anything. After all, you are a trained marshal."

That evening, Marcy was pleased that cooking Dan's enchiladas with her chicken divan in the microwave didn't ruin the flavor of her dinner. But the pungent odor of the chili-seasoned tomato sauce rode roughshod over her nostrils all through the meal.

Without being told, she fixed Dan his after-dinner coffee, and they sat in the living room together with their cups and cordial glasses of Frangelico—she, on the sofa, and he, in what was obviously going to be *his* easy chair.

"Push the arms forward," she told him. "The footrest will come up."

He did so and leaned back. "This is nice," he said, and there it was again—that caressing tone in his voice. "Dinner was perfect, coffee's perfect, liqueur is perfect." For a while he just looked at her, the waves in his short dark hair catching the golden light from the table lamp. His hazel eyes glowed gold and silver; his lips were poised perfectly, just asking to be kissed. They moved slightly to form a tempting smile. "You're not half bad yourself."

Marcy glanced down at her cordial glass as she turned it in her fingers. "You seem to be in a perfect mood."

"This seems to be a perfect time, a perfect place," he told her, his eyes languidly roaming over her face and body.

It was happening to her again. There went that insistent tugging at her heartstrings that occurred whenever Dan was attentive, seductively pleasant. A part of her seemed to be awakening, a part that had lain dormant for too long. *Why couldn't circumstances be different?* she wondered.

"You're a thousand miles away, Marcy," he whispered over to her.

His voice and the gentle tugging at her heartstrings were one and the same, she suddenly discovered and smiled. "Oh, I was just thinking."

"About these calls?" he asked, and then he answered for her. "It'll all be over soon."

Soon, she thought, *and then you'll be gone.* She looked up at him. "And then I can go on being Marcy Keaton."

Dan tilted his head a little. "Is Marcy Keaton so different from Patricia Keppler or Patricia Dodd?"

"I hardly remember Patricia Dodd," she told him, a trace of sadness shading her words.

"Tell me about her," he suggested.

Marcy angled her legs on the sofa and smoothed her dress over her knees, and then she leaned her head backward a little. "Patricia? She was an only child and a lonely child. Neither of her parents had a lot of time for her. They were too busy working hard at being strangers to each other. It was one military base in Europe after another. She learned not to make many friends at any of them. It was too difficult to keep saying goodbye to them."

Moving her fingers over the arm of the sofa, she continued. "The general lost himself in work, and her mother lost herself in drink, trying to numb herself against loneliness and boredom. They divorced, and Patricia was shipped off to a series of girls' schools, first in Switzerland and then in Italy. When she was eighteen, she was packed off to the general's sister in California. Then it was school again."

"University of California, wasn't it?"

"Santa Barbara," she told him.

"A major in journalism."

Marcy felt strange, his knowing so much about her, but then she supposed that there were things that couldn't possibly have been in her file. "Yes," she continued. "They were better years for Patricia. Graduation, her own apartment, and then a job with a newspaper. They were her best years." Her expression darkened. "And then she met Robert Keppler."

"Why'd you marry him, Marcy? It just doesn't seem to fit . . . you and him."

She got up, crossed her arms as though to warm herself from a sudden chill, and began to pace. "Why does any woman marry a man? I was in love." She faced Dan. "Why is everything always so much clearer when we look back at what's happened to us, at things we made happen?"

Turning away, as though probing her own thoughts, she said, "I guess maybe all those years of constantly moving and changing friends made me yearn for a real home, for some stability in my life. I wanted so badly to be loved."

Dan said, "We all do, Marcy."

But he said it very quietly, and Marcy didn't seem to hear him. "Robert said he loved me." Her brief laugh was low and nervous. "And he was handsome. You know, the California type . . . blond, suntanned. And he was wealthy. Prince Charming had arrived, and he swept me off my feet. During the first year I was unbelievably happy. I felt loved for the first time in my life."

Running one finger along the edge of the mantel, she said, "We had a spacious home overlooking the Pacific, and I was Mrs. Robert Keppler. I finally belonged somewhere, to someone.'' Her eyes lowered. ''And I thought someone finally belonged to me, but the more successful he became, the more Robert changed. He became obsessed with having power, became greedy, experimented with drugs, even, and I became just another fixture in the strange world he created for himself. Then I was alone again.''

''You're not alone now, Marcy. I'm right here to help you in any way I can.''

For how long? she thought. *You'll leave, too!* She turned with a quick movement. ''Dan, I think you should move back to your apartment.''

The non sequitur startled him. ''What?''

''I think it would be better if you did.''

''Mind if I ask why?''

''Yes, I do mind.''

''You know I can't do that, Marcy,'' he said firmly.

She turned away again, not wanting to listen. ''No, I don't know it.''

Suddenly she felt his hands on her shoulders, felt their warmth penetrating her arms, felt his hot breath near her ear.

''Marcy, things are going so well. We just need a little more time. Why mess up what might—''

''Dan, they're going too well.'' But it was useless for her to resist his touch. Her body rested against his; her head lay on his shoulder.

As she stood cradled against him, his arms circled her body. The intoxicating aroma that was specifically hers filled his nostrils. His arms tightened as he kissed her hair and he moved his face over the silky mass. Just the feel of her made every muscle in his body tense, made him mad with desire for the wanting of her, for the sheer joy it would give him to explore her body, to taste her mouth, to give her pleasure and to receive from her—to make her feel loved once more.

"You know you don't want me to leave, Marcy. You're lying to me, but what's worse, you're lying to yourself, and you're buying it."

Her fingers slid over his arms; the strength of them made her feel safe, made her feel desired, made her want to reach out to him and accept what she knew he was offering her—himself.

"I'm frightened, Dan," she said softly. "I can't control my thoughts anymore."

Just as softly, he asked, "Why do you have to?"

The beating of her heart was growing stronger. She was having trouble organizing her thinking. Trying to make sense of her confusion, she answered, "Self-preservation, maybe. Self-respect." The warmth of his breath on her ear tormented her.

"You're a marvelous mystery, Marcy Keaton, or whoever you are. It would take a lifetime to learn all there is to know about you." His arms pressed against her; his voice became husky. "Leaving you now is out of the question."

He held her tightly against his chest, and she could feel the thudding of his heartbeat. She looked up into his eyes and saw the fire in them, saw the desire there.

Strong fingers lifted her chin...and she closed her eyes. Her body swayed slightly, and then she sank into his embrace. Her fingers eased their way up across his chest—nervous fingers, searching fingers. Her arms slipped over his shoulders...and she leaned against his hard body.

Their forms merged as one as he brushed his lips across hers gently, slowly, tantalizingly. With unsteady fingers, she traced the strong line of his jaw, and then they moved upward over his cheek, back over his ear, and then slipped through the soft hair at his nape. Pulling his head closer, she opened her lips and welcomed his feverish tongue.

Oh, the taste of him! The sensual flavor of his breath, the feel of his lips against hers, the strength of his arms around her. Was she dreaming? No...life had been cruel to her, but it would never be so cruel as to take the reality of his embrace from her. It would never—

The harsh ring of the phone put a sudden stop to the beautiful moment.

CHAPTER SIX

FOR ONE BRIEF MOMENT they both just stared at it. Then Marcy said, "I'm not going to answer it."

"You have to," he told her firmly. "The more we can get on tape, the better."

Cautiously Marcy picked up the receiver. Dan was at her side, listening. Closing her eyes, she said, "Yes?" knowing what she would hear in reply.

A muffled voice, low and insidious, said, "Your time has just about run out. Goodbye, Mrs. Keppler. Pleasant dreams."

Marcy's fingers froze around the receiver. Dan pried them loose and then watched as she slowly took several steps away.

He put the receiver down and was about to say something, but Marcy spoke first. Her voice was filled with tension. "Goodbye? Dan, when is it going to stop?"

He went to her and took her in his arms again. Holding her in a protective embrace, he said, "Soon...soon," in an assuring tone of voice. "Right now, I don't have any answers as to why he's doing this, and to tell you the truth, I'm a little shaky on the questions. But one way or another, it'll end soon." He felt her go slightly limp in his arms. "Listen, why don't you go on to bed. A good night's sleep will help. I'll stay up awhile, keep an eye on things."

Once in bed, Marcy lay on her back very still, staring up at the ceiling, "the voice's" words echoing in her ears: *Mrs. Keppler... Mrs. Keppler... Mrs. Keppler.* The very name had been and still was a curse to her. She wished, as she had many times before, that she had never heard the name, had never met Robert.

A twisted smile accompanied her reddened eyes, a tortured smile brought on by recalling that when she'd married him, she had thought her life was finally going to change, that at last she was going to find real happiness.

Happiness. The years of happiness she'd experienced could be counted on one hand. Three years with the newspaper and her first year of marriage to Robert—a total of four years. Maybe that was all that some great design had allotted her.

She'd been sent to interview him. His firm, Silbide, Inc., had been one of the newest and shiniest in Silicon Valley. She had been led into his office by his secretary, and all the fanciful dreams of her girlhood days seemed to be wrapped up in the man who was introduced to her as Robert Keppler.

He had been truly a golden-haired Adonis; not merely blond, but golden. His hair had sparkled from the sun streaming in through the window behind him, and his skin had been tanned to a golden hue. His nose was sculpted to perfection; his lips were indecently sensual. But it was his eyes that were so unusual, so captivating. They were the color of a clear sky after a springtime rain, and they sparkled with an almost electric vibrancy that startled her.

Patricia Dodd hadn't at all been prepared for Robert Keppler. Nothing in her upbringing had trained her to protect herself from a man like him, nor, God forgive her, did she want to be protected. One look at him and she'd been smitten. She never quite understood why he'd been so taken with her. Her innocence, perhaps? Did devils relish preying on the uncorrupted?

Whatever the reason, being in his office was like being caught up in a whirlwind of fantasies. He was charming to the point of entrancement, gallant, sensual to the point of making her blush, and when he told her shortly afterward that she would marry him, Patricia Dodd felt herself to be the most fortunate of women.

"The most damned!" she murmured as she lay there in the darkness. She began yet another attempt to suppress her memories of Robert Keppler. If she thought about it, she'd go mad.

She rolled over onto her stomach and rested her fingers on her cheek as thoughts of Dan drifted into her head. It was true he made her feel vibrant, but she wasn't sure if happiness lay in becoming more involved with him than she already was. She was almost overwhelmingly attracted to him, but so had she been attracted to Robert at first. And what did she really know about Daniel Elliott? Why had his wife really divorced him? No, she would have to be extremely careful where Dan was concerned. She was much too vulnerable. What if the phone hadn't rung just minutes ago? How far would things have progressed between them? Would she have been alone at this moment?

Again she tossed about on the bed, restless and agitated. She had thought of leaving Florida, of using the name Patricia Dodd and starting anew, and now, grasping at wisps of ideas, she thought of returning to Europe for good. But that would be running away, and she was tired of running.

The night was long for Marcy. Her sleep was intermittent and troubled, but dawn finally did come, and the light of day did have a soothing influence.

Possibly because her sleep had been so erratic, Marcy awoke later than usual. It was almost eight-thirty. When she went down into the kitchen, she saw Dan's note taped to the refrigerator. He'd left early in his car and had taken her car keys with him. His scrawl told her to "stay put" until he returned. She tossed the note into the garbage can.

After pouring herself a glass of orange juice, Marcy sat down at her desk. She reached down into the side drawer, having decided to work on her article for *Interface Update*, a trade magazine for the microcomputer industry. But as she reached for the file, her eyes landed on the material on Oceanview Villas she'd gathered thus far. She took that file out of the drawer. In it were the notes she'd made at the library when she'd come across the article on the interstate land-fraud scam.

She glanced at her wristwatch, finished her juice, and then got her spare set of car keys from her bedroom upstairs. Minutes later she was heading toward the county courthouse to try to find out just what the commissioners knew about the Oceanview Villas project and Mark Godette.

"I'm sorry, Miss Keaton," the secretary told her, "but the commissioners are at the Southwest Florida Water Management District meeting in Hillsborough County today."

"Oh...well, perhaps you could help me. Oceanview Villas has hired me to do an article on their proposed development on Pine Island, and I need to know the status of their application for a permit to begin their operation."

"Pine Island?" The secretary's expression told Marcy that nothing was registering. "Are you sure it's Pine Island?"

Marcy said, "Yes," and watched as the young girl went to a file cabinet behind her desk and began fingering some folders.

"Nothing pending for Pine Island here. Why don't you check with the Construction Licensing Board on the third floor."

Marcy thanked her and left the office. The licensing board clerk was of little more help. He told her that no application for a license was on file from an Oceanview Villas, Inc., but that it wouldn't be until a preliminary okay had been received from the county commissioners' office.

She shuttled from office to office—Planning Department, Zoning, Community Development and Official Records—but no evidence of any inquiry had been made by any firm for a development on Pine Island. As far as the officials in the county courthouse knew, Oceanview Villas, Inc., didn't even exist.

Marcy's nose started itching again.

As she sat in the small luncheonette on the first floor of the courthouse, she sipped her iced tea and made notes on her legal pad. *To do: check rental office of building where Oceanview is located. How do they pay—by check? Which bank? Call Better Business Bureau, state attorney's office* She crossed that off. *Not yet.*

A quick check of her wristwatch told her it was almost one o'clock. After one last sip of her iced tea, she headed back to the parking lot across the street from the courthouse. Oceanview Villas would have to wait. *Interface Update* was still a paying customer, and their article was due in the mail tomorrow.

When Marcy returned home, she was relieved to see that Dan's car was not there. However, she had just closed the front door when she heard a car door slam in front of the house. She glanced out the window and saw a cab pull away. Dan started up the walkway, carrying another suitcase. Quickly Marcy put her handbag and notepad on the desk.

As Dan entered, she turned and smiled. "Are you preparing for a long siege?"

"No sense running back and forth to my apartment every other day for clean undies, and before you ask—yes, I do know how to operate a washer and dryer." He started up the stairs with his suitcase, but then stopped. "When I come down, I want the other set of keys to your car. I felt the hood. It's still hot."

With one hand on the bottom post of the stairway and her other hand on her hip, she said, "It's *my* car, Elliott."

Dan set his suitcase on the step above him. He sat down and said, "C'mere a minute."

She did, wondering all the way up the steps why she was answering his beck and call. When she reached where he was sitting, she glanced down at him, intrigued by the shiny waves in his dark brown hair and the whites of his eyes that reminded her of new snow as he looked up at her. Then he took hold of her hand and pulled her down to sit beside him. His arm went around the back of her shoulder...and she felt the gentle pat of his hand.

"Marcy, think of it this way. I am a guest in your home. That makes you my hostess. Be nice."

The next thing she felt was the warmth of his lips on her cheek. As he bounded up the remaining steps with his suitcase, she raised her fingers to her cheek to catch the feel of his lips before it faded, to hold it there for as long as possible. For a moment she just sat there, listening to the whistling coming from his room, and then she eased her back against the wall, wondering what was happening to her.

One nut case was phoning her and scaring her to death. Another nut named Mark Godette might have put her on the trail of something illegal. And now, the biggest nut of all had moved in on her, was up there whistling, putting his underwear in the dresser drawer. It couldn't be everyone else, Marcy told herself. Everyone couldn't be crazy except her. Maybe she was becoming flaky and just didn't realize it.

But no, there was nothing flaky about the way she had felt when Dan had just kissed her. It wasn't really a kiss: it was just a friendly peck on the cheek. A friendly peck? How could that set her entire body in a frenzy? How could so quick a touch send hot flashes rushing through her? Why had she wished he had turned her face toward his and kissed her properly, longingly, passionately? So much for her being careful around Daniel Elliott.

She heard a closet door close and sat upright. She stood quickly and hurried down the stairs.

Immediately she began working on the *Interface* article. Her own computer was tied in to the company's main terminal, so it was just a matter of retrieving the latest statistics and updating her material. Her knowledge of computers was the one good thing that had resulted from the time she had spent with Robert in California.

There was no more talk about car keys when Dan returned to the living room carrying his attaché case.

He settled in his chair, and, using the case as a portable desk, he began filling out what he told her were reports for the Service.

As she worked at her desk, she couldn't help but notice the shape of Dan's arms in his polo shirt; nor could she help but see how well his form-fitting pants suited his trim body. And she couldn't quite control the surges of agitation that swept over her when he would get up and use the phone, or walk by her to go to the kitchen to get them a cold drink. But she was determined not to be affected by his presence.

Then there were those moments when he'd just suddenly glance her way. She'd wonder what he was thinking when he looked at her like that. It wasn't a smile he'd give her, but it certainly wasn't a frown. It was almost as though he wanted to say something and couldn't quite make up his mind whether or not to say it. She was determined not to be affected by him, but she had to admit to herself that she liked the quiet in the room, liked the comfortable silence between them.

Suddenly her stomach growled, and she realized she hadn't had breakfast or lunch. "Dan," she asked, "how does lasagna sound for dinner?"

He looked up from his paperwork and inquired, "Who's cooking?"

She asked, "*You* could handle lasagna?"

"If it's frozen. Sure."

"It's frozen," she told him.

And he did handle it. Even a tossed salad was not beyond his culinary prowess. After dinner, as they sat in the living room, Marcy turned the conversation to something that had nagged at her during the night: Dan's divorce.

"Believe it or not," he said, "I work hard at my job. That was one thing Hope never understood. It's important for me to be good at what I do. I'd come home beat, and she'd start in on me. I never took her anywhere. We never had enough money to do anything. If I even mentioned that I'd had a bad day, she'd say I asked for what went with the job...tell me I could make more money doing something else."

He had the footrest raised, and now he leaned his head against the back of the easy chair. "It was never peaceful like this... just the two of us talking reasonably. And then she'd tell me I had no time for her or my son, little Danny. God, I miss him!" He grew even more pensive. "Hope and I just couldn't live together. The situation grew from bad to worse. And then when I was gone for a few days, she decided to get even with me—as though we were trying to see how much we could hurt the other—and she found someone else to take my place."

He shook his head slowly and then said, "Funny, looking back, I thought I was right, and she thought she was right. Now I know no one was right, and no one was wrong. Something was just missing between Hope and me: something had died."

"Understanding?"

His thoughtful eyes looked over at Marcy again, and he said, "Love, maybe."

In those eyes, Marcy thought she saw a certain pleading, a searching, a reaching out toward her. She had believed that Dan had never known an insecure moment in his life, that he was totally self-reliant; but in his eyes she saw that he, too, needed love, although she wasn't certain he ever would or could ask for it.

"Enough about me," Dan told her. "What did you do this morning? Where did you—"

The phone on the desk sounded its by-now hated shrill ring. Dan jumped up to make sure he had the recorder on. Then he waited for Marcy to lift the receiver.

"Yes... oh, yes, Faye." Dan saw the instant relief on her face as she listened. "Now? Well, I have a guest." She shrugged her shoulders toward Dan. "All right. We'll be right over."

Dan asked, "'We will'?"

"My neighbor, Faye Thompson. Her mother is visiting, and she wants me to meet her before she leaves. We're both invited, but we won't have to stay long."

"Informal?"

"She said to come as you are."

Marcy and Dan crossed the palm-lined lawn to the Thompsons' next door. Faye was a rose fancier, and the garden in front of her home was strewn with blooming yellow, pink, red and white roses that filled the night air, and their scent competed with that of the night-blooming jasmine that grew up and over the white wooden trellises that bordered their Florida room.

Once inside, with introductions made—Dan introduced himself as Charles Winters—Faye's mother, Irene, asked Marcy if she was a Florida native.

"No," she told her, "I'm originally from New York."

"I'm from California... Los Angeles."

Marcy's heart skipped a beat.

"I'll be returning home tomorrow," Irene said. "Have you ever been to California, Marcy?"

"No," she said, "but I imagine it's a lot like Florida."

Irene laughed softly. "Oh, no, no, no. Sand and water, maybe, but life here in Florida is much calmer." For a few moments then, she seemed to be examining Marcy's face, and her perusal became quite obvious. "I don't know what it is, Marcy, but you look familiar. Yet you've never been in California."

Dan had been talking with Faye's husband, Jack, about the current drought and the water conservation program, but he'd also been listening to Irene and keeping an eye on Marcy. He saw her pale slightly and realized that Marcy was probably thinking that the older woman could have seen the numerous photographs taken of Marcy during the trial two years ago. He excused himself to Jack and joined Marcy.

"Charles," Irene said, "I was just telling Marcy that I have the strangest feeling I've seen her somewhere before. I'm really good at faces. It'll come to me"

"Mother," Faye said, "Marcy has a complexion every woman would love to have. You're probably confusing her with someone you've seen in a magazine."

Marcy tried to look nonchalant, but inside she was experiencing it again—that fear that one day someone would recognize her. Living a lie had become a daily trial, a constant fear that around any corner, in any store, there was that possibility of being found out, of being exposed for who she really was. And the longer she had had to deny her real self, the more anxious she had become.

Dan said, "Marcy, I think we should leave." Before anyone could object, he added, "Irene, it's been a pleasure meeting you." To the Thompsons he said, "I'll be visiting here awhile longer, so I'll see you around." And then they returned home.

Dan locked up and then sat down next to Marcy on the sofa. "It's not easy, is it?"

She shook her head. "She was from Los Angeles. Did you see the way she was looking at me? Dan, I've been thinking about leaving Florida."

Moving his finger over the seam at her shoulder, Dan said, "It could happen anywhere else, too. Why don't we sit this one out together and wait until we hear what the FBI finds out?"

"The FBI? Are they in on this now?"

He nodded. "The Marshal Service works with them when necessary, and vice versa, and the Feds have a bigger source of manpower and can cover a lot more territory.''

Marcy had placed one of the sofa cushions on her lap. Absently her fingers had been rubbing across the smooth velvet material, but suddenly her inner tension mounted, and she tossed the cushion over the arm of the sofa. It landed next to the end table.

''Dan, I'm tired of being involved with the FBI, the United States Marshal Service and everything! I just want to live a normal life!''

Dan got up and went over to the end table. He was leaning down to pick up the cushion when a silvery sparkle caught his eye. He knelt down, slipped his hand under the table and removed a small object.

He stood up and put a finger to his lips. Marcy started to say something but followed his instructions to remain silent. He held up the object for her to see. It was a circular piece of metal the size of a quarter, but thicker, and it had a needlelike protrusion that stuck out of it.

Dan pulled a tissue from the box on the desk and wrapped the metal object in it. Then he placed it in the drawer next to the gun.

Marcy rose from the sofa and asked, ''What is it?''

''A bug: an electronic wireless microphone-transmitter,'' he told her.

''You mean someone's been listening to everything we've been saying?''

''Probably, and there may be more around. I'll get a debugging team in here tomorrow.'' He leaned back against the edge of the desk and began a thoughtful massaging motion at the back of his neck. "There's something not right here. A sicko wouldn't go to all this trouble, and if it is for revenge, it's pretty mild. I wouldn't bet on it being the syndicate or the Moray boys."

Marcy moved next to him. "What could possibly be right about any of this? The man's obviously insane. Weird phone calls...bugging my house. What's he after? If he wants me scared, I'm scared!"

"Why the bugging?" Dan said. "What information could you have that someone would sneak in here and plant that thing?"

"I don't know, Dan. And it *has* to be someone from California. Who else would be calling me Mrs. Kepler?" An ugly thought crossed her mind. "You don't happen to have a disgruntled employee at the Witness Protection Program who might have gone off the deep end?"

"No," he said, "I know them all. What about this writing business of yours? Any serious problems?"

At this point, Marcy could hardly think clearly. She currently had seven clients, and she tried to sort through them in her head, but with the phone call and the incident with Irene next door still in her mind, she couldn't concentrate. She shook her head.

"What about that land development project? That's big stuff, isn't it?"

"I'm no longer handling it," she told him and quickly added, "Dan, I'm going to bed. My head is killing me."

"Take something for it," he suggested, indicating his concern for her. "Tomorrow morning I'll get the bug and the tape to the service lab boys and find out if they've gotten anything on the Moray kids yet." He went to her and took her by the shoulders. "Try not to worry, Marcy. We'll see this thing through together."

Marcy tossed for what seemed like hours. Her half asleep moments were filled with questions, fears and confusion.

Suddenly she bolted upright in bed and quickly realized she'd sensed the reverberation of an explosion. She saw a red-orange glow dancing outside the window of her bedroom and she jumped up and ran into the hallway. Looking down, horrified, she saw that the front door had been unhinged. The drapes were in flames.

Dan came rushing down the hallway. His gaze shot toward the fire and then back to her. "Are you all right?"

"Yes."

He charged downstairs, rushed into the kitchen and came out with the small red fire extinguisher he'd seen there. He jerked the pull pin loose from the spray lever. The doorframe and the drapes over the wide front window were ablaze with snapping orange-yellow tongues of fire.

He quickly assessed the situation and moved in closer toward the flames. The intense heat washed over his face and his bare chest. He aimed the nozzle at the base of the drapes and squeezed the handle. A powder stream shot out, and he began a quick side-to-side sweep. The flames flared up momentarily on contact with the chemical; fumes and hot smoke caught in his throat. Quickly he moved back and started on the other end of the drapes, which were now a pillar of roaring flames. The sheer panels under the drapes all but melted away.

Marcy had already rushed to the downstairs bathroom and had soaked a large towel. Back in the living room, she saw Dan trying to control the flames around the doorframe, but the fire had begun to burn its way along the wooden baseboard and up through the fabric of the entry hall wall covering. She swatted the flames with the wet towel, but then she, too, began to cough.

"Marcy!" Dan hollered, "Your nightgown! Get back!"

She looked down and saw that the hem had caught a spark and was burning. Quickly she smothered it with the wet towel and moved backward as Dan used the extinguisher on the wall.

Marcy stepped farther back and used one corner of the towel to wipe her eyes. They were burning from the vapors and the smoke that filled the room. Looking over at Dan, she saw that he was wiping his eyes, too.

He'd controlled the leaping flames. The fire was out, but the fumes and smoke remained.

The sound of a siren pierced the quiet night. As it came closer, Dan told Marcy, "Get dressed and pack a few things. We're getting out of here now."

MARCY SAT HUDDLED in the front seat of her Thunderbird, watching Dan as he stood at the pay phone on a corner in downtown Clearwater. After talking with the firefighter in charge at the house, he'd tried to call the Marshal Service, but he'd found that Marcy's phone was dead: the wire had been cut. Now she watched as he finished one call, wrote something down, and then punched the buttons again. The second call was much shorter than the first, and she felt better when he was again sitting beside her, driving south along U.S. 19.

"Where're we going?" she asked.

"Someplace where no one will find you."

"Where's that?"

His smile was purposeful. "I'm not going to say...just in case your car's bugged."

She hoped he was kidding, but she wasn't sure. "You're being very careful, aren't you?"

"Right. I hate the idea of either of us spending any time in traction."

She said, "I've an idea."

"Lay it on me."

"Write everything down."

"Bad idea," he told her. "Get some shut-eye. We've a few hours' drive ahead of us."

Marcy leaned back on the headrest and closed her eyes, and she had to smile to herself when she heard Dan mumble, "Damn bucket seats." Moments later, she was asleep.

Dan turned down the soothing music on the car radio and began the ascent up the Skyway Bridge over Tampa Bay. Traffic was minimal, but every now and then he glanced in the rearview mirror and then over at Marcy. *Why the hell would anyone want to spook a nice lady like her?* he wondered. And she was nice; she was more than nice. She was the kind of woman any man would be proud to take home to mother. He looked over at her again. Periodic lamppost lights sent flickers of yellow-gold across her face. *It's a pretty face,* he told himself. *No, it's a beautiful face.* And the body he'd seen at the beach was just what he liked in a woman.

Get a hold on yourself, Dan, he ordered. *I've been through the romantic scenario, and it fizzled out. Let's not ask for that hell again.* His eyes turned toward the sleeping Marcy. *That's not hell you're looking at... That's heaven.*

He drove on in the night, and a few hours later he turned west to head over the bridge to Esteban Island off Florida's southwest coast. Once on the island, he'd look for the Whitesands Resort Hotel, the one the Service had recommended when he'd phoned and told them that he thought it best to get Miss Keaton out of the area for a few days. The marshal on duty had told him the Whitesands had above-average security. Dan's second call had been to make reservations.

He looked over at Marcy. He hated to wake her when she was sleeping so peacefully, but he stroked her hair and said, "Wake up, sleepyhead. We're almost home."

"Home?" she repeated, covering her yawn with the palm of her hand. "Where's that?"

"Right here." He pointed toward a new high rise with an enormous blue canopy suspended over its imposing entrance. Tall palms graced the sides of the building; plant-studded terraces permitted a view of the softly lit atrium that soared up the center to the top floor.

"This is home?" she asked as she ran her fingers through her hair, trying to obtain some semblance of order in it.

"It will be for a few days."

Suddenly recalling the bombing, Marcy pulled the jacket of her white linen suit a little closer around her body. "Dan, phone calls are one thing, but—"

He said, "Don't start worrying until I tell you to, Mrs. Davidson."

"Mrs. Who?"

"That's how we're registered. Mr. and Mrs. George Davidson."

Marcy pressed one thumbnail onto the other. "Dodd, Keppler, Keaton...and now Davidson. When is it going to end, Dan?"

"What's in a name?" he said as he looked over at her, but Marcy wasn't smiling. She was still too unsettled, too frightened by the chain of events of the past few weeks. And now there was another name to get used to, another false front behind which to hide the woman she really was.

CHAPTER SEVEN

THEIR TENTH-FLOOR SUITE was elegant, furnished in tropical style. In the living room, two white matching sofas stood in front of the gas-log fireplace. Maori-type rugs were scattered over the highly polished wood floor. But it was the bedroom that caught Marcy's immediate attention. There was no door or wall between it and the living room. It was a step up from the main room with only two large carved columns separating it from the living room. The king-size bed loomed out at her. Over the bed was some artist's attempt to be Gauguinesque.

Marcy stepped up into the bedroom and cast a furtive glance around. There were two sets of white carved doors, which she assumed were closets, a sitting area in front of floor-to-ceiling sliding glass doors, a cocktail table that looked like a large wicker basket, and matching chairs on either side. Her eyes flicked back to the huge bed, and then she slid open the glass door and walked out onto the balcony.

Sunrise had begun only seconds before. The sky far out over the Gulf of Mexico was still a blue-gray color, but even as she watched, streams of yellow-gold and orange splashed from overhead behind her and etched their way to the far horizon. Except for the earnest screeching of hungry sea gulls, all was quiet.

Dan was closing the door behind the bellhop when she reentered the bedroom. Nervously she fingered one of the plastic cards they'd been given when they checked in. It looked like a credit card and they'd been told it opened not only the door of their suite, but also the inner entrance door of the hotel. A doorman kept watch over the outer entrance. She remembered Dan asking how often the cards were recoded. He had seemed satisfied when the clerk told him it was done weekly.

Whistling, Dan strode past Marcy and went to the luggage rack where he opened his suitcase and pulled out a pair of pajamas.

She asked, "What are you doing?"

"Going to bed. I'm beat. Remember, I've been driving half the night." He took off his jacket. Marcy's eyes widened when she saw that he was wearing a shoulder holster; it wasn't empty.

"Are you always going to wear...that thing now?" she asked.

He patted the .45 and smiled a devilish grin. "Not when I'm taking a shower...or making love." He pulled the multicolored spread from under the four stacked matching pillows, and then he looked over at her. "Are you coming?"

"Are you kidding?" she retorted. Her eyes darted toward the sofas and then back at him. "And what makes you think you're getting the bed?"

"I'm paying for it."

"Uncle Sam is, and I'll reimburse him for my half," she informed him.

Dan sat down on the bed and half turned his body toward her. "You don't have to do that. You're a tax-paying citizen. You're entitled to certain rights, and protection is one of them in your case."

"You take the bed," she told him. "I'll take one of the sofas." She stalked out of the bedroom and plunked herself down on the sofa facing the wide windows overlooking the beach. She just sat there looking straight ahead, watching the sky brighten with the early morning light.

From the bedroom came, "You know, Marcy, you're more intellectual than I am."

"You want an argument?"

"You know, Europeans have different ideas about sex than we do."

She turned and saw him begin to unbutton his white dress shirt. Quickly her eyes darted back to the sunrise. "What brought on that great insight?"

"I'm being intellectual."

"I know Europeans better than you do."

She didn't see his wicked smile. "That's what I'm hoping."

"Don't you wish," she mumbled. Then, over her shoulder, she said, "You think you're quite a ladies' man, don't you?"

"I charmed a few in Brooklyn in my youth."

Silence hovered over the suite momentarily.

Then, from the bedroom, she heard, "You're not much on confrontation, are you?"

Her determination to remain silent vanished. Without looking in his direction, she asked, "Is that a plus or a minus?"

"Marcy, Marcy, Marcy. What am I going to do with you?"

"Nothing, Dan, Dan, Dan. Nothing!"

Why was it so quiet? She jumped when she felt his hand on her shoulder. From the corner of her eye, she could see his cream-colored pajamas hanging over his arm.

"Look, I need to get some sleep. I'm going to go in there and take a shower, and then I'm going to get into that bed. You do whatever you want to do, as long as you do it here. You leave this room, and I'll be after you with a pack of wolves. While I'm sleeping, I want you to write 'I will listen to Dan' a hundred times. Neatness will count."

His hand left her shoulder, and the sound of his footsteps grew softer until there was silence—for a few moments. Then she heard the shower door slam shut and the spray of water. She sat there for a few minutes trying to figure out if she was tired. No, she really wasn't. After all, she'd been the one who had slept during the entire drive. Suddenly she thought of Murphy. She'd have to phone her, tell her not to come by on Monday. She knew the housekeeper was worried about her, and if she saw the damage in the house . . .

Marcy looked around the room and saw the white phone on the desk by the far wall. Her hand had just lifted the receiver when another hand with wisps of dark hair on it covered hers and forced the receiver back onto its cradle.

"What the hell do you think you're doing?"

She turned. There he stood, holding up his pajama pants with his other hand. His bare, broad chest was heaving slightly; little drops of water dripped down the line between his well-developed muscles.

"I...I was just going to phone Murphy. Let her know I'm all right. She'll be worried."

"You're not going to be *all right* if you touch that phone again, Mrs. Davidson. Remember, you're here in-cog-ni-to. That means no one...I repeat...no one is to know you're here."

She watched as he fastened the snap on his pajama bottoms.

"That's inhuman," she told him. "She'll worry."

He ran long-suffering fingers through wet hair that stuck to his forehead. "I told the office to call her and let her know you went away for a few days."

"Oh."

"Please, Marcy...please. Can I go to bed now? I'm so tired my brain's screaming for REM time."

Quietly she said, "Go to bed," and turned away.

"You'll be good and stay put?"

"Yes."

"You won't use the phone?"

"No."

"You won't call room service?"

She looked back at him. "What if I get hungry?"

His arms went out to his sides. "I'm not going to do a Rip van Winkle number on you. Just let me have two hours in the sack, and then we'll go downstairs. You can gorge yourself."

She mumbled, "Go to bed, Elliott," and watched him plod off to the bathroom to finish drying off. Moments later she heard him slip under the sheets, heard his deep sigh of contentment echo through the suite, and then all was quiet.

She yawned, kicked off her pumps and curled up against the sofa's plush pillows. She realized she was exhausted from the events of the past few weeks. Little by little her eyes closed, but her sleep was light, and occasionally she would wake, remember where she was and then doze off again.

During one of her waking moments, she heard a quiet moan coming from the bedroom. It grew more distressed. She sat up and looked over at Dan. He was tossing in his sleep. Suddenly he shot up in the bed and yelled, "Marcy!"

"I'm right here," she said anxiously as she ran to him.

The look on his face frightened her. There were beads of perspiration on his forehead and cheeks.

"Marcy?" he repeated more calmly and took hold of her in his arms. "My God! I saw you at the door just before the explosion."

"It was a dream, Dan, only a dream. I'm all right. We're both all right," she comforted him. Then she went into the bathroom and dampened a washcloth. Gently she wiped his face and neck. He hadn't put on his pajama top, so she eased him back onto the pillows and ran the cloth over his shoulders and chest. His breathing was still heavy; his eyelashes still flickered nervously, and she wondered if his sleep was often so troubled. *The job, maybe,* she told herself.

As she started to rise from the bed, he reached out and took hold of her hand. "Stay with me, Marcy. Please . . . just a little while."

"I will, Dan." She sat on the bed and leaned her back against the cushioned headboard. "I'm right here beside you."

Dan nestled his head on her lap and placed one arm across her as though he were afraid of losing her again. With gentle fingers, she brushed back the dark waves that were disheveled and then began a soothing stroking motion on his shoulder. She saw the scar from his bullet wound, and suddenly she realized what Hope must have gone through. How many nights had she tried to comfort him like this? What Marcy didn't understand was how his ex-wife could have left him to go through something like that alone. *No one should have to face terror alone.* She had done it, but then Dan had come into her life. Now, however temporary the situation might be, she felt needed, important to him, and it was a wonderful feeling.

For a while she held him, stroking the smooth, warm skin under her palm, and for the first time in her life she experienced the comforting joy of intimate contact with a man—innocent yet intimate contact. His breathing slowly became even, deeper; she could feel the undulations of his chest as it moved rhythmically against her thigh.

She looked down at his peaceful face and gently ran her fingertips over the stubble of his beard. As his hold on her loosened, she realized he was asleep once more, so carefully she eased out from under his grasp, placed his head onto the pillows and pulled the sheet up over him.

She glanced at him for a moment longer, and then she moved quietly toward the glass door to the balcony, where she turned and looked back at him. His sleep was now peaceful, but she was troubled.

Slowly she slid the glass door open and stepped out onto the balcony. The sun was not yet directly overhead. She looked down at the white sand along the beach dotted with colored umbrellas, and then her eyes took in the vastness of the emerald-green Gulf. White puffs of clouds made the blue sky seem even bluer. Her eyes followed the gaily colored parachutes that were being pulled by motorboats...and she watched the people dangling high in the air under the chutes. She smiled at the youngsters frolicking in the easy waves near the shore, and then wondered if the people windsurfing really enjoyed it when their surfboards overturned, landing them in the frothy waves.

Why would anyone ever court danger? she wondered. Life was filled with it already, or at least hers was. She scanned the beaches again, but try as she did, she couldn't keep her mind occupied. She could no longer avoid thinking about what she'd been trying to push into her subconscious—her growing feelings for Dan.

This is crazy! she told herself. *We're so different. I'd drive him up the wall, and he'd age me long before my time.* She rambled on mentally, telling herself all the reasons she could think of to stop things between them before it was impossible to do so, but then an echo of his voice filled her ears, and she knew it was already too late. She was falling in love with Daniel Elliott, and there wasn't a thing she could do to change that.

Her lips twitched slightly as she recalled his kiss and the feel of his strong arms as they held her in that firm embrace. She crossed her arms in front of her and held her shoulders tightly, trying to relive the feel of his arms about her. Oh, the lovely—

"Hungry?"

His voice startled her. She turned quickly to see him standing by the open glass door, still wearing only his pajama bottoms, one arm raised and propped against the door. She looked at his face in amazement. He appeared totally rested, as though he'd had a full eight hours' sleep. His eyes glowed like opals; his smile, formed by those beautiful lips of his, exposed the brightness of his teeth.

She commanded her voice to sound casual. "Starving."

AT BREAKFAST, in the hotel dining room, she watched as he covered his scrambled eggs with black pepper.

"You must have a stomach like cast iron," she muttered as she began on her English muffin. For some reason, she had lost her appetite. She was having a difficult time thinking about anything other than him.

"Pepper is good for digestion," he said, "but these eggs aren't as good as yours. Toast isn't, either." He glanced at her half-eaten muffin. "I worry about you."

"Why?"

"You don't eat enough."

She said, "You should see me when there's shrimp in sight."

"Good. We'll have it for dinner tonight. They've got a shrimp fleet right here. Should be fresh."

"Anything but Mexican food," she told him.

"You don't like Mexican?"

"Not really."

He looked at her strangely. "And if I don't switch to watercress sandwiches, you'll withdraw your love? What do you want? A man or a trained dog?"

She put down her muffin. "What brought that on? All I said was—"

"We could compromise," he interrupted. "Do you like Italian food?"

"Yes."

"Good. I'll give it a whirl."

"Dan," she suggested, "maybe you didn't get quite enough sleep. What's this 'withdraw your love' business?"

He wiped his lips with his napkin. "You're a woman, right?"

"You noticed."

There was that erotic glint in his eyes again, that golden sparkle that sent electric shivers rushing across her skin. "I noticed." He chewed thoughtfully as he looked at her, and then he continued. "Women are always trying to change men, right?"

"Wrong. At least not this woman."

"You think I'm okay the way I am?"

"Except for occasional demented delusions, I think you're . . . so-so."

"So-so? What the hell does that mean?"

She took a sip of her black coffee and then put her cup down. "You're unpredictable and so—"

"Lovable?"

She warned, "Dan, don't start."

He stared directly into her eyes while, with closed lips, he ran his tongue over his upper teeth. Then he placed his elbows on the table, clasped his hands and rested his chin on them. "I think you're lovable, Marcy Keaton. In fact, I think I'm falling in love with you."

Marcy's palms flattened on the white tablecloth. Her heart skipped a beat, and she heard herself ask, "You think?"

"You'd rather I lie and say I couldn't live without you?"

She felt as though he'd just dashed her face with ice water. "No, Dan, I don't want you to lie to me. I don't want you to say anything to me. You're just like any man . . . not happy unless you feel some woman can't live without you."

A silence hung over them, a poignant hush during which Marcy ached inside. She'd wanted to hear him tell her that he loved her; he almost had. She'd wanted to hear him say he couldn't live without her; he hadn't. She'd wanted to hear—she wanted, but what did he want? It seemed obvious to her that she'd never find out; for, whenever they spent a few minutes talking, they ended up snapping at each other. The sad thing about it was that she'd been right: they were too different.

Dan finished his coffee and asked, "Are you always so testy in the mornings?"

"It's not morning, and I'm going for a swim."

She started to get up, but he grabbed her wrist and pulled her back down. "Not without me, you're not."

"Why? I thought we were safe here. Why are you being so cautious?"

"Every once in a while I'm wrong."

"Did I hear right?" she asked. "You're admitting you're not perfect?"

"Your memory's bad." He pointed his finger at her. "I told you that once before. You have to start paying more attention to what I say."

A slow burn started at Marcy's waist and worked its way up to her eyes. His finger was the fuel. Her father used to point his finger at her while dictating orders. Robert had had the same nasty habit. And now this U.S. marshal was pointing his finger at her, telling her what she could and could not do.

Her slow burn tempered somewhat, though, when she looked into Dan's eyes. She reminded herself that he wasn't her father; nor was he her ex-husband. He was a man who had just told her that he thought he was falling in love with her.

Gently she took his extended finger and curled it inward. "Dan," she said calmly, "do I have your permission to go for a swim? I like to swim."

"Sure, soon as I'm finished. Sit." Unwillingly she did. Dan took a last sip of coffee and wiped his mouth with his napkin. He felt awkward suddenly, almost embarrassed. He was sorry that he'd admitted he thought he was falling in love with her. He guessed that the ex-Mrs. Robert Keppler was laughing at him inside. With the high life she'd known, why the hell would she care if a civil servant was falling in love with her?

His voice took on a slight edge as he said, "You know what, Marcy? I bet all your life you've never lived more than fifty feet from a swimming pool. Bet you had a huge one in that home of yours in California. I can picture you walking around in that house, a showplace of understated opulence, I'm sure. Mrs. Robert Keppler, one of the so-called beautiful people of this world."

That hurt, and Marcy couldn't understand why he was suddenly being so cruel. She realized now that he was a fighter at heart; she knew she wasn't. Her eyes blinked rapidly, and her voice shook a little when she quietly told him, "Even the beautiful people of this world have problems, Dan."

Then she got up. This time he didn't even try to stop her. He just sat there cursing himself silently, remembering how wonderful it had been to rest his head on her lap when he'd had that nightmare. He remembered the touch of her hand stroking his back and shoulders. And the knowledge that they were worlds apart was maddening; she, with her annuities, tax-free municipal bonds and whatever the hell else made her the wealthy woman he knew her to be, and he, with his civil service paycheck and child-support payments.

Worst of all, he was jealous of a dead man.

CHAPTER EIGHT

MARCY ACCEPTED the cold drink Dan handed her. They'd been at the beach for about an hour. She swam and he swam, and they said very little to each other. His words at breakfast still stung. She couldn't understand the enigma called Daniel Elliott: so comfortable to be with one moment, and so hurtful the next.

Maybe it was her, she thought. Perhaps recent events were taking their toll on her tolerance level. Maybe she was only half listening, half understanding. Maybe she hadn't already fallen in love with him. No. That thought quickly disappeared.

"Ever been parasailing?" he asked, breaking into her self-examination.

"No," she said, looking up at the people hanging from parachutes over the water.

"C'mon, let's try it." He stood up and put his hand out to her.

"I'll try tacos again first," she said, happy that they were talking again.

"Always one to keep your feet on the ground, aren't you, Marcy?"

She shielded her eyes from the sun and looked up at him. "Go fly a parachute, Dan." Then, concerned, she asked, "Are you good at it?"

He chuckled. "I don't know. I've never done it before."

"Oh, great! And you want me up there experimenting with you."

He kneeled down beside her and spread his fingers on his tanned thighs. "Not if you don't want to." He glanced up. "Looks like fun, though. I'd hate to miss out on this chance to try it."

She asked, "What's stopping you?"

Tapping the tip of her nose, he asked her, "If I'm up there, who's going to look out for you down here?"

Smiling, she said, "Trying to lay a guilt trip on me is not going to work, Dan." She lay down on the blanket.

"How about making you admit you're just afraid to try it?"

She shot up to a sitting position. "Afraid?" She looked at the parachutes again and swallowed. "Who said I was afraid?"

"Well, I just assumed that—"

"You assumed wrong. Let's go parasailing."

Dan jumped up before she could change her mind. He took hold of her hand . . . and Marcy found herself jogging down the beach toward the chutes lying in readiness.

Minutes later, after instructions from the young man who had fit her into a harness that was attached to the parachute, Marcy looked over at Dan. His harness was being fitted. Grinning, he gave her a thumbs-up sign.

"Okay, ma'am," her instructor told her, "here you go!"

Marcy took a quick look at the cable line that attached the parachute to the waiting motorboat offshore, gulped, and took the few leaping steps she'd been told to take as the boat pulled away. The chute behind her blew open with an awesome snapping noise, and in seconds she was airborne. To her surprise, the sensation was breathtaking, just the reverse of the feeling one experienced on the downward plunge of a roller-coaster ride. With eyes still squeezed shut, she began to loosen her hold on the harness. Her feet and legs tingled in the nothingness. The wild rush of air that had brushed across her face subsided a little.

She took a deep breath, and through a slit of an opening in one eye she peered at the clear blue sky. The other eye opened, and she dared a glance down at the green water and the motorboat dragging her behind it.

After another deep breath she looked down to her right, down at the white sand and the dots of people on the beach. And then it happened.

She thought she was falling and let loose a scream that no one but she heard. Her knuckles turned white with the strain of holding on to the harness for dear life. But no, she wasn't falling. It was the motorboat; it was turning in the water.

She looked to her right again and saw Dan flying by in the distance. He was waving his arm at her, and although she couldn't see his face, she knew he was smiling at her. She watched as he dipped one way and then the other.

He waved at her again, and it took every bit of willpower that she could muster to release her right hand from the harness and quickly—very quickly—wave back to him.

The tingling in her feet became a throbbing sensation as her boat turned once more. Her heartbeat had slowed down somewhat, and her breathing had calmed, but she still felt as though she'd been soaring in space for an eternity. In reality, it had only been a matter of minutes.

She glanced around, looking for Dan again, but the wind covered her eyes with loose-flowing strands of hair. There were several other chutes flying over the Gulf, and she wasn't sure which one was Dan's.

Then the boat slowed down and headed toward the shallow water. She felt a sinking feeling in the pit of her stomach at the sensation of slowly falling toward the water, but it was a smooth fall.

The water seemed to be rising up toward her, and remembering the instructions the young man had given her, she began trying to run as soon as her legs hit the water. It worked! Then the boat stopped, and Marcy's legs gave way.

Dan and her instructor were there in seconds. She felt herself being pulled up by the arm as she spit out water.

The instructor told her, "You did great, ma'am... just great."

Her soaked hair hanging over her face, she tried to aim her weak "Thank you" toward him.

In a jolly tone, Dan said, "That wasn't so bad, was it?" Then he took hold of her arm and started to lead her out of the surf onto the beach.

Trying to catch her breath, Marcy said, "It was... fun."

"Fun? It was incredible! Just like a bird's view of the beach."

Back at their blanket, he handed her a towel, got his, and began to rub his face and body with gusto. Marcy sank down on the blanket, spread her fingers through her hair and smoothed it back over her head. Her sensibilities returning to normal, she looked up at him and said, "This is your idea of looking out for me?"

"You're still in one piece, aren't you? And you said it was fun." Drying his legs, he added, "You've got to admit it was exciting." He lay down next to her on the blanket, rolled over on his back and clasped his hands behind his head.

Marcy looked down at him. At his expression of satisfaction, she realized that he needed excitement in his life, that flying through space and looking danger right in the eye gave him a feeling of heady power. It was a feeling that she could never share with him.

"You know," Dan said as he gazed up at the cloudless sky, "I've never told anyone this, Marcy, but someday I want to go to Tahiti. Not alone. That wouldn't be any fun, but, I really want to go there."

"Why Tahiti?" She was truly interested.

"Damned if I know. Maybe it's just the way the name sounds." His voice caressed the word. "Ta-hi-ti. Maybe it's just having a secret goal, a dream that will probably never come true."

Still looking at his contented face, she leaned down on her elbow. "It will if you really want it to."

Angling a look at her, he admitted, "I don't dream much any more. Dreams are too elusive." He looked back up at the sky.

Marcy wanted to tell him to dream. To dream about her. Instead she asked, "What were you like as a boy, Dan?"

He gave her a quizzical look and then turned over on his stomach. He reaching out for a handful of white sand and held it in his palm for a moment. Then he made a fist and let the sand slip out from the bottom. "I was your everyday, average, rotten kid. I used to get into a lot of trouble. All of us kids in Brooklyn did. Nothing very serious, really, but I guess even then I needed to live on the edge of danger."

He scooped up another handful of sand, but this time he spread his fingers and let the sand slowly slip through them.

Marcy asked, "And your parents?"

He didn't say anything at first. Finally he told her, "They had a saying about going to the beach. 'April and May stay away. June and July swim till you die.' I always had to sneak off to go to Coney Island in March."

"Wasn't the water cold?" she asked, trying to picture the young Dan hiding a wet bathing suit.

"You'd better believe it." He looked at her. "But I did it, anyway."

"Rebellious, huh?"

"No, I don't think it was that so much. More like asserting my independence."

Marcy suggested, "And that's why the thought of any woman trying to change you drives you crazy."

His sunlit hazel eyes bore into hers. "Maybe the right one wouldn't."

Marcy looked away. She believed he meant what he just said; at least, she wanted to believe it. She changed the subject. "From the way you were flying up there, I'm surprised you're not a pilot...one of those daredevils who goes around the country putting on shows."

"I was in the air force for two years," he told her, "after Brooklyn College and some accounting at Columbia. I spent two years in military police, special investigations."

"Is that how you became interested in the Marshal Service?"

He rested his chin on his hands. "Naw. I wanted to do police work ever since my first Saint Patrick's Day Parade in New York. All those shiny buttons...the applause from the crowd. I got hooked early; it was just a matter of finding my niche. The Service was being expanded, and it seemed the logical place... either that or the FBI."

Marcy was listening attentively, but she was also looking. She liked the way his hair was reshaping itself into those soft dark waves, liked the way the sun was giving his smooth back a burnished glow and liked the way he kept picking up sand in those strong hands of his and letting it go again.

He turned his head toward her...and for a few tense moments their eyes met, examined and inquired.

Those eyes of his! Marcy felt as though her entire self was being drawn into them. Again she forced herself to avert her eyes from his steadfast gaze, and she changed the subject.

"So, you like police work. What else do you like?"

He leaned his cheek on his folded hands and flashed her a winsome smile. "Words that start with the letter *s*. Words like serendipity, simpatico...sex."

"I had to ask," she said playfully. Then she raised her knees and circled them with her arms.

"Want some advice, Marcy?" Dan asked as he continued to study her.

She laughed. "From you?"

"Forget about blond guys with suntans."

"Why?"

"Trust me."

Tugging a shiny lock of his hair, she asked, "Anything to do with your having dark hair?"

"Sharp, aren't you?" He reached up and took hold of her hand and slowly placed both their hands on the beach blanket.

It was such a simple gesture, and she honestly believed that he would never in a million years understand what it was doing to her inside. How could he, when she herself didn't understand it? With his touch came a feeling of being reborn, renewed.

Softly his thumb caressed her fingertips. His voice was low, musical. "Amazing what just touching someone can do to a person." He lowered his eyes. "My fingers touching yours, and I can feel a reaction throughout my entire body."

He did understand! Realizing that, Marcy also realized she had never felt as vulnerable as she did at this very moment. She wanted to pull her hand from his, but at the same time she didn't want to. She couldn't. Trying to maintain some sense of control, some sense of sanity, she said, "Don't say things like that, Dan. Please don't."

Quietly he asked, "Why not?"

She felt his fingers tighten around hers, and then she told him, "Because I don't believe in dreams anymore, either."

"Have a little faith, Marcy Keaton."

"In whom? You?"

"If not me, who?"

She eased her hand from his. Dan sat up and leaned his arms on his raised knees. She'd rejected him again. Staring out over the water, he said, "Americans spend some twenty-six billion dollars a year gambling." He paused and then he glanced over at her. "What's it going to cost you to take a chance on loving me, Marcy?" Her silence tore him apart. "What is it? Do you resent the fact that I can't give you the things that Robert Keppler did?"

The man's name jarred her and sent a surge of disgust tearing through her. "No, Dan," she said quietly as she started to gather her things. "I resent the fact that I've already fallen in love with you." Then she started back toward the hotel.

"Dan," he muttered to himself, 'vour worst enemy is your mouth."

Later in the afternoon, Dan stood by an extremely quiet Marcy at one of the boutiques on the first floor of the hotel. At one point he called the Marshal Service in Clearwater from a pay phone in the lobby, keeping one eye on the door of the fashionable shop Marcy was in. He wasn't too happy upon hearing that the California people hadn't reported on Dirk and James Moray's whereabouts yet, and he was even less happy to hear that the bomb at the door of Marcy's home had been wired to go off when opened but something had malfunctioned. "They mean business now," he told the man on the other end of the line as he glanced through the boutique window and saw Marcy smiling at the saleslady. "You say it looked pretty professional?'' He listened. ''Yeah, well those Moray boys are into electronics. We know that.'' Again he listened. Some good news. The door on Marcy's house was being replaced.

Dan gave him the false names they were registered under as well as the suite information and told him to let him know the minute California had information on Ed Moray's sons. Then he hung up, thinking that ''the voice'' could still be anybody—someone they hadn't even thought of.

THE DINING ROOM was elegant, with soft music, a tiered fountain, luxuriant tropical plants and attentive service for genteel guests. Dan looked across the table at Marcy. She was stunning. Her shopping spree had resulted in a silky aquamarine cocktail dress. The color gave her blue eyes a lovely sparkle of green, and the cowl collar, he deduced, was one that could be pulled down in front or back, depending on the wearer's mood. Obviously she wasn't in the mood to expose anything to him right now. Each time he'd tried to bring up their conversation on the beach, she'd cut him off. Just as that collar did. It dipped down at her back, only adding to the look-but-don't-touch appearance of her upswept hairstyle. The only jewels she wore were small emerald earrings and a matching piece at one side of her hair.

''You look beautiful,'' he told her as he lifted his Scotch on the rocks to toast her.

"I don't feel beautiful. I feel like I'm thirty-one going on ninety." She didn't, really, and after her earlier shopping, she had decided to forget the conversation she and Dan had had on the beach—forget that she had admitted that she loved him, forget that at brunch he had said that he *thought* he was falling in love with her. These were tense times, she'd told herself, and people did and said strange things under stress. Yes, she'd decided to forget. She could do it. Sure she could. He was a man and she was a woman, and the only thing they were doing was having a pleasant dinner together.

But her will was short-lived. Suddenly, as she looked into his eyes, she felt as though she were twenty-one. She lifted her champagne glass to return his toast. "Anyone ever tell you that you have nice eyes, Dan?"

"They came with the mouth and the nose. Anything else you want to know about me?" he asked with a flirtatious smile.

Now Marcy felt eighteen—playful, desired. "Something unusual I should be aware of?"

"My adrenaline level is particularly high this evening."

Returning his piercing stare, she sipped her cocktail. "My guess is that you thrive in high-adrenaline situations."

He rested his forearms on the edge of the table, exposing the sparkling silver cuff links just under the sleeves of his dark blue suit. "If they're the kind I'm going through this minute."

"Maybe it's the Scotch," she suggested.

"No, it's you. You're mystery, temptation and earth mother, all wrapped into one glorious package. I'm thinking of having your name tattooed on my tongue."

Her laugh was soft. "Your tongue?"

"Just so I can run it over my lips every now and then."

That unnerved her a bit. "Dan, may I say something candid?"

"Be my guest."

"That idea lacks finesse."

"You can do better than that."

She became serious. "We have to remember that you're just doing your job, that—"

"So I'm a marshal. Does that mean I've given up the right to be a person, a man?"

She ignored his interruption. "That when your job is over, you'll go your way and I'll go mine. We should forget some of the more personal things we've said. I already have."

"That's a convenient little trick, this forgetting business. You do it well, but then I imagine you've had lots of practice. Most women I've known would have—"

"Dan, that man over there." His eyes followed hers. "The one signing for his check . . . the one sitting by himself."

"I see him. What about him?"

"I've seen him in the building where Oceanview Villas has its offices. I know I have!"

He was all business now, remembering the phone calls to the Service he hadn't told her about, realizing that everyone was a suspect at this point. "He could have followed us, Marcy. Not likely. I was checking all the way down here, but he could have. I've got to find out what he's doing here."

Marcy steeled herself inside. She was tired of running, tired of being threatened and forced to flee her own home. She'd had enough. Removing the napkin from her lap, she placed it on the table. "I'm going to find out right now."

"Wait a minute, young lady. I'm running this production."

"Correction, Dan. We're in this together. Besides, being a woman, I have ways of getting information out of him you'd never have."

"I could beat it out of him. Could you?"

"And if he's not following us, what do you do then? Apologize? No. Leave him to me."

He leaned back in his chair, admiring her spunk. "Think you can play like you're on the meter?"

" 'On the meter'?"

"A hooker."

"Don't be crass. I know men."

"So do I."

"I'll be casual."

"But explicit."

"How explicit?" she asked, frowning.

"Make him think you're offering him the heavens."

"For God's sake, I'm just going to talk to the man. I'm not trying to be included in his will."

He lowered his voice. "Listen, you want to be a marshal? Lower that collar. You can, can't you?"

Narrowing her eyes, not sure if he was putting her on, she nodded and gently adjusted the collar of her dress, exposing the valley between her breasts. "Do I look like a marshal now?"

Dan's eyes rolled upward, and then he said, "Don't promise *too* much, just titillate him a little."

"A little," she repeated and stood up.

Glancing up at her breasts, he said, "Only a little, and don't worry. I'll be right behind you...just in case."

She leaned down and whispered, "Dan, isn't this entrapment or something?"

He whispered back. "You want to rid the world of sewage, don't you?"

"Not personally. I just want to get whoever this nut is off my back." She straightened up, adjusted her collar and went off to follow the man into the lounge.

Ten minutes later, she was sitting across from Dan again. He asked, "His voice. Could it be—"

"No. It's too...wishy-washy. But he knew I was with you. Kept asking about you and what kind of work you did. He was more interested in you than in me."

"Well, what did you find out?"

"He's a fashion designer. He has an office in the same building as Oceanview. He's here for a break from the 'horrible, horrible world of business.' "

"I suppose you told him I was a ski instructor in Aspen, Colorado."

"As a matter of fact, I did. What's wrong with being a ski instructor?"

"Never mind. We've got more important things to think about. Like how long that bug might have been in your living room and just who might have heard what was said."

Marcy thought for a moment and then said, "We talked about practically everything that's been going on."

Dan nodded. "Right. All about the crazy phone calls you were getting, the fact that I'm a marshal and that the FBI is in on this case now."

Marcy blushed a little, thinking more of all the personal things that had been said between her and Dan.

Blaming himself for not having had the house gone over, Dan knitted his eyebrows in self-recrimination. Then he said, "Let's order."

After dinner, Marcy suggested dancing in the lounge, but Dan headed her straight back to their suite, telling her he was expecting a phone call. They sat quietly for a while, and then he suggested playing cards. When she agreed, he got the deck from his suitcase and asked, "Poker?" She shook her head. "Knock Rummy?" Another shake. "Pinochle?" The same. "What can you play?" he asked in desperation. "Fish," she told him.

"Do you want to learn another game?" he asked hopefully.

"To tell you the truth, Dan, card games don't appeal to me that much," she said regretfully.

The cards went back into his suitcase.

Dan had taken his coat off and tossed it over one of the sofas. Marcy eyed the shoulder holster he wore as he went behind the bar opposite the fireplace.

"Drink?" he asked.

"No, thanks," she told him, going over to the electronic unit that was built into the wall. She turned on the radio and tuned it until she found a station playing soft music.

For a few moments, Dan stood by the bar, drinking his Scotch, watching her sway her body along with the music. He swallowed quickly, and then he moved to the center of the room and extended his arms to her. "May I have this dance?" he asked quietly.

Her smile was soft, alluring, and her steps were graceful as she went to him. After a few slow steps, she stopped. "Do you have to wear that thing?"

"Habit," he told her and took off his shoulder holster.

Once again she was in his arms, her body following the direction of the strong arm around her waist. They were both quiet as they danced, and little by little he held her closer until her head rested on his shoulder. Relaxing music lulled their movements.

She felt so comfortable in his arms—too comfortable, really—and her heart blocked any message her brain might have wanted to send to her. His dancing was smooth and easy to follow. She could feel the warmth of his body and her nostrils were filled with the essence of lime. The effect was intoxicating, and she inhaled deeper as her fingers again discovered the softness of the hair at his nape.

Dan sighed deeply and whispered, "I want you so badly my teeth hurt."

Without opening her eyes, she softly suggested, "Maybe you should see a dentist."

"I don't want to make love to a dentist. I want to make love to you, Marcy Keaton."

Still holding on to him, she murmured, "I'm Mrs. George Davidson. Remember?"

He squeezed her. "Yeah, my wife." His hand slipped down from her back and traced the curvature below.

Quickly she returned his wandering hand to her back, telling him, "We're dancing, not wrestling."

"What have you got against wrestling? We're consenting adults."

Her eyes opened. "I'm not consenting to anything."

He stopped dancing and just stood there holding her as he rocked her gently. "You said you loved me," he reminded her in a whisper.

"And you said you *thought* you were falling in love with me. Let me know when you decide." Was she getting dizzy or giddy? Both of her arms went around his neck for support; both of his tightened around her for sheer pleasure.

"If I say I love you, is that enough?" he asked strangely. "Or do wedding bells have to be included?"

Dreamily she responded, "I'd think about it."

He stopped rocking her, took her by the shoulders and then stepped back from her. "You put a high price on yourself, Marcy Keaton." He went back to the bar and took a drink of Scotch. Then he faced her. "What have you got against making love? Bad memories?"

She didn't feel dreamy any longer. "No, Dan. It's all a matter of timing, and yours stinks."

"Timing? Isn't that a lot to ask for a chance at a little happiness?"

"Is that all you want out of life? A little happiness every now and then?" She went to the electronic panel and switched off the radio. Turning, she said, "Dan, I've been lumbering from one crisis to another. Life and time are passing me by, but I'm going to hold out for the gold ring. The brass is not good enough...not for me."

His drink went down fast; he poured another. "With all the women in the world, I get stuck with one who's got principles."

Marcy wondered at his uncanny ability to say exactly the things she didn't want to hear. She took a few steps to the sofa in front of her and placed her palms on the back of it. "I'm sorry you're stuck with me,

Dan, stuck with the job they handed you, but I'm also a human being. And right now I'm a tired and frightened human being who just happens to be a woman." She lowered her voice. "A minute ago I felt desirable, feminine, and it was a wonderful feeling, but I don't imagine you'd understand that."

He gulped down more Scotch and said, "I understand this. A man puts his arms around a woman, and right away she hears wedding bells." His arm went out, and his index finger pointed directly at her. "I've been through that bit, Marcy, and it still hurts. It hurts like hell. I've got a kid who doesn't recognize his father and an ex-wife who treats me like a stranger!" He tossed her a thumbs-up sign. "But I'm making it, Marcy...the hard way, but I'm making it!" He poured himself another drink.

Now she understood what was eating at him, why he was hesitant about committing himself, but she didn't like his mood. It frightened her. "Dan," she said quietly, "don't you think you've had enough to drink?"

Angry eyes glared back at her. "Don't worry, *Mrs. Robert Keppler*. I'm not your enemy."

Sorrowfully she asked, "Just what are you to me, Dan?"

He stared at her for a minute with dulled eyes, and then he licked moisture off his lip with his tongue. "I'm your keeper. Now, why don't you get yourself away from me and go to bed."

With unsure steps she went toward the bedroom. She was about to go up the one step, but then she turned toward him. Her voice was controlled, quiet. "Dan, you're so sure about everything...everything except whether or not you want to take another chance at loving and losing. Look at your life, though. What do you really have to lose?" She turned away and went into the bedroom.

IT SEEMED LIKE HOURS before the living-room lights went out. Lying in the big bed, Marcy felt more alone then she ever had in her entire life. Helping Dan work through his bitterness seemed impossible now. She couldn't even help herself. With tears in her eyes, she muffled an ironic laugh in her pillow. She tossed some more and then heard Dan's heavy breathing coming from the living room. Sleep for her had been elusive.

Quietly she got up and put on slacks and a top. She started toward the living room, but then remembered to take her security card. Stealthily she made her way through the living room. Dan was lying on one of the sofas. He hadn't bothered to undress. The soft light of the new moon covered his sleeping form, giving his face a pearllike glow. *I didn't want to love you, Dan,* she thought sadly, *but, God help me, I do.* Very carefully she opened the door and closed it noiselessly behind her.

The beach behind the hotel was deserted. Marcy walked to the water's edge and sat down, hugging her raised knees, wondering just what sin she had committed to be handed the life she had known so far. Would it ever be different? Would there ever be another Dan? She tried to remind herself of all the mean things he'd said to her, but it was useless. How could she blame him when he was apparently suffering as much as she was? They had both tried marriage; neither of them had been fortunate. Yet she was willing to chance it again—with him. He wasn't. *Maybe,* she thought, *men hurt differently than women.* Then she thought of his son. Yes, she decided, Dan's loss had been greater. He'd loved his wife and still loved Daniel Junior, and he'd lost both. And Robert? By the time he had died, love had no longer been a force in their lives. By that time, she'd almost hated him. Or pitied him—she wasn't sure which.

She gazed up at the sky and watched the myriad of stars sparkle against the black backdrop and suddenly she felt insignificant, like one little speck of dust in the universe. *But this little speck has a heart,* she told herself, resting her head on her knees, *and my heart is breaking.*

"Marcy!"

The call was faraway, but she knew it was Dan's voice. She looked up at the building behind her. He was standing on the balcony, looking down at her, motioning for her to return to the hotel. She stood up and started to walk out onto the wooden fishing pier that jutted out into the dark water. The sandals she wore were silent as she slowly moved across the diagonal planks. He'd yell at her; she knew he would, but she didn't care, as long as he never looked at her again with so much hatred in his eyes.

She'd reached the end of the pier when she heard him running onto it. There was nowhere for her to go. There wasn't even a railing at the end of the pier. His running steps came closer, and she braced herself for the tirade she knew would follow. Glancing upward, she saw a cloud floating under the crescent moon. It darkened momentarily.

"For crissake, Marcy—" he started. Then there was silence. The cloud had passed, and the moonlight suddenly revealed a man, and sparkled on something he held in his hand.

Marcy felt herself being jerked down to the wooden walkway. She heard a couple of quick hissing sounds and saw the wooden side railing just above her head splinter. In a second, Dan pulled his .45 from his shoulder holster. The next thing Marcy knew, she was falling into space. Gunshots echoed in her ears.

CHAPTER NINE

MARCY'S REAR END HIT the water first. It wasn't a very dignified way of falling, but it was safer than many of the other ways she could have gone after Dan had pushed her off the pier. When her head bobbed up from the murky water, she sputtered, went under again and then resurfaced. The shooting had stopped. She heard splashing sounds; a body was cutting through the water near her. In moments, strong arms were holding her.

"Are you okay?" Dan asked anxiously as he treaded water next to her.

She was still spewing water from her mouth. "I think so."

"Thank God," he muttered, and then he started swimming toward the shore, his right arm arched around her throat in perfect lifeguard form.

Surprised by the strong grip around her throat, Marcy swallowed more water. Gasping for breath, she tried to speak. "Wh...what do you th...think you're doing?"

Dan began treading water again. "I'm saving your life, damn it!"

She pushed at the wet strands covering her eyes. "Dan, I *know* how to swim. Did you have to push me off the pier so hard?"

"Marcy, I'm not going to spend the rest of my life in here trying to grow gills explaining it to you. Didn't you hear the shots? He was using a silencer."

She looked over at him. "Thanks, Dan," she said.

"C'mon, let's get out of here."

"You're sure he's gone?"

"I hope he is, but someone's bound to have heard my shots and phoned the police. The last thing we need is publicity."

He told her to follow him at a distance, and they swam to shore.

Up in their suite, Dan showered first. It made sense since he'd be quicker, Marcy had told him. But once he had assured himself that Marcy was really all right, his blood began to heat up, and while she was showering, he boiled over. Into the bathroom he stomped, wearing only his white briefs.

"Lady, if you ever try that solo crap again, I'll kill you!" He paced to-and-fro in front of the steam-laden glass shower doors, waving an angry arm in her direction. "If anything happens to you, I'm going to have to live with it the rest of my life!"

From behind the shower doors came, "Dan, get out of here!"

"Not until I'm finished. Now hear this, Marcy Keaton. From now on you don't even go to the bathroom without my permission."

"I *am* in the bathroom, and so are you. Get out!"

Dan stretched one arm up and leaned it against the wall; his other hand rested on his hip. "You're not listening to me again," he said patiently. "Look, the guy after you is a killer. Mr. Nasty won't care how many holes he plugs into you."

"Get out, Dan. I mean now, and close the door after you."

She waited for the sound of the door closing, but all she heard was his electric razor. She knelt in the corner of the tub and let the water from the shower head pummel her body. Not until she actually heard the door close did she get up, finish her shower, and blow-dry her hair.

When Marcy emerged from the bathroom, she was wearing a long white terry robe; her wet hair glistened as did her angry eyes. She took a quick glance around to find her target. He was standing at the bar in his short beach robe, pouring something into two small glasses.

"What am I, Dan? A nonperson? How dare you—"

"Marcy, be quiet," he said calmly. He walked over to where she was standing, just in front of one of the sofas, gave her a little push, and she plopped down. "Drink this. It'll ward off pneumonia."

She refused the glass. "Funny, isn't it? You make all the rules."

He glared down at her. ''I don't *make* the rules, but I am paid to shove them down your throat.'' He held the little glass out to her again.

''What's this you're trying to shove down my throat now?''

''Scotch. It'll warm up your insides.''

Marcy finally succumbed, and they drank together in silence. When they had finished, he placed their glasses on the bar and returned to the sofa next to her. Gently he placed his arm around her and pulled her closer to him. ''Marcy, I can't take much more of this being at odds with each other.''

She didn't want his arm around her to feel so good, but it did. She looked at him. ''Were we ever at evens?''

''The night I kissed you we were.''

She cringed inside, not wanting to remember that, not wanting to think of the way his lips had felt. She started to pull away from him, but his arm was like iron. ''There's nothing worse than someone who will take advantage of another person's vulnerable moments,'' she said quietly.

Again she tried to move; again he tightened his grip on her. ''Dan,'' she said uncomfortably. ''This isn't fair.''

''Why not?''

She snuggled closer and began toying with the end of the belt of her robe. ''It makes it more difficult for me to stay mad at you.''

''Why would you want to do that?''

Because I have to, for my own sake, she said to herself, but to him, she said, "If I didn't, you'd walk all over me with your orders."

"You've got to do what I tell you. I'm a trained marshal."

An easy smile formed on her lips. "Can I get a second opinion on that?"

Looking down at her, he ran his fingers over her lips. "Don't smile like that."

Marcy felt his hand move slowly up and down her arm and decided it was time to change the subject. "Dan, that man on the beach. He was trying to kill me, wasn't he?"

He kissed her hair and held her a little tighter. "He didn't, though."

"When you fired back, were you able to get a good look at his face? Was he the man I saw on the beach or the man I talked to in the lounge?"

"No, in both cases. The guy that shot at you was younger than the man in the lounge, and he had dark hair. Male Caucasian, about five-ten, one-sixty, wearing a safari shirt. He was left-handed."

Marcy felt her throat tighten. "Dirk?"

"Could have been. I didn't see his face. It was too dark, and he ran like a lizard when I shot back. Until we hear from the California office, we're going to have to be very careful." The lines in his forehead deepened. "I get this feeling, though, that the guy who shot at us was hired muscle—the silencer, the way he picked just the right time, no witnesses. . . ."

Marcy sat up straight and looked into Dan's concerned eyes. "You said 'us.' I thought he was after me."

He brushed back a lock of stray hair that had fallen over her eyes. "If he had just wanted you, Marcy, why didn't he take you when you were sitting alone on the beach?"

The thought of herself getting shot was enough to petrify her, but the thought of Dan getting killed because of her almost froze her blood.

Dan said, "What I don't understand is how he knew we were here. I was so careful on the way. I was sure we weren't being followed. If we had been, I should've seen headlights in—"

Suddenly he jumped up and ran into the bedroom. Marcy watched as he put the .45 into the pocket of his robe and shoved his security card into the other pocket.

"Stay put," he told her. "I'll be right back. And don't open this door for anyone."

In five minutes he was back, carrying a small metal box in his hand. "An electronic beeper," he told her, holding it up. "It was under the back of your car." Then he was busy punching digits on the phone. Seconds later, she listened as he gave a concise report of what had happened. Then she heard him say, "Still no word from California? Damn! I'm getting her out of here. I'll contact you when I'm sure I have a clean line." He hung up. "Get packed, Marcy. We're moving on."

"At two in the morning? Whatever happened to a good night's sleep?"

"Now, Marcy."

She placed both her hands on the edge of the sofa cushion and leaned forward. "Dan, can't we just forget this whole thing? I'll go live somewhere else, become someone else." Again she felt the sting of fear at the thought of his getting hurt.

He was already busy packing his own suitcase. From the bedroom, he called, "You don't just walk away from a killer. Now, pack!"

She joined him in the bedroom. "Dan, I don't want you getting shot at anymore because of me."

"And I don't want you getting shot at at all." He tossed one of her suitcases down from the luggage rack. "Start packing, or I'll pack for you. You've never seen me pack a woman's suitcase. You wouldn't like it, Marcy. It's not a pretty sight."

"I thought you said this would be an easy case, Dan," she reminded him as she began to take some things from a dresser drawer.

"I lied. Hurry up."

"I suppose if I said I wasn't going, you'd force me to."

"If that's what it takes, my little marshalette. Get the picture? Now pack . . . nice and peaceful like."

Fifteen minutes later, they were driving south. She insisted that she drive, after telling him that with all that Scotch in him, he'd fail any breath test, and also that he needed sleep since he now had two people to protect.

"Don't dillydally," he told her as he leaned back to catch a few winks. "Just follow U.S. 41 south and then east."

About an hour later, his eyes snapped open as he felt the car lurch far to the left. Marcy was passing a semitrailer. He glanced over at the speedometer. She was doing eighty. His hands dug into the dashboard. "For crissake, woman, slow down!"

"You said not to dillydally."

They both heard the blare of the trailer's angry horn as she pulled in front of it and continued down the highway.

Stoically, he said, "Pull over, Marcy."

"Why? I'm not tired."

"Pull over," he repeated, "or I'll tear the gearshift out of the damn car."

She knew he would, so she started to pull off the road. Quickly he grabbed the wheel and steered the car back onto the highway. "Not here!" He forced a calm voice. "Didn't you see that sign back there...soft shoulder? Just wait until we see a side road."

A few minutes later, he said, "There's one. Turn off." She did. Once the car was stationary, he looked over at her and smiled. "Well...we cheated death once again."

With Dan behind the wheel, they started down U.S. 41 once more, going a little slower this time.

Marcy asked, "Where are we headed now?"

"The only place I can think of where you won't be able to go wandering off without me."

"Where's that?"

"You'll see."

CHAPTER TEN

"WHAT HAVE YOU GOT AGAINST graceful dining, Dan?" Marcy asked as she glanced around the noisy and crowded delicatessen he'd chosen for breakfast once they'd reached Miami.

"We're eating on taxpayers' money. Gotta watch the pesos. Splurges bring out the beast in the guys in accounting...the Whitesands bill is going to short-circuit their adding machines."

"Lunch is on me, then," she said as she peered at the menu.

"Might not have to worry about that," he told her and then suggested, "Try the buffalo sausage or alligator tails. They're fabulous."

Her face contorted. "For breakfast?"

"Sure. You can't spend the rest of your life eating scrambled eggs every morning."

"I happen to like scrambled eggs, unless they're camouflaged under black pepper the way you eat them." She paused and then asked, "What did you mean when you said we might not have to worry about lunch?"

"We're going on a cruise," he answered casually.

"Who is?"

"You and me, that's who."

"What if I don't want to go on a cruise?"

"You do."

"Who says?"

"I do," he told her firmly. "As soon as we order, I'm going to visit the travel agency next door and see if I can get us out of here today."

Patiently she asked, "Dan, why this sudden desire for an ocean voyage?"

"Necessity is the father of invention."

"The mother," she corrected.

"Whoever. With miles of water around you, I'll know where you are. You won't be getting into trouble running off to a library or onto a dark pier in the middle of the night."

Marcy thought about it for a moment, and suddenly her features softened, and the corners of her mouth curved upward just a tad. The idea of a cruise with Dan didn't seem all that bad. Not at all. In fact, the more she thought about it, the more she liked it. There'd be lots of dining and dancing and moonlight walks around the deck. Yes, it was beginning to seem like a smashing idea.

Her glee was short-lived, however. After they ordered, Dan went next door to the travel agency. His face wasn't at all enthusiastic when he returned to the table a few minutes later.

"You don't look happy," she told him. "Problems?"

"The clerk laughed at me. All those cruise ships lined up out there, and the soonest we can get on one is next week."

"Not even one stateroom?"

He started in on his alligator tails. "They have one, all right . . . a cancellation for what he called a 'penthouse suite.' Has its own living room, a TV . . . even a refrigerator. That's more than I had in my first apartment."

"What's wrong with it? It sounds great to me. Why didn't you book us?"

Dan wiped his mouth and stared at her. "For a week, it costs more than I make in a month. The guys in accounting would go to the moon, and I'd wind up pasting in mug shots somewhere in South Dakota for the rest of my life if I sent in a charge like that. That's why."

"Oh." Her mind clicked away furiously. What if the man on the pier had shot Dan? Deciding that one scar from a bullet was enough for him, she picked up her handbag and stood up.

He dropped his fork and asked, "Where do you think you're going?"

"Somewhere you can't come with me." Pointing to his plate, she said, "Wrestle with your alligator. I'll be right back to see who wins."

After ten or so minutes had passed, Dan started to get nervous and was just about to get up and head toward the ladies' room when he saw her walking toward their table. She had the look of the proverbial cat who'd just done away with the canary.

"Your eggs are cold," he said, not liking the gloat of satisfaction on her face.

Marcy picked up her fork and snatched a piece of alligator tail from his plate. She rolled it around inside her mouth and enjoyed his suspicious expression. Finally she chewed and swallowed. "Not bad," she commented and quickly washed it down with a sip of black coffee. "Do you get seasick, Dan?"

"No, do you?"

"Sometimes."

He had that gut feeling again. "What's with the medical history, Marcy?"

She sipped some more coffee and said, "You'd be no fun on a cruise if seasickness was one of your shortcomings."

He lit a cigarette and blew a stream of smoke off to the side. "But we're not going on a cruise," he reminded her.

"But we are," she corrected. "I just booked us for the penthouse suite. We leave at four-thirty this afternoon. Give us plenty of time to—"

"To sober up! I told you the Service won't pay for a luxury junket."

"This one's on me, Dan," she informed him with a gleam in her eyes.

He gave his cigarette a final crush in the ashtray. "Please, don't tell me you're carrying that much money on you."

"Not quite, but a checkbook and a quick phone call to my bank worked just like magic."

He still didn't like it. "Marcy, spending that much money makes me crazy."

"Treat it as a learning experience," she told him, thinking, *This time you'll take orders from me, Daniel Elliott!*

THE PENTHOUSE SUITE was aptly named. It had a living room, full bath with shower, a vanity console, TV and a refrigerator. Marcy eyed the huge bed and then the small sofa. Her eyes returned to the bed before she looked over at Dan.

"Isn't this something?" Dan remarked as he looked around the elegantly appointed rooms.

Marcy began unpacking the things she'd brought with her from the hotel, one of which was a gift she'd bought for Dan. She'd picked out a short gold chain with an anchor on it, a token she would give him when the time was right.

"We stay in here until the ship leaves," he told her, still peering out the wide window that overlooked the water.

Cheerfully she said, "You're the boss."

He turned. "When did you start becoming so agreeable?"

"Why fight fate?" she said sweetly as she hung up one of her new purchases, a white chiffon cocktail dress.

"Fate?" He glanced around the suite. "When I phoned the office, the guys called it luck." He laughed. "I'll bet right now someone in Clearwater is trying to get a fistful of court orders to check out my apartment and gym locker. They probably think I've been on the take and have millions stashed away." In reality, when he'd phoned the office, he'd been given several alternative places to stash Marcy Keaton, and he'd had to convince them the ship would be the safest place for her just now. The fact that she was paying for it didn't hurt his argument. Yet, in his heart, Dan knew the real reason he wanted to go on the cruise was that he wanted to be somewhere with her where she couldn't run from him. And unless she walked on water, this was the place.

Marcy looked at his reflection in the mirror over the vanity. "Didn't you tell them I was paying for it?"

He looked back at her in the mirror. He had reported that fact, but he told her, "Listen, the guys can see that I'm okay looking, but they don't think I'm good-looking enough to be taken on a cruise by a lovely lady."

Yes you are, her heart whispered silently as she continued to study him in the looking glass. Suddenly her thoughts were filled with him, with concern for his happiness and his safety. *Please, God,* she prayed silently, *let him love me as much as I love him.*

Dining on the cruise ship that evening was a complete success as far as Marcy was concerned: there wasn't a taco in sight. Their dinner companions were genial, and she enjoyed her duck *à l'orange*. Dan attacked his lobster thermidor with gusto.

After dinner he suggested trying the casino or catching the singer in the main lounge, but Marcy opted for a walk on deck. She told him she loved the feel of a clean ocean breeze, but in her heart she knew she didn't want to share him with so many people on their first night at sea.

The evening was perfect. The moon showered the smooth water of the Caribbean with silver jewels. The ship's pace was easy; the drone of the parting water sounded more like leaves rustling in a soft breeze. The tangy smell of the salt air mingled with the aroma of Dan's lime after-shave. Marcy was content.

She stopped and leaned her arm on the railing. She gazed up at the stars, her face bathed by the light of the moon. The night breeze played with the tips of her hair and teased her white chiffon dress.

Dan stood beside her, leaning his forearms on the railing as he looked out over the peaceful water. Marcy had never seen him look so elegant. His dark blue suit emphasized his perfectly proportioned body, and his white dress shirt highlighted his ruddy complexion. The ocean breeze ruffled the waves in his dark hair, and the moonlight graced it with a sheen that tempted her to run her fingers through it.

"Do you go on cruises often?" he asked her, interrupting her reverie.

"No," she said after a pause. "I had enough traveling when I was young to last a lifetime."

"That's right. You were an army brat," he recollected as he slowly turned toward her, thinking how beautiful she looked in the moonlight.

She smiled, "Let's just say we moved around a lot."

"It's never really stopped for you, has it?"

Her smile faded. "No, not really."

They were both quiet, and Marcy's thoughts drifted backward in time, back to her father, the general, who was always too busy for her. Her mother had been just as neglected by him. She'd been a sweet, gentle woman who had changed a lot after she'd taken to escape through drinking. Marcy had watched her parents become strangers to each other, and she'd been almost happy when her mother had obtained a divorce. Contact with her, then, had been minimal, and when her mother decided to remarry, Marcy had said goodbye to her in her heart.

The ocean breeze picked up a little, and the wind against her face returned her thoughts to the man standing beside her. "You were fortunate to grow up in one place with a family," she told him. Her smile became a pleasant admonishment. "Even though you insisted on swimming at Coney Island in March."

He didn't return her smile. "They weren't really my parents," he said, looking out over the water that was becoming choppy. "They were foster parents. I had several sets of them. I wasn't exactly your model kid. I moved around a lot, too."

"Just like me," she said, almost to herself.

"I ran away twice. Once I got as far as South Carolina and spent the night in a crummy jail. I was all of twelve. Jail's not a nice place for a kid."

There was silence for a few minutes, and Marcy asked, "What happened to your parents?"

Dan entwined his fingers as he leaned on the railing. "My dad died in Korea the year I was born, and a few years later my mother just took off."

She asked, "No relatives to raise you?"

"None who wanted to. Nobody offered, anyway."

Marcy had often thought that she'd had to face life alone, but now she realized just how solitary Dan must have felt—how alone he must feel now. Yes, they were really quite alike. How sad that neither of their marriages had filled the void in their lives. She looked over at his profile as he stared up at the night sky, and she marveled at his strength. At least she had never experienced financial problems while growing up. There had always been more than enough money, perhaps too much. Dan, on the other hand, had made it on his own, with very little help from anyone. Was that why he so cherished his own independence now? No wonder he hesitated to commit himself. First his mother abandoned him, and then his wife.

She sighed, more for him than for herself. "Loneliness is an awful thing, isn't it, Dan? As hard as we try, I guess we do carry around a lot of baggage from our early years. It seems as though some people start out with a better chance at happiness in life than others. It doesn't seem fair."

He moved his body sideways to better see her. The ethereal quality in her voice, the soft musical tone was so soothing. "I like the sound of your voice," he told her.

Marcy looked into his eyes, saw the fire burning in them and wanted to be lost in them forever. She wanted him to take her in his arms now and hold her gently. As though he read her thoughts, his arms reached out to her.

She felt her shoulders tremble under the touch of his hands, felt her entire body vibrate with the warm sensations that flowed through it. She wasn't certain who moved first, but suddenly she was close to him, looking up into his wondrous face, that face she had grown to love. It moved closer to hers, then closer still, and her lips quivered with anticipation.

Their lips joined, and she reveled in the savory taste of him. She felt her body go limp against his, felt his strong arms support her and hold her securely in a tight embrace. Was there anything in the world as real as this moment? she wondered. No, she told herself. All that mattered was that she was in the arms of the man she loved. His breath flowed into her, and hers into him. His warmth penetrated her, engulfed her like the sweetest of cocoons.

The separation of his lips from hers seemed cruel, but then she felt him lean her head on his shoulder and shuddered at the sensation of his warm breath on her ear.

"Marcy," he whispered, "you're hurting, and I'm hurting. What are we going to do about it?"

"I'm not hurting, Dan," she answered softly. "I've never felt as wonderful as I do at this moment." She nuzzled closer against him. "I love you so much. You could never hurt me."

Still whispering, he said, "Then there's only one thing we can do."

She raised her head slowly, saw the tension in his jawline and the need in his eyes. Very slowly she nodded, and then she thought she saw a hesitation in his eyes.

"Marcy—" his voice faltered slightly "—you're sure you won't regret this?"

Her eyes shone. "Tomorrow, maybe, but not tonight."

In their suite, Marcy sat on the bed, watching Dan step out of his briefs. She was not prepared for the enormity of her excitement as he stood there like a bronzed statue bathed in the softness of the moonlight streaming through the large windows.

Instinctively she knew that whatever did happen now, it would not be rushed. She could tell from the expression on his face, the placidness in his eyes. She felt it when he undressed her slowly, kissing her tenderly all the while. He savored the shedding of each garment as he caressed her and moved his lips over her body, and then he drew back the covers and lay her down on the bed.

For a moment he stood there, tall and proud and tempting, and then he lay down on the bed next to her. She heard a gasp slip from her lips as Dan's face came toward hers. His breath was warm and sweet; his lips moist and soft. She felt herself being pulled against his body and pleasure shot through her as flesh touched flesh.

His caressing hands moved over her back and descended farther. A lightheadedness began to overtake her. Her arms moved up across his firm chest and moved over the wide breadth of his shoulders, then her hands traveled to his nape and her fingers lost themselves in his soft hair.

It had been some time since she'd held a man in her arms, but she had never held a man she'd cared for as much as the one she was holding now; she'd never experienced the inner sweet agony that was playing havoc with her body and her mind. She wanted to give him everything she had to give. She was determined to take everything he had to offer.

She felt her chest heaving for air. She gasped and pulled her face from his. Arching her body slightly, she cupped his head with trembling fingers and guided his face to her bosom. For moments she felt a gentle nudging between her breasts, and then his taunting ministrations to her tender peaks. Her lips parted, and she drew in needed breaths as he continued his ardent attentions. And then a sudden coolness wafted over her.

Now she wished that he would rush, that he would carry her to the moment of ecstasy that she knew awaited her. But it was not to be. She opened her eyes partially to see him lying next to her, leaning on his elbow, his chin resting on his curved fingers.

His eyes were bright with golden light and emerald flecks as he softly told her, "You're more beautiful than I ever imagined in my fantasies."

His gentle fingers traced her features: her brow, her cheek, her lips. She felt his caressing hand move slowly down over her throat, across her shoulder and to the swell of her breast. Then it moved down her side, down over the curvature of her hip and inward to begin a tantalizing torment.

Was the exquisite agony being caused by his lips and tongue? Yes, oh yes! And now the sounds of his contentment reached her ears. With her palms pressed against the bed, she arched her body up to meet his fervent probings.

She felt the tremor begin in her toes, sensed it work its way up her legs as it built to a shudder that shook her entire body. Another gasp. A deeper moan. And she soared heavenward. Through flickering lids she saw the man she loved loom over and then slowly lower his body onto hers. The next sensation was a joining of such power that it caused her to sigh deeply.

She raised her arms to encircle his body and welcomed the feel of his warm and satiny flesh. At his low moan of satisfaction, her palms swept downward, and she began to urge him on, moving with him in even undulations. They moved as one, and together they became lost in each other.

Later, Marcy lay cuddled in Dan's arms, feeling like the happiest woman alive. Her palm brushed the stubble on his cheek, and then her fingers retraced the path they had followed numerous times already. Down they slipped over his strong neck and found their way over his broad shoulder and firm arm. Then her palm thrilled at the soft wisps of hair on his warm chest. She let her fingers dally, let them rest against his still-hard nipple. Downward still she guided her hand over the firm musculature of his stomach until it slid over the velvety arch of his hip.

She had never realized that lovemaking could be so marvelous, so reciprocal, so divine. She knew she would be content with only the memory of the past few hours, and if life offered more, she wasn't certain that her heart could bear the joy.

Dan breathed deeply and then asked, "Marcy, what are you trying to do... drive me crazy?"

She slowly moved her lips over his chest, kissed it, and then rested her cheek on its warmth. "If that's what makes you happy," she said as she continued to taunt him with easy caresses. She paused for a moment and said, "Do I make you happy, Dan?"

"If I get any happier, you know what's going to happen, don't you?" He raised himself up onto his forearm and looked down at her, his eyes taking in the way her shiny hair flowed around her smiling face. Then he lowered his eyes to her plush white breasts and he guided his thumb across them. Gently he kissed each one, fondled them for a moment, and then his palm began a tantalizing caress between her thighs, "Yes, Marcy Keaton," he told her, his bright eyes searing into her, "you make me happy."

With soft hands, she cupped his face and drew it down to hers. Their breaths mingled, their tongues danced, their excitement rose in pitch. They both sighed when their bodies united once again, and as they soared together, each held securely on to the other, as if to hold fast to the dream they had found.

Again, Marcy lay in Dan's arms, a sweet exhaustion making her feel languid and peaceful. Dan glanced over at the digital clock on the vanity: it was a little after midnight. Carefully he eased Marcy's head onto a pillow, got up, put on his briefs and a short beach robe, and quietly left the suite.

A few minutes later he was back, carrying a tray. He flicked on the light switch, filling the room with soft indirect lighting. He glanced over at her on the bed and almost dropped the tray. There she sat, her eyes wide, pointing his .45 at him.

She asked, "What was this doing under your pillow?"

His Adam's apple bobbed; he swallowed his heart and waved his hand to the wall of the bedroom. "Don't ever point a gun at someone unless you mean business."

She aimed the barrel toward the wall. "Do you always sleep with . . . this?"

"It's a habit," he told her as he put the gun under his pillow again. Then he sat on the bed next to her, put the tray down and crossed his legs yoga-style. "Chow time."

Marcy leaned back against the headboard. Looking down at the tray, she said, "Pizza?"

"You said you liked Italian."

"How can you eat now?"

"I'm hungry!" He spread a napkin across her lap.

Automatically Marcy pulled the edge of the sheet up over her bare breasts.

"Don't do that," he told her as he pulled the sheet down.

She pulled it back up. "I feel odd sitting here with . . . well, you know what I mean."

He stood up and removed his robe, then sat back down in a cross-legged position. "There, now we're like two peas in a pod."

She eyed him strangely. "It's not the same, Dan."

"You women never will be equal until you're free to walk around like we guys do. You know that, don't you?" He tugged at the sheet, but she held firm. "Here, have some pizza."

She reached for the slice, and as she did, he pulled the sheet down again. His eyes remained riveted on her breasts and the small birthmark on her left side.

She said, "My birthmark makes me feel self-conscious."

He said, "That's not a birthmark. That's a beauty mark."

"Glad you think so."

"I think so." He kissed it.

Trying to be as casual as possible, she chewed her pizza, but finally she said, "This isn't going to work. I feel ridiculous."

With a lecherous smile, Dan said, "Don't worry. If you drop an anchovy, I'll take care of it."

Up went the sheet.

"Naughty, naughty," he admonished.

Marcy took another piece of pizza. After she'd swallowed, she mumbled, "Look, Dan, I'm a bright, aware, contemporary woman, but habits don't change overnight."

"Our relationship has."

Now that's what she really wanted to discuss. "How has it changed?" she asked, trying to be circumspect.

He stared at her. "Boy, either you're short on memory, or I'm short on performance."

"Neither," she told him. "My memory is improving with age." She reached for another piece of pizza.

"So's your appetite." He quickly took the last piece.

With her mouth full, she asked, "Where'd you steal this?"

Again he stared at her and then said, "You know, in spite of what you think of my ethics, you've got a face I could look at every morning."

Suddenly Marcy was having a difficult time swallowing the pizza. Yet a casual approach seemed better than pressing. "So, you did steal it."

"Uh-uh. They've got a pizza party going on at the pool. Disappointed?"

"In what?"

"That I didn't steal for you?"

She saw the strange glow in his hazel eyes, but she had no way of knowing that he was thinking of Robert Keppler. Not realizing that, she said, "Dan, you're sick."

"Is being in love ever a normal state?"

She averted her eyes. "You're in love with me?"

"What happened to that fabulous memory of yours?"

"Not a thing," she said. "You just seem to be having a difficult time coming out with the words 'I love you.'"

"Actions speak louder than words," he told her.

Still she didn't look at him. "Wouldn't hold up in court on a breach of promise suit."

He let her wipe her lips with her napkin, and then he got up and took the tray over to the vanity. With his back to her, he said in a low voice. "Don't talk court to me, Marcy. I've been there once...the divorce court. I didn't like it one bit."

Marcy winced at his remark and felt a sharp pang in her heart. His words didn't bode well, not at all. She was disappointed, but not sorry. No, never in her life would she ever be sorry that she loved him with all her heart. It was that love that prodded her to say, "Dan, you know what your problem is? You're a family man without a family."

She watched as he lit a cigarette at the vanity, his back still to her. In the mirror she saw his reflection, his downcast eyes, the drawn features that but a moment ago were smiling. He glanced up and saw her sitting looking at him. His eyes met hers. "Look, I'll send you flowers, bring you gifts, the whole bit, but—"

"Dan," she softly interrupted, "do me a favor. In the top drawer, there's a little white box. Would you bring it over here?"

"Sure." He tucked his cigarette in the groove of the ashtray and brought her the little box.

"Sit," she told him and handed him the box. "It's for you."

He looked puzzled and then chanced a smile. Opening it, he found a short heavy gold chain with a small gold anchor on it.

"No sailor should be without one." She wanted to smile, but the quizzical look on his face stopped her. "Don't you like it?"

"It's great, but why?"

"I wanted to. It made me happy."

"When did you get this?"

"While we were shopping yesterday." She glanced quickly at the clock and added, "The day before yesterday, rather. Put it on so I can see how it looks."

He did, and she smiled. "Now you'll be safe, even in rough waters. You've got an anchor to keep you from drifting far away."

Dan's fingers slid along the heavy gold chain. "This must have cost a few bucks."

Marcy didn't like the tone of his voice. She eased the sheet up a little more. "My having money really bugs you, doesn't it?"

"No, but my not having it does. I've got all my money tied up in this month's rent back in Clearwater. My cash flow is a trickle." He went to the vanity, snuffed out the cigarette butt and lit another. He turned around and leaned back on the edge of the console. "People with hearts of gold worry me. They often have feet of clay."

Marcy knew that he was thinking about her husband, and the fact that he had made money dealing with the syndicate. He was doing it again—confusing her. Quietly she said, "I didn't buy it with dirty money, Dan. The money I do have is rightfully and honestly mine."

His face took on a prove-it-to-me look that she found annoying. "As a reporter, you saved your pennies, huh?" His voice was taunting.

She tried to remind herself that this was the man she loved, but all she wanted to do now was to jerk the chain off his neck and throw it out the window. Instead she composed herself, having learned that Dan had a cynical side to him, one brought on by his job, she supposed, and by life, as well. "My grandmother left me some money, Dan," she began calmly. "Then, when my father had his heart attack, there was money from him. Robert was part-owner of Silbide Incorporated, a legitimate firm—"

"And there was money from that," he added sarcastically.

"Dan, the attorneys worked everything out. They assured me that the sale of my interest in the company had absolutely nothing to do with the money Robert was making on the side illegally."

He seemed to believe her. She saw it in the softening of his face.

"The money kept coming in, Dan, but I'd have exchanged it at any time . . . all of it . . . for honest affection."

"That's so easy to say when you have it."

"Would giving it all away prove anything to either one of us?" she asked, dismayed that what had started out as a blissful evening was winding up with a stupid argument about money.

Dan switched off the lights, picked up the ashtray and lay down on his back next to her on the bed. He held the ashtray on his stomach and puffed at the cigarette in his other hand. In the darkness, the tip of his cigarette glowed.

She tilted her head toward him. "What happened to the discussion we were having?" she asked tentatively.

"I need time, Marcy," he said in a tight voice.

Without looking at him, she said, "Time passes quickly."

His voice was dull. "Time is only a measurement."

"Of our days, Dan . . . and our nights."

CHAPTER ELEVEN

MARCY LAY on the blue-and-white lounge chair on the crowded deck and watched Dan's smooth strong strokes as he swam toward her. He reached the side of the pool and grabbed it with his tanned hands. His usually wavy hair hung straight down over his forehead, and beads of water ran down his smiling face. The gold chain he wore sparkled in the morning sun.

"Come on in!" he yelled to her, but she shook her head. He swam back to the opposite end of the pool.

She leaned back, breathing a little easier now than she had last night. Their conversation had placed an emotional barrier between them that neither wanted there, but, at the time, neither had been able to cross it.

Sometime during the night, she had awakened to find his arm over her, his strong leg tucked between hers. He had been sleeping, but her startled movement had woken him. "Honey?" he'd said in his half sleep. Then he'd pulled her closer to his body, cradling her in his arms. Soon he was asleep again.

In the morning, Dan had been the first to open his eyes. When Marcy did awaken, it had been to the soothing strokes of his warm hand over her body, a stroking that had led to gentle kisses, soft caresses, and then to passionate embraces.

Marcy watched Dan lift himself out of the pool and smooth his wet hair back from his forehead. Yes, she admitted silently, she wanted to be his lover, but in her heart she wanted so much more. She wanted this man coming toward her to be hers forever, just as she wanted to be his—only his.

Easing himself down on the lounge next to hers, Dan let his head fall backward and let loose a deep satisfying sound of contentment. Marcy looked over at him just in time to see him turn his head toward her. The sun made little diamonds of the droplets clinging to his dark eyelashes.

"Know what?" he asked as his eyes roamed over her face.

She felt his hand take hold of hers, and suddenly all seemed right with the world. There were no problems to contend with, no past to justify, no future to fear. Quietly she asked, "What?" and returned his smile.

"I am the envy of every man on this ship."

His thumb brushed across her fingers, creating a wonderful sensation that shot up her arm, a sensation so strong that it caused her to shudder. She took a quick breath and asked, "Fact or opinion?"

"Fact," he told her without taking his eyes from hers. "I've noticed the men looking at you... some furtively, some downright hungrily." He raised himself up onto his right elbow. "Can't say as I blame them. You're a pretty classy lady."

"If you think you're going to get an argument on that one, Dan, you're wrong."

An unexplained tenseness clouded his smile as he lifted her hand slightly. His thumb continued stroking her fingertips. Without looking at her, he said, "You deserve the best, Marcy, the very best."

Her other hand covered his. "I already have the best there is . . . the very best."

That day, they enjoyed some of the cruise ship's offerings. He shone at trapshooting and basketball, while Marcy outdid him in golf putting and volleyball. Aerobics was a tie, and they both welcomed a sauna and massage in the health spa. They went their separate ways to the beauty salon and barber shop, but their holiday mood continued throughout dinner and the Las Vegas revue afterward.

"A nightcap?" Dan asked as they strolled on deck.

Marcy smiled her assent, and Dan led her to one of the quieter bars where he ordered white crème de menthe and soda for both of them. While waiting for their drinks, he saw that her attention had been drawn to the pianist, who was playing a soothing Gershwin medley, saw that her head was moving almost imperceptibly in time with the music.

He extended his hand. For a brief moment their eyes met, and then he rose and guided her to the small dance floor.

Again she was in his arms, and all seemed right. She felt secure in his embrace, loved the soothing warmth of his body, the firm caress of his hand at the small of her back. As he pulled her closer, she rested her temple against his cheek, and the warmth of him spread across her face as she drifted along, easily following his smooth guidance.

Hearing his low, melodic humming of the tune the pianist was playing, Marcy closed her eyes and said, "You're constantly surprising me, Dan Elliott."

His hand moved slowly up her back as he softly asked, "How so, Marcy Keaton?"

Snuggling even closer, she replied just as softly, "At times you can be such an ogre, and then at times...like this... such a delight."

He placed a gentle kiss on her forehead and suggested, "Maybe it's because you bring out the beast and the best in me."

Marcy's hand, which had been extended, was now tucked against Dan's chest, with his hand over hers. She could feel the steady beat of his heart, and it sounded like the sweetest of music to her. The song ended then, and Dan led her back to their table.

Raising his glass, he toasted, "To smooth sailing."

IT WAS A LITTLE AFTER EIGHT the next morning when the ship docked at the little city of Charlotte Amalie on St. Thomas in the Virgin Islands. The day was perfect. The early morning sun bounced off the row of white cruise ships and the myriad of sailboats and yachts moored in the placid harbor.

The sprawling town set at the water's edge was crammed with white and pink low-rise buildings. Their reddish roofs contrasted brilliantly with the blue-green Caribbean water and the azure sky. The tropical city was jammed with tourists. Neither Marcy nor Dan was interested in browsing through the duty-free shops, nor did they want to take a guided tour through the island's historic buildings, so they decided to go off on their own.

Dan rented a car, and they followed a road that curved along the coast of the small island, bypassing beach areas that were dotted with tourists. Farther up the coast he spotted a small inlet almost hidden by lush tropical vegetation, but not so much that he was unable to see a brief span of white sand.

Carefully he pulled over and parked, and minutes later they had climbed down the hillock. Directly ahead was the clear water that seemed to stretch out infinitely. Except for the soft swish of the gentle surf and the easy rustle of beach ferns in the breeze, all was quiet.

Marcy removed her sandals, which she had purchased on the ship, and walked a few steps in the powderlike white sand, her eyes scanning the wide expanse of sky and sea.

"Nice, isn't it?" Dan said as he watched the sea breeze blow against Marcy's fuschia sundress.

She turned toward him and raised one hand to brush away the strands of hair that flowed across her face. "More than nice. It's awesome. So immense and yet so peaceful." Again she looked out across the water.

"It makes me feel as though we're the only two people on earth."

Dan moved behind her and encircled her in his arms. "This is what I imagined Tahiti would be like. Soft sand, clear water, blue skies . . . and someone like you with me."

A pause and she said, "See, dreams can come true."

Slowly moving his palm down her arm, he told her, "You're not a dream. You're very real."

The word "real" triggered a restlessness in Marcy, and she began wondering if anything in her life was real. She thought about her future. What would it be like? Would she ever be Patricia Dodd again? Would she always be Marcy Keaton? And what about the future? Would Dan be in it? She had honestly thought he might propose marriage after their intimacies aboard the ship, but he hadn't.

She was surprised when she heard herself ask, "Dan, what do you want out of life?" She felt his hand tense on her arm, and then he moved away from her. Turning, she saw him walk under the shade of a palm and rest against its curved trunk. She went to him.

After lighting a cigarette, he told her, "That's a big question." He gave a low laugh. "You mean other than Tahiti?"

She said, "Seriously."

A flight of small white terns swooped down over the water's edge and then flew out of sight. After another puff on his cigarette Dan answered, "I don't know.

Sometimes I feel like two men. One part of me just wants peace and quiet. The other part wants what most men want . . . a home, a family." There was another forced low laugh. "A mortgage."

Marcy leaned against the trunk of another palm and looked out over the water. "You haven't had much luck with women, have you?"

"About the same luck you've had with men."

After removing her sunglasses, she faced him, saw the tenseness in his jaw and lips. Uncertain whether to continue or not, she did, anyway. "I think there's a difference between us, though. I think I've finally forgiven the men who have disappointed me, but I'm not sure you've forgiven your mother for abandoning you or your wife for divorcing you. That kind of disillusionment can eat away at a person, cheat you of that peace and quiet you're searching for. It can also make trusting someone else all but impossible."

His hazel eyes bore into hers. "Trust?" He crushed his cigarette in the sand and said, "When your job deals with the darker side of humanity, you learn not to trust anybody."

She asked, "No one?"

A gentle finger lifted her chin up a little. "I trust you," he told her, and then her eyes brightened again.

They drove back to the edge of town and found a quaint Danish restaurant. It was cozy, smelled of seafood, pungent spices and salt spray, but, best of all, the luncheon rush hadn't started yet.

Over cold beer, Marcy tried not to think about the phone calls, the bombing and the man shooting at them in the dark of night; but she knew she was going to have to face reality soon. Ocean cruises had a way of eventually coming to an end. Her greatest fear was that more than this brief trip would come to an end.

Dan ordered Kobenhavner omelets for both of them, and Marcy quietly asked, "Dan, do you really think it's Dirk or James Moray doing all these horrible things?"

He hoped so, but that awful nagging in the pit of his stomach told him otherwise. He wanted to lie, but he couldn't do that to her. "I don't think so, but before we go back to the ship, I'll phone the office in Miami to see if they've had any word yet. Then we'll know for sure."

"For sure," she echoed softly. "Then it will all be over."

Dan didn't say anything.

She waited for a few moments and asked, "What about us, Dan? Will that be over, as well?"

He took a long sip of his Danish beer and said, "Marcy, I make a good crutch to lean on." He found himself biting his lower lip after he'd said it.

Slowly turning her glass on the paper napkin in front of her, she told him, "I don't want you for a crutch, Dan. I want you for forever. I love you, and I think you love me."

He snuffed out the cigarette he'd been smoking—a little too forcefully. "The damn thing about it is that

I've got a great talent for loving, but not for marrying. I'm not ready to handle that right now...not again."

Although it was quite warm, a sudden chill swept through her. Then she told him, "I'd try to settle for the loving, Dan."

"You would?" he questioned dubiously.

"I would," she repeated. "Maybe you were right. Maybe I am a nice-girl-gone-tough."

"Sure you are...about as tough as whipped cream."

Their omelets were served, but Dan didn't feel like eating, which was rare for him. He tried to take a few swallows, but all the while he kept thinking that he was suddenly being pressured into a commitment. He didn't like the feeling. He glanced quickly at Marcy and remembered her telling him that she'd "try" to settle for the loving. Her new attitude worried him.

How long would she settle for just that? Was she just using words to cover the sound of imminent wedding bells? How long would it be before she'd wrap him around one of those pretty fingers of hers? He'd been curled around one before, and the memory of the experience still hurt.

He glanced at her again. *But this one's a real lady,* he reminded himself. *She wouldn't play the games that Hope had.* Yet women with money probably played other kinds of games. Money was power; that much he was well aware of. He didn't know if he could live with being second in command. No, it wasn't his nature. He did know he didn't want to go to Tahiti on her money, and Tahiti was a symbol of all the secret dreams he had—dreams he needed to achieve on his own. He didn't want his dreams bought for him.

It was almost three o'clock, and the ship was scheduled to leave at four, so Dan took Marcy to the pier, told her to go on ahead and that he'd follow after phoning the Service in Miami.

On board, in their suite, Marcy busied herself putting away the few souvenirs they'd purchased in Charlotte Amalie, and then she decided on a quick shower. It had been hot on the island, and she knew the shower would be refreshing; it might also help clear the confusion in her thinking.

Under the cool spray she wondered about her telling Dan she'd try to settle for the loving, not press him into marriage. She knew Patricia Dodd would never have settled for that, nor would Patricia Keppler have. Was Marcy Keaton so different?

She tried to convince herself that loving Dan as she did would make everything all right, that in time he would want to marry her, need to marry her. It would all just be a matter of time.

When Dan did return to the ship, Marcy was out of the shower and dressed, waiting for him, but she didn't like the look on his face nor the dullness in his eyes.

"What's the matter, Dan? Didn't they find Ed's sons?"

He closed the door behind him, went to the small refrigerator and took out a bottle of beer. "Want one?"

She shook her head and watched as he snapped off the top, wiped it with his palm and then took a hefty slug. "They found them," he told her as he walked over to the long vanity and leaned against it. "They picked James up last night. So far he's admitted to being in Florida. Dirk is and has been in Australia for the past year."

Marcy sighed what should have been a sigh of relief, but the sigh seemed to stick in her throat. Why wouldn't Dan look at her? Why was he avoiding her eyes? She said, "That's good news, isn't it?"

"It's good news," he told her. "They'll question him some more today. He'll sing."

She was standing in back of the sofa, and now she leaned forward and rested her hands on the back of it. "Do they think James was capable of...of doing everything? Do you, Dan?"

He took another swig of beer and said, "He might just have been nutty enough, but he had to have had help. The guy that shot at us had dark hair." Finally he did look over at her. "Don't worry, Marcy. They'll stick with him until it all comes out."

Her smile was weak, unconvincing. "Then it really is almost finished...all of it." She looked into his eyes, and she knew instantly that everything between them would indeed be over. Quietly she said, "Our time is up, isn't it, Dan?"

He dropped his empty bottle in the garbage can and took out another beer from the refrigerator. "It wouldn't work for us, Marcy. I'm not ready for commitment, and regardless of what you say, I don't believe you'd go along for the laughs without a promise from me."

The thudding in Marcy's heart echoed in her head as she walked around to the front of the sofa and sat down slowly. Unfortunately she knew he was right, and the knowledge of that was suffocating her.

Dan went back to the vanity, pulled the chair out and sat down. "We're too different, Marcy. You're Park Avenue. I'm Main Street. If we argued, and there would be times we would, you could take off for the French Riviera. I'd be lucky if I could afford a trip to Coney Island. No, we've just been playing wishful games."

"Games," she repeated quietly, and then she looked up at him. "Was everything a game to you, Dan?"

He stood up quickly and went to the window. Shoving his hands into his pockets, he stared out at the water. "Everything's a game. My job's a game. Life's a game."

Softly she asked, "And love's a game?"

He faced her and hated the sadness in her expression, hated himself for having put it there. "No," he answered just as softly, "love's the only thing I don't like to play at. I always lose." He went back to the vanity and picked up his beer. "There's an opening coming up in the Miami office. I'm gonna take it."

It was all over. Marcy tried to compose herself, but the dizziness was increasing. "I guess it is safer to be the loved one and not the lover," she whispered.

"Loved one? Lover? What difference does it make?" He undid the gold chain around his neck, looked at the little anchor one more time, and then he went over to her. He took hold of her hand, placed the chain in her palm and then closed her fingers over it. "Save this for the right guy, Marcy."

She wanted to beg him not to end it, and it was all she could do to say weakly, "I'd like you to have it, Dan."

"How about we settle for a tie, Marcy?" he suggested, and then he quietly left the suite.

For minutes, Marcy sat there in a state of shock, her fingers toying with the little gold anchor on the chain. Carefully she wiped away the teardrop that fell on it. Then, with moist eyes, she looked around the empty room. Only silence was there with her. She was alone once more.

DAN SAT at one of the bars on the ship and ordered another double Scotch. The bartender watched him from the other side of the bar as Dan conducted a private conversation. "She'll say—" his voice rose in pitch "—'You don't have to feel guilty about making love to me.'" It lowered. "And I'll say, 'I don't *have* to feel anything!'" He took another swallow of Scotch. "And she'll say, 'Goodbye, Dan.' And I'll say, 'Goodbye, Marcy Keaton,' and then she'll walk away... and I'll never see her again." He lit another cigarette, although he had a lit one burning on the edge of his ashtray. "So then I'll yell after her, 'Good luck!' but she won't even hear me." He held on to the edge of the bar with both hands, trying to swallow. Then he tried to laugh, but no sound came out. "Good luck, Dan... all fools need luck," he mumbled and pushed the bar stool out from under him.

Outside the door to the suite, he straightened up and pushed back his hair. After steadying himself, he turned the knob and lunged forward into an empty room. "Marcy," he called, then checked the other room. Instinct told him to look in the closet. Her clothes were gone

MARCY PEERED OUT the window of the jet flying over the waters of the Caribbean. The emerald-blue waters were dazzling under the hot sun.

She tried not to think during the three-hour flight from St. Thomas to Miami. Yet, the memories came, one overshadowing the other: memories of Robert Keppler, Edward Moray and Daniel Elliott. Robert, the man she'd loved at first, then learned to hate. Dan, the man she'd almost hated at first, then had grown to love. Ed had been too much of a friend to love or hate.

Her thoughts drifted back to that night several weeks before the shooting when Ed had come to dinner. Ever since his wife Ellen had died the previous year, Marcy had made it a practice to invite him often. Grief had remained with him longer than anyone had anticipated, and James's being away at school hadn't helped. In a way, helping Ed had helped Marcy; for she, too, had sustained a loss. Her husband Robert, the golden-haired boy of Silicon Valley, had died for her when she'd found out about his penchant for suntanned beachgirls and beachboys. She'd seen him pick them up along the shore their luxurious home overlooked, seen him make contact with strangers and walk down the beach with them.

She'd denied the facts to herself for as long as she could, but as he became more flagrant with his obsession, as his touch became unbearable to her, she'd confronted him with her suspicions. He hadn't bothered to deny anything; he'd just laughed at her and told her to busy herself with the house, make a baby or two to keep herself company.

Robert laughed a lot, but that night when Ed had come to dinner, he hadn't laughed. Something had been disturbing him, and Ed had been furious. Over martinis they'd argued; during dinner they'd argued, too, but they'd been so circumspect that Marcy never could understand what the real problem was. It was during coffee in the library that Robert had asked her to leave him and Ed alone for a few minutes.

She'd done so, but soon their muffled shouts had carried onto the terrace by the pool. Then she'd seen Robert come storming out of the library. He'd rushed past her without saying a word; his face had been beet red. She'd watched as he headed toward the bathhouse on the far side of the pool. She'd known that he'd don swimming trunks and would soon be prowling the beach again.

"What's going on Ed?" she'd asked as he'd come up behind her.

"Just business, Patricia," he'd told her and then he'd asked for a brandy.

It had all happened a little more than two years ago, but Marcy remembered it as though it had only been yesterday....

"HE'S A BASTARD, isn't he?" Ed said.

Attempting understanding, she said, "He's a troubled man, but he refuses to get professional help." She handed Ed his brandy and joined him.

"Let's face it, Patricia; he's rotten. He's causing problems at the company, and if he's doing what I think he is, I'll—" He saw the distress in her eyes. "But it's what he's doing to you that I can't tolerate. He's putting you through a living hell. Why do you put up with it?"

She leaned against the grand piano and stared down at the beach through the wide window. "I can't, Ed. I just can't put up with it any longer. I know I made a promise to God for better or for worse, but I can't handle this. I'm going to file for a divorce."

"Patricia, God would never blame you for leaving that... that—"

Quickly she turned. "Don't say it, Ed. Please."

He put his brandy glass down, went to her, and placed her glass down on the table near the fireplace. Then he held her in his arms. "Patricia, when Ellen died, I thought something in me had died, too. Maybe a little of me did, but I can see the skies getting bluer again.'' He lifted her chin a little and looked into her sad eyes. ''With Robert, your skies would only get blacker.''

For a moment their eyes searched each other's. Perhaps it was the tension she'd been living with, or maybe it was the kindness, the understanding in Ed's eyes; but for whatever reason, she accepted the tender kiss he gave her, welcomed the feeling of his arms around her....

THE RATIONALE she'd used with herself was that she and Ed had both suffered loss in their lives: he, the loss of his wife; she, the loss of a true husband. Sharing their losses had made her feel that a terrible burden had been lifted from her. It had been some time since she'd felt as feminine as she did at that moment when Ed kissed her.

Thus had begun the deeper friendship between her and Ed Moray. It had grown through several meetings for lunch, a few cocktails together and smiling glances at dinner parties. It ended, however, one day when he'd asked her to meet him at his home. Mrs. Robert Keppler had been unable to go through with that final charade. She hadn't loved Ed, and not loving him, why would she have even stopped to wonder if he'd really loved her?

AS MARCY CONTINUED to stare out the plane window, a terrible thought crossed her mind. What if Ed Moray had loved her? What if his killing Robert *had* had something to do with the way he had felt about her? No, she didn't even want to think that! It had been an accident. They'd argued because he'd found out that Robert had drifted into crime and was about to take Ed and the company down with him. It had had nothing to do with her.

But Dan would never believe that. He was too cynical. And this money business bothered him, too; he was obsessed with being independent.

Marcy gave a soft, bitter laugh as she gazed out at the puffy white clouds in the distance. Loving a man was one thing, and living with him was another, she thought. The woman who chose to try to break through Daniel Elliott's cynical shell had a difficult job cut out for her. The task would be all but impossible; he had encased his emotions in an armor of self-protective indifference. Too many people had already given him cause for mistrust.

She glanced down at the little gold chain she held in her fingers, and then she granted that the task would be immense, but the rewards superlative.

CHAPTER TWELVE

YESTERDAY, Marcy had just made it off the cruise ship before it had left the pier at St. Thomas. There had been no over-the-shoulder glances at the ship as it had moved out of the harbor. She'd taken a taxi to the Carib Beach Hotel just across from the airport after she'd found out that the first plane to Miami wouldn't leave until nine o'clock the next morning.

She hadn't been concerned that Dan would come after her. He'd told her the case was all but wrapped up, and he wouldn't want to see her again, anyway. She'd also known that the cruise ship would be at sea the next day and wouldn't land at Nassau until the following morning.

She'd eaten little for dinner in the hotel restaurant, and her attempt at sleep that night had been unsuccessful.

The next day when her plane arrived at Miami International, she took a cab to the parking facility where she and Dan had left her Thunderbird before setting out on the cruise, and late that evening, exhausted and depressed, she pulled up in front of Murphy's house in Clearwater. She knew it was inconsiderate of her to disturb her housekeeper at this hour but Murphy was more than that; she was her friend and confidante—insofar as she was able to confide in her. The thought of going directly to her own house was unbearable. She had to talk to someone.

Murphy's White Fantasy wasn't all that bad on the rocks—lots of rocks, Marcy decided as she brought her friend up-to-date. She related almost everything about the past few days: the "accidental" fire at the house, the stay at the Whitesands on Esteban Island, her first encounter with alligator tails and the disastrous Caribbean cruise. What she left out—the more intimate details—Murphy filled in for herself as the two women sat in the small but neat kitchen sipping on Murphy's private stock.

"I got the phone call saying you were going away for a few days, so I've been picking up your mail for you, and there are notes from some of your friends to call them. But this trip of yours, I thought it was a tryout for a honeymoon."

"Hah! That will be the day," Marcy said coolly, her attempt at disinterest not quite convincing enough for Murphy.

"Listen, Marcy, Dan's got some very nice qualities."

"Such as?"

"He's a man and he's got a job. Not to mention a pair of legs I'd kill for."

"I like his eyes," Marcy said softly, beginning to feel the benefits of her hostess's beverage. Then, quickly catching her dreamy mood, she added, "He does not have a job. The job has him."

"Yeah, that's the only fly in the ointment. He'd be good at whatever he decided to do, but this U.S. marshal bit could have its drawbacks."

Marcy sipped and said, "He's not only good at it; he's great at it."

Murphy said, "Pity. A fair cop might make a great husband, but a great cop might only make a fair husband. It's not like he has a nine-to-five job."

"And it's dangerous. He's already scarred. Did you know he's been shot once?"

Smiling her White Fantasy smile, Murphy asked, "How would I know? You were the one on the cruise with him."

"Murphy!"

"Marcy!"

They both smiled knowingly and sipped.

Tapping her curved finger on the kitchen table, Murphy said, "It's in the stars for you."

"What's in the stars?"

"Dan is."

"Have you been reading tea leaves again?" Marcy asked lightly.

"Don't discount the tea leaves so quickly. In the old country, my mother read them and my grandmother read them. In fact, it was my grandmother who told me I'd be taking an ocean voyage and would marry three times. And it was in the tea leaves that I saw you and Dan getting together."

Resting her chin in the curve of her palm, Marcy said, "You really believe in them, don't you, Murphy?"

"When an Irish woman believes in something, all the devils in hell can't shake her belief."

"Did you see your last husband in the tea leaves?"

Pouring herself a little more of her fantasy juice, Murphy shook her auburn head. "No, no. My grandmother saw him. I just scratched his fender."

"You did what?"

"Well, I had to get his attention. He was the bashful type. It was when I was a flag girl for the county highway department. We were working on the beach causeway." Murphy's green eyes sparkled in reminiscence. "Jacob used to drive by daily. Then one day I noticed that he'd circled the block to get another peek at me. The next day I waved my little red flag at him." She laughed. "He got redder than the flag. A half hour later he was driving by again. Well, I thought, this can't go on forever, so when he slowed down by our construction trucks, I hit his fender with my flag stick."

Marcy asked, "And that endeared you to him?"

"He was furious! But he had to get out of the car to read me the riot act. We were married two weeks later . . . rest his soul."

"I think with Dan I'd need more than a little red flag," she said almost to herself. Then to Murphy, she added, "That is *if* I were interested."

"'If'? Listen, Marcy, when you talk about Dan, your eyes glow like you think the guy changes his clothes in a phone booth."

Marcy groaned. "Oh, Murphy, I do love him, so very much, but he's not the marrying kind. One woman gave him a hard time, and he thinks every woman would."

"So? Boys will be boys. You're a woman. You're supposed to know that. Use a little chicanery."

"I will not. There's no way I'm going to try to trap him or beg for happiness."

"Bull! Happiness is filling out your training bra. Making a man realize he can't live without you is something entirely different. Look at it this way. You're doing him a favor. Just don't let him know it."

"You're a better woman than I am, Murphy Rabinowitz," Marcy told her, dubious about the advice she was being given.

"Adele O'Rourke Shaughnessy Murphy Rabinowitz," she reminded her guest and added, "Well, you gotta do something. Look at you. You're miserable without him."

Marcy sighed in agreement, thinking that Murphy had as many names as she did. Then she asked, "How long does it take to get over someone?"

"It takes as long as it takes. But you either love him or you don't. Don't whine about it. Do something."

"I'd have to get him to listen first, wouldn't I? Besides, he's planning to transfer to the Service in Miami."

"Oh." Murphy leaned forward. "What have you to do is—"

The ringing of the phone in the living room cut her off. Marcy looked at Murphy. Murphy stared back.

"Who'd be calling me at this time of night?" she asked as she started to leave the kitchen.

"Murphy!" Marcy called after her.

The older woman turned. "Will you stop worrying that every phone call's gonna be him." She picked up the receiver, but cautiously. "Hello," she said in her husky voice. "Yes, operator, it is." She shrugged her shoulders and waited. "Yes . . . oh! . . . Dan."

Marcy began to wave her hand frantically, trying to tell Murphy not to let him know she was there.

"Where are you calling from?" She listened and then covered the mouthpiece with her hand. To Marcy she whispered, "Somewhere in the middle of the goddamned ocean." She removed her hand. "Good to hear from you...yeah...yeah... Yes, she's here...just fine." Murphy pointed to Marcy and then to the receiver. Marcy shook her head violently. "Can't Dan. She's upstairs sleeping. Poor thing was a wreck when she got here. I put her right to bed. Gave her a pill. Yeah . . . yeah . . . keep her right here," she repeated. "You'll be in Nassau tomorrow . . . plane to Tampa. Okay, Dan, we'll see you then. Oh, Dan, she's worried sick about you, so be careful. Bye, Dan."

The second Murphy put the receiver down, Marcy asked, "Why did you tell him that?"

"You are worried, aren't you?" She smiled that Irish smile of hers. "You should be. He's coming after you, Marcy. I'm to keep you right here until he can get his hands on your throat."

Unconsciously Marcy's fingers moved to her neck. "When is he arriving?"

"Late tomorrow. He's flying from Nassau, but has a stopover in Miami. He says I'm not to let you out of my sight, and you aren't to go near your house. What's going on, Marcy?"

"I wish I knew," she answered, knowing that she couldn't tell her friend the entire story, not even in the strictest of confidence.

"Well," Murphy said, "you'd better go on upstairs and get some sleep. Don't want you making a liar out of me."

"Humph!," she grumbled as she climbed the stairs. "He's out there in the middle of the ocean, and he still thinks he can order me around."

Once settled in the bedroom next to Murphy's, Marcy could barely keep her eyes open. A hot shower after Murphy's potent concoction had done the trick. Yet her brain wanted to sort things out. Why was Dan coming back into her life? The FBI had caught up with James Moray, and he'd admitted that he'd been in Florida. In her half sleep, her mind tortured her with replays of her last conversation with Dan, the one they'd had before she left the ship.

She thought everything had been settled between them. She'd been playing for keeps, and he'd just been playing. He wouldn't give her any guarantees, any promises. At least he'd been honest, brutally honest. And now he was coming back into her life. Why? To torment her again?

Her eyes closed, and she reached over to the empty pillow next to hers. "The man is a devil," she mumbled incoherently. "A fallen angel, at least...a brute...such lovely eyes...strong arms—" Sleep finally won out.

Murphy let Marcy dream away past noon. She knew how exhausted she'd been, and she knew just what the chances were of keeping her there until Dan arrived.

And Murphy had been right. As soon as Marcy had had some coffee, she wanted to go home.

"But, Marcy, Dan said not to go near your house."

"He said, he said. Well, I'm tired of men telling me what I can do and what I can't do! They've been doing that all my life, and that's finished as of now."

No matter, Murphy decided. If Marcy wasn't there when he showed up, he'd make her house his next stop. And Murphy wasn't about to miss that scene; they'd need a referee, anyway.

Marcy was thankful that Murphy insisted on going with her. It was her day to work at the house. In her heart, Marcy didn't want to be left alone with Dan—not ever again. Her loving him as she did gave him the enormous power to hurt her. And as for Murphy's advice on catching a man, Marcy had decided to stop banging her head against the wall. If Dan was determined to be a bachelor the rest of his life, so be it.

When Marcy pulled into her driveway, she couldn't help but notice the scorched bushes the explosion had caused, and she saw that the door had been replaced. She wondered at the mentality of a man like James Moray, wondered at the hatred that must have consumed him to do such a thing.

Having been closed up for a while, the house still had the odor of burned wood and drapes, so, while Marcy unpacked, Murphy turned on the air conditioner and sprayed air freshener in the intake panel of the system. Soon the entire house had the slight aroma of a pine forest, a pleasant woody scent.

When Marcy came back downstairs, she took one look at the drapeless front window and decided that it had to be fixed temporarily. Since the windows in her dining room faced the rear of the house, she and Murphy took those drapes down and hung them over the front window. Then, as Murphy busied herself, Marcy made several phone calls to friends who had left notes in her mailbox. The story was always the same: there had been an accidental fire, and she was visiting briefly while repairs were made. Gloria asked about Charles Winters and was disappointed to hear he had returned to Aspen.

It was a little after six in the evening when Dan arrived.

Upon hearing the taxi door slam shut, Marcy made a beeline upstairs, telling Murphy, "I don't want to talk to him!"

Murphy shrugged her shoulders and opened the front door. She took a long look at Dan's haggard appearance. His eyes were bloodshot, and there were grayish circles under them; his usually ruddy complexion was also a pallid gray. "You look like your hair hurts," she pronounced bluntly.

"It does," he mumbled, leaning against the doorframe. "That's why it's not combed."

Stepping aside, she said, "Come on in. I'll fix you some coffee... or would you rather—"

"Not the thermos, Murphy," he pleaded. "Just coffee, lots of it." He walked to the center of the living room, looked around and asked, "Where's the lady of the house?"

Murphy tilted her head up toward the staircase and went into the kitchen.

"Miss Keaton," he called sweetly. He got no answer. He moved to the bottom of the stairway and bellowed, "Get your tail down here... now!"

A door opened quietly, and Marcy slowly started down the stairs. "Oh, Mr. Elliott—" her voice was calm, cultured, pleasant "—what brings you here? I would have thought you'd be enjoying the rest of the cruise."

For a moment he just stared at her, his eyes sending golden daggers into her cool blue ones. Then he said, "If you weren't enjoying it, what makes you think I was?"

Marcy heard the depth of fury in his voice. Unconcerned, she asked, "You were angry because I left?"

"I skipped anger. I went right to rage. Why did you do a damn fool thing like that?"

"You are upset," she commented casually.

"You noticed."

She moved past him and sat down on the sofa, angling her long legs gracefully. "You spend a great deal of your life being upset, don't you, Mr. Elliott. In any case, I thought you had said all there was to be said just before I left the ship."

He started to run his spread fingers through his dark hair, but the pain in his head made him stop. He went to the easy chair across from her and let his body fall into it. "Since when did you start listening to me? I told Murphy to keep you at her place."

Her smile was generous. "What makes you think anything you say now would be important to me?"

He leaned forward and pointed his finger at her. "You're going to listen to me whether you like it or not, lady."

Just then, Murphy brought in Dan's coffee and gave it to him. She checked his face and then Marcy's. She innocently asked, "Marcy, would you like some?"

Marcy leaned back and crossed her arms. "I'd drink with the devil himself first."

Dan put his cup down on the table next to him a little too noisily. "What makes you think he'd want you to?" He glared at her with fire in his hazel eyes. It seemed to him they were back to square one.

Marcy sighed and said, "Nothing's changed, has it, Dan?"

He picked up his cup, but before drinking, he said, "What happened on the cruise ship changes a lot of things."

Marcy watched him drink, trying to assess just what he'd meant by that. Had he been referring to the times they had made love together? Or had he been reminding her that they had no permanent future together? She wasn't certain. Looking down at her fingers, she said, "As far as I'm concerned, nothing happened."

"Sure, Marcy," he said aloud. To himself, he said, *It happened. You know it, and I know it. It's right here between us now.* Finally he said, "What the hey. I'm a pussycat. Remember?"

"When a beautiful woman is involved," she added.

"You remember."

"Everything. Particularly the part when you told me we'd both been playing wishful games, that everything was a game to you."

"So much for honesty," he said, getting up to pace. He ran his fingers through his hair and winced. At the kitchen door, where he knew Murphy was listening, he asked, "What do you think, Murphy?"

Opening the door a bit, Murphy gave Marcy a scolding glance. "I see it's still business as usual with you two." Looking up at him from her five-one height, she added, "You don't look like you're going to last through the cocktail hour."

Dan groaned at the thought, remembering how he'd tried to polish off all the Scotch aboard the cruise ship.

A light went on in Murphy's head. "Oh. So, you party with the best of them, eh, Dan? Well, I've got just the thing for you. Step in here a minute." She shut the door and pulled him into the kitchen. As she went to the refrigerator, she whispered, "Are you seriously interested in her or not?"

Leaning over the sink, he whispered back, "I'm interested, but—"

"But nothing. Now go in there and stop yelling at her. Be nice. I'll bring you something that'll fix you up."

When he returned to the living room, Marcy asked, "Feeling better?"

"Doctor Murphy hasn't started treatment yet."

"You're in good hands," she told him.

"It's not her hands I want to be in."

Sadly she said, "It's too late, Dan. You can't have it both ways. You were right. I'm not the kind of woman who can go along for the laughs."

Just then Murphy came in carrying what looked like a small glass of tomato juice. Handing it to him, she ordered, "Drink this down in one swallow."

Cautiously he took the glass from her. "What is it?"

Smiling her Irish smile, she told him, "A Bloody Mary. What else?"

Down it went. After his ashen face turned pink and then scarlet, he grabbed at his stomach.

Pointing across the room, Murphy said, "The bathroom's in there."

Dan lunged toward it, and Marcy asked, "How do you make a Bloody Mary?"

"The usual way, but I added some cayenne pepper and ipecac. He'll be okay...all he needs is his stomach cleaned out. You know, Dan reminds me of my second husband. I worked in a bar then. One day he came in and drank—"

"Murphy, now is not the time. I think United States Marshal Daniel Elliott is going to want some more coffee when he's finished cleaning out his stomach."

"Gotcha," she said and headed for the kitchen.

Fifteen minutes later, a not-so-steady-on-his-feet marshal emerged from the bathroom. His suit coat and tie were dangling from one hand, and his eyes were glazed over. "Ever thought of loaning Murphy to the CIA? We wouldn't have a sober enemy left in the world." He literally fell onto the sofa and groaned.

Marcy shook her head, and then a smile escaped from her lips. She took the jacket and tie from his hand and laid them across a chair. Then she sat down across from him again and watched the heaving of his chest. A moment later she was up and soon returned from the bathroom with a wet washcloth that she placed over his forehead.

He murmured, "God, that feels good."

Sitting opposite him again, she said, "That should teach you to go looking for trouble."

With closed eyes, he said, "Don't talk troubles. We still have them."

"What are you referring to?" she asked suspiciously.

"Who put the bomb on your doorstep and who shot at you on the pier... we can rule out James Moray."

With wide eyes, she leaned forward, feeling a surge of fear rush through her body. "But you said that he admitted being—"

"He admitted to the phone calls. That's all. He did see that pretty face of yours on TV, and yes, he hates you for what he thinks you did to his family. But he's not a killer. Airline tickets and eyewitnesses place him in California the night of the bombing. When he said 'goodbye' on the phone, he meant it. He figured he'd spooked you enough, and then he headed home."

Marcy clutched her arms, and she slowly sat back in the chair. "Are they certain he couldn't have flown back? Are you?"

Patting his abdomen, he said, "I feel it... in here."

"That could be Murphy's Bloody Mary."

His unsteady fingers lifted the corner of the wet washcloth from one eye. "I know the difference. I'm a trained marshal."

"So you keep telling me. Just what are you trained in?"

The washcloth covered the eye again. "Hell, I don't know anymore."

"Did you ever?"

"Yes. Before I met you."

Half thinking about another crazy man out there somewhere and half trying to carry on her conversation with Dan, she said, "I guess that's a compliment."

"No, it's a confession."

She thought a moment and then asked, "Dan, are you trying to tell me you're still in the protection business?"

"Until we find out who's after you now, I am."

"How's the patient?" Murphy asked, bringing coffee for them. Both Marcy and Dan wondered how much she might have heard about bombing and shooting, but the woman's face gave no hint. She handed Marcy her cup and then pulled Dan up by the arm. "See, you're gonna live after all."

Sitting up, still holding the by now warm cloth over his forehead, he admitted, "That's what I'm afraid of."

She took the cloth and handed him his coffee.

Dan looked up at her. "Is there anything in this besides coffee?"

She brushed his hair back from over his forehead. "Trust me."

He glanced over at Marcy for confirmation. She gave him a noncommittal expression.

"Now this is nice," Murphy complimented. "You've both been in the same room for more than five minutes and nothing's been broken." She saw Dan and Marcy exchange subtle smiles. "Listen, Dan, I want to ask you something."

He looked up at her again.

"Are you really happy living the single life?"

"Murphy!" Marcy yelled.

The older woman turned to her, raised her palm and whispered, "This requires a little tact." She looked back at Dan. "Are you going to ask Marcy to marry you or not?"

His eyes peered at Marcy as she jumped up, took Murphy by the arm and led her to the entry hall. "Goodbye, Murphy. I'll see you later." She handed the woman her purse and opened the door.

With green eyes sparkling, Murphy sent Dan a smile. "Look out for her. She's an endangered species." She winked at him and left.

Dan said, "That one's a class act, isn't she?"

"With a big mouth," Marcy returned.

He said, "I like her."

She said, "I love her."

Instantly Marcy wished she hadn't used the word "love," because when she did, their eyes lingered on each other's. Marcy forced herself to ask, "Are you feeling better now?"

Dan stood up. "I need you to feel anything."

"Don't say things like that," she told him.

"Why not?"

She picked up her cup and then his. "Because relationships based on need aren't very successful." She was about to go into the kitchen, but she stopped suddenly and faced him. "I needed Ed Moray at the time, but I didn't love him." She lifted her shoulders slightly. "And after your divorce, you needed someone. Your job threw us together, and need took over.

I couldn't have meant very much to you, Dan. Not really."

With certainty he said, "You're right up there with oxygen."

She went into the kitchen. From the corner of her eye she saw him lean against the kitchen door, watching her. Quietly she told him, "I thought we'd settled all this on the ship."

"When I found out that you'd taken off, I nearly went crazy." He started to make imaginary circles on the cabinet near the door. "Everything I said seemed to make sense to me when you were right there, but when you weren't . . . nothing made any sense."

"Like I said, Dan, you can't have it both ways. If you think you can, you're deceiving yourself, fantasizing." She started to rinse the cups.

"Fantasies . . . dreams," he said, then paused.

Marcy didn't want him to say anything else; she didn't want to hear the sound of his voice. It was too warm and comforting. But Dan continued.

"You know, when I was a kid, I used to actually dream about being locked inside a big department store." His laughter was halfhearted. "For the whole night, I could have anything I wanted . . . all those goodies just for me. But I always woke up the next morning, and the dream was gone."

Marcy finished rinsing the cups, but she still didn't look at him. Softly she said, "Dreams slip away from us sometimes."

"You're not a dream, Marcy. You're real, and once you said you loved me."

She wasn't going to cry. She wasn't. "We're just trouble for each other, Dan."

"I thought you were used to trouble."

She dug her heel into the floor, forced a pleasant expression, and then faced him. "I'm not masochistic." Quickly she walked past him and went into the living room. He followed.

"Marcy, if we both—"

"Dan, when you first showed up on my doorstep, you told me you were here to do your job. If we both remember that, maybe we can get this business over with...and then you can go after your dreams, and I'll search for mine."

"That's how you want it?" he asked.

"That's how it's going to be."

Dan rubbed his fingers over his jaw, and then he nodded. "Right," he said. "Business first." He sat down on the sofa, where she usually sat, and draped his arm over the back of it. She sat in the chair where he usually sat. "Business," he repeated, as though to discipline himself. "Ooookay, the first line of business is to get you out of here again." He stood up.

"Wha—? Dan, I just got back in!"

"You want business? You get business. One: James Moray did the phoning. Two: Someone else bugged your house. Three: That someone else tried to spread you all over the lawn with a bomb. Four: That someone else also took potshots at you on the pier. Five: We don't know who this someone is, Marcy, but if Mr. Someone finds out that you're back here, what makes you think he's now a kissing cousin?"

She looked up at him to see him standing there with his knuckles planted on his hips. She had to agree that there was a certain logic in what he was saying. "No Whitesands," she told him.

He shook his head in agreement.

"No cruise."

Another shake.

"Where, then?"

"You're coming to my place."

She jumped up from the chair. "Your place? What's wrong with a hotel?"

He reminded her, "We tried that."

"I...I...I could stay with Murphy," she stammered.

Seriously he asked, "Do you really want to put her in that much danger?"

He was right; she knew it the minute he said it.

"Believe me, Marcy, you'll be safe there. I promise."

Dan's apartment was just off the curve of Gulf-to-Bay Boulevard in Clearwater; in the Rose Garden complex. Marcy looked for the roses, but there weren't any. The U-shaped building was neat looking, but a fresh coat of paint would have helped. His apartment was on the second floor.

Once inside, Marcy looked around the living room. It was rather small, and the furnishings didn't quite match; it seemed as though he'd gotten a piece from this set and a piece from that. It was clean, but a little reorganizing would do wonders for it, she thought. Her attention wandered to the colonial love seat that was set at an odd angle to the wall.

Dan noticed and said, "Have to keep it that way to watch TV."

"Oh," she commented.

He picked up her suitcase again, after having locked the door behind him. "The bedroom's in here."

Following him in, she noticed that there was only one single bed in the room; again the furniture seemed mismatched.

"You can have the bed," he told her. "I'll bunk in the living room."

"On the love seat?"

"Not on your life. I've got a sleeping bag." He chuckled. "Used to have a camper to go with it. Hope got that." After he placed her suitcase on the bed, he said, "Bathroom's right here." She watched as he removed the towels and tossed them into a hamper by the sink. "I'll get you some fresh ones." He started to leave the bedroom, but then he turned. "Have you had dinner?"

Quietly she said, "No," realizing just how much she was really putting him out.

"Let's see," he pondered. "We can have frozen macaroni and cheese and sausage, or we can have sausage and macaroni and cheese. Which sounds good to you?"

Marcy felt her lips curve upward as she looked at him standing in the doorway, waiting for her selection.

"You choose," she said. "They both sound good to me."

He asked, "How about a cold beer while I get my chef's hat?"

"Give me five minutes to get organized and freshened up."

"You got it," he said and went through the living room toward the kitchen whistling, but then he was right back to clean out a top drawer of the dresser for her to use.

When he left again, Marcy unpacked, and as she did, she noticed a framed photograph of a boy about two years old on the dresser, a dark curly-haired boy with hazel eyes. Dan's son. There was no picture of his ex-wife in sight.

The sound of soft music came from the living room, and when she entered, she noticed that he had repositioned the love seat and had straightened up somewhat. The little coffee table, which had been loaded with magazines and books, had been cleared off and placed in front of the love seat. Another chair had been moved to the other side of the table.

"You've been busy," she told him.

He said, "I don't get much company up here. Makes a guy lazy about appearances." He set her glass of beer down on a coaster. "No microwave," he told her. "Hope kept—" He stopped himself, then said, "Dinner will take a little while."

"No problem," she offered and sat down on the love seat.

Dan stood there for a moment, just looking down at her, and then he picked up his glass from the table, held it up in front of him and said, "Here's to being roomies again." Then he took off into the kitchen.

Marcy sipped from her glass, wondering just how safe she would be, but also wondering just how safe she really wanted to be.

Soon the pleasant odor of baked sausage wafted into the room, and Marcy began to feel quite cozy in Dan's little apartment. The music coming from the stereo was soothing, and the beer, which always made her drowsy, was having its pleasant effect. And then Dan was back with a can in his hand, and he refilled her glass, saying, "A little longer."

Dinner, when ready, was served on the small round table that was in a corner on the opposite side of the living room. Neither of them wanted to discuss the problem that weighed heavily on both of them, at least, not while they were eating. After dinner, though, they did discuss Marcy's situation.

"Down to business," Dan said almost apologetically, sitting in the chair across from the love seat where Marcy was seated. "Marcy, Moray's sons are in the clear, and the syndicate is just not my choice for villain in this scenario. Is there anyone else you can think of who would want you dead?"

"Or you, Dan," she said, reminding him of the possibility that he was the target.

"Let's stick with my premise for a minute. Is there anyone you can think of who just possibly hates your guts enough to want to kill you?"

"Of course not," she answered firmly.

He asked, "What about this multimillion dollar project you were doing public relations for? That much money has a way of attracting trouble."

Marcy had to think about that. True, something had been bothering her all along about the Oceanview Villas setup—but Mark Godette attempting murder? It was laughable, and she found herself grinning about it.

"What?" Dan asked.

"Mark Godette and Oceanview Villas. I mean, Mark fired me, but that wouldn't give him reason to—"

He snapped his fingers. "That's right—he fired you! But why?" His interest piqued, he got up, walked around the coffee table and sat down beside her on the love seat.

"He wouldn't give me a good reason, but I suspect it had to do with the background research for a story that I was doing on the development his corporation is planning. He didn't think it was necessary, and he became quite adamant about my not doing it. Then, when I told him I was going to use it for a free-lance submission, he blew."

Dan's head tilted quizzically. "Since when is free publicity frowned on in the business world?"

Shrugging her shoulders gracefully, she said, "That's what I thought was so strange, Dan."

He leaned back against the corner of the love seat. "How'd the guy find you? Going through the yellow pages? And why wouldn't a project like that warrant a bona fide PR agency?"

Somewhat resentful, she told him, "I'm good at my job."

Dan was busy thinking. "Probably too good. My guess is that he thought you'd be easier to handle than a regular PR firm with a large staff, didn't realize just how thorough you'd be in your work."

The compliment made her feel better. With a sudden burst of enthusiasm, she absently placed her hand on his knee. "There's more, Dan."

He glanced down at her hand and felt his Adam's apple jiggle. Raising his eyes to hers, he asked, "What?"

"Well, because Mark was acting so strangely, I started to do more research on the progress of the land development, but when I went to the county courthouse, none of the offices had any record of even a request for development on Pine Island—that's where Mark's brochures show the project."

She began a rhythmic tapping of her fingers on Dan's thigh. "Why would they have had brochures printed when the project hadn't even been approved by the county yet?"

Dan let a strained breath slip through his lips, and he tried to keep his mind off her fingers, which were setting his body ablaze with male energy. Casually he placed his arm in back of her on the love seat and inched closer to her. "Keep talking, Marcy. I think you're onto something."

Wide eyes looked up at his. "You do?"

Inhaling that intoxicating scent of hers, he said, "I certainly do."

Her index finger poked his chest. "What if Mark is misrepresenting what the Oceanview Villas project is all about? What if it's all some kind of racket behind a respectable front?"

While she'd been talking enthusiastically, Dan had maneuvered his head closer to hers, and now his lips were quite near her ear. "You're making all this sound very suspicious, indeed." He slipped his arm around her. "Tell me, was this Mark guy—"

"Mark Godette," she said.

"Was he ever in your house?"

"Yes," she told him, wondering why he was asking, trying not to think about why she had cuddled up when Dan had pulled her closer. "Why?"

Dan's other arm went around her. He closed his eyes and moved his cheek slowly over her hair. "Were you with him all the time?"

After thinking for a moment, she answered, "Yes," and started to toy with the top button of his partially opened shirt. Now she was fully aware that Dan was slowly and gently moving his hand over her back; she was also fully aware that she didn't want him to stop. Her fingertips eased into his shirt to the flurry of soft hair on his chest. His masculine scent flowed into her nostrils, creating a pleasurable feeling of light-headedness. She found her lips being drawn to the side of his neck.

Dan sighed deeply at their touch, but being a dedicated marshal, he persevered. "Did you keep your eyes on him all the time he was there?"

Marcy softly asked, "What?"

"Was he out of your sight—" his hand moved down over the swell of her hip "—even for a little while?"

"Umm...let me think." She tried to. And succeeded. "When I went to retrieve the background material he'd given me, and again when I went to get the stationery he wanted back," she murmured, really not caring about Mark or his project at the moment. Dan was doing marvelous things to her body and to her equilibrium.

"That's when he could have done it," Dan said in a hushed voice.

"Done what?"

"Planted the bug."

Marcy's eyes shot open. She sat up, and with both her hands on Dan's chest, she asked, "Why would he do that? What would he expect to hear?"

He told her, "You said he was uptight about your digging into his organization. What's he hiding?

Maybe he had to find out how much you knew already.''

''Dan,'' she said as he gently pulled her back down against him, ''I don't know anything.''

''Maybe he doesn't know that. Maybe he got bits and pieces of our conversations . . . heard U.S. Marshal Service and FBI and figured you were planning to bring the federal agents down on him. I don't know. There are lots of maybes.''

Resting against him again, Marcy said, ''The bombing, and the man shooting at us . . . Mark?''

''Probably not. My guess is hired guns. The guys in the front office of big operations don't do the dirty work.'' He thought and then told her, ''You must have really scared him and his boss.''

She asked, ''Why do you say 'his boss'?''

''From what you've told me, I'd say your Mark is just a well-paid office boy, but he's our number one lead right now. Tomorrow I'll get the Feds to check for wants and warrants and do a C and C on your ex-employer.''

''A C and C?''

''A credit and criminal check.''

Dan had conquered Marcy's resolve to maintain her distance from him. She wasn't protesting the fact that she was in his arms again.

Quietly she asked him, ''What do we do now, Dan?''

He unfolded his arms from around her, rose from the love seat and extended his hand to her, saying, "We get a good night's sleep. Coming, Marcy?"

She looked up into his shining eyes and reminded herself that she'd told him she would try to settle for the loving. Maybe she could. Without further hesitation, she slipped her hand into his.

CHAPTER THIRTEEN

BREAKFAST FARE AT DAN'S consisted of scrambled eggs à la Marcy and leftover sausage from the night before. This morning, Dan's apartment seemed charming to her. The furniture was wonderful; the minikitchen was wonderful; Dan was wonderful.

And for Dan the world had tilted right side up once more. He'd even forgone covering his scrambled eggs with pepper, just to please Marcy.

He was having a cigarette with his coffee when Marcy asked, "Dan, this land fraud business, how does it work?"

"There are varieties upon varieties," he told her. "People with larceny in their hearts will always figure out a way to beat the system. Sometimes it's done all on paper. An innocent real estate agent can get a phony clean title search and pass the property on to buyers who think they've got clear title, only to find out that they don't really own the property, even though they've paid the full price for it." Crumbling his cigarette in the ashtray, he continued. "But that's usually on a small scale, a local operation. It's the out-of-state guys who are harder to catch up with."

Marcy wondered about Mark's corporation. She asked, "Why's that?"

"Usually you've got someone up on top of the operation who's pretty important, well-heeled. He runs a legitimate business with branches throughout other states, and plants a few not-so-legal operations here and there, always careful to use other names for them so they won't be connected to him or his legitimate branches. Naturally the bogus ones disappear immediately after the kill."

"You think that's what Mark is involved in?"

"If he is, it's a biggie."

Marcy took their plates to the sink; then she turned and asked, "Why can't the FBI stop them? That would come under their jurisdiction, wouldn't it?"

"Manpower," he told her, "is the biggest problem the FBI and the Marshal Service have. The units that handle land fraud are also responsible for handling bank fraud, embezzlement and public corruption. And when federal agents do crack a case, we find ourselves stuck in the federal court system—it's choked. Look at what's going on now. The court's ordering counties to release prisoners because of overcrowded jails. The big guys know this, and they're willing to take chances."

Marcy was just about to say something when the phone rang.

"Yes... yeah, just got in last night," Dan said. "What's up?" To Marcy, he whispered, "My boss." He listened a while longer, and then a frown settled on his face. He glanced at his watch, and he asked, "Has Ted left there yet...? Ask him to stop by my place and pick me up. We'll ride over together... No, I haven't checked another car out yet... Okay, see you later."

Sitting back down at the table, Marcy asked, "Where are you going?"

He reached for his suit jacket and told her, "There's a big drug bust going on at the Port of Tampa. Some Panamanian ship was hauling in cocaine. There's a call out for all Spanish speaking agents to help screen and process the crew. It's top priority." He leaned down to kiss her. "Sorry, but I gotta run. I'll be back as soon as possible." He was halfway out the door when he glanced back over his shoulder. "I hate to leave you alone. You will stay right here, won't you?"

Marcy nodded and watched Dan close the door behind him.

As she did the dishes, she began thinking of what Dan had said about land fraud operations. She was still not totally convinced that Oceanview Villas was a sham. After all, Mark had wanted publicity about it. Why had he hired her in the first place? It was true that the news releases she'd written on Oceanview hadn't been passed to the press yet; nor had the radio and TV spots been aired, but the master schedule had been revised so that nothing would be released until next month.

Questions, and more questions. She had to have some answers, and the library was as good a place to start as any. Minutes later she was in her Thunderbird, parked in Dan's spot, and then she was taking off for the main library, feeling somewhat guilty about deceiving Dan.

Again she was seated in front of the microfilm screen with the *New York Times* film threaded in it. She rolled it forward, remembering that article on the interstate land fraud case had been dated March tenth or eleventh. Searching, she found it on the front page of the March eleventh edition.

FBI PROBES INTERSTATE LAND FRAUD
N.Y. BUSINESSMAN INVOLVED

She rescanned the article. Victor Lasky, whose Wall Street firm dealt with comparative market analysis and nationwide development investments, had been questioned regarding allegations that his firm was connected with a Fort Lauderdale, Florida, company that had been selling nonexistent homes.

"Sounds familiar," Marcy told herself, thinking of her conversation with Mark.

She forwarded the microfilm to page seven for the continued story and read that the Fort Lauderdale company had issued brochures and new releases describing the proposed development throughout the southeastern states, and that after receiving monies from down payments and the sale of bogus securities, the company had closed its doors and vanished. The evidence tying in Lasky's New York firm was circumstantial. No charges were filed.

Marcy tapped her fingers on the counter holding the screen for the microfilm. "That would explain the reason for wanting local publicity about the proposed development," she said softly. Then she wondered about that Victor Lasky character.

She unthreaded the microfilm, and returned it to its round can and placed it on top of the filing cabinet she'd taken it from. Then she went into the reference room, over to the shelves that held phone directories from all states. She pulled out the New York City directory and went to one of the tables in the room. The listings under real estate were overwhelming, and she could find none under the name "Lasky." But she did find a Victor R. Lasky listed in the white pages, and she jotted the number down.

After replacing the phone directory, she went to the public phone in the hall of the library. She had the call charged to her home phone and waited as she listened to the ringing at the other end.

"Mr. Lasky's residence," a woman's voice said.

Marcy tried to sound businesslike when she said, "This is Mr. Godette's secretary in Clearwater, Florida. Mr. Godette is calling for Mr. Lasky."

"I'm sorry. Mr. Lasky isn't here at the present."

Marcy asked, "May I have his office number, please?" She wrote it down as the woman gave it to her. And then she placed another call to New York.

"Nationwide Analysis and Appraisal," a woman's voice said.

As Marcy wrote down the name of the firm, she again said, "This is Mr. Godette's secretary in Clearwater, Florida. Mr. Godette is calling for Mr. Lasky."

"Mr. Lasky is out of town. May I take a message?"

"No, thank you," she answered and hung up. "Out of town," she repeated, and then a dark thought crossed her mind. She dialed again, this time a local call.

"Oceanview Villas."

Marcy knew the voice to be Mark's secretary. She said, "This is Mr. Lasky's secretary in New York. May I speak to Mr. Lasky, please?"

"He's not here right now. One moment."

"This is Mark Godette . . . hello . . . hello!"

A stunned Marcy held on to the receiver for a few frightening seconds. Then she quickly returned it to its cradle on the wall.

In his office, Mark asked his secretary, "Who was that who called?"

"Mr. Lasky's secretary in New York."

He ordered, "Call her back . . . right now."

Marcy sat in her car in the library parking lot for a while, trying to put all the pieces in place. It was too much like a nightmare. "Patricia Dodd," she told herself, "you were born to attract trouble." Her frenzied thoughts raced on. Dan had been right. It must have been Mark who had placed the bug under the end table, and when he had heard mention of the FBI and the U.S. Marshal Service, he must have reported it to

Lasky, who'd rushed down to see how serious matters really were. There was probably too much money at stake to just pull out. Besides, what crime had been committed so far? Proposing to build some houses on an island? All they would have to do now was file an application with the Board of County Commissioners, and everything would be legal.

But they were worried about her and the investigative story she'd told Mark she was going to pursue. That was bad enough, but they could have killed Dan. What if he had opened the door? What if he had taken the shots meant for her on the pier? She knew she could run away now, leave the state; but Dan, now that there was proof that Mark was the one out to get her, would probably rush head-on to certain death.

Her face muscles tightened, and a firm resolve settled on her features. The wheels of her car screeched as she tore out of the parking lot and headed for the shop where she'd purchased the gun. An unloaded gun wouldn't be much protection against the likes of the Lasky-Godette duo.

An hour later Marcy was back at her house, loading the clip with bullets, following the clerk's instructions. The gun felt hard and cold in her hand, and she didn't think she'd ever really be able to use it on anyone, but if it meant saving Dan's life, she'd find the strength somehow.

She placed the leftover bullets back in the cardboard box they'd come in and put it in the drawer of her desk. The gun went into her handbag.

Not knowing how much longer she'd be at Dan's apartment, she went upstairs and put a few more things in another suitcase, and then she went into the kitchen and bagged some items from the freezer and some canned goods, knowing that Dan's cupboard was almost bare. It was late afternoon when she arrived back at his apartment, but Dan hadn't returned yet. She charmed the manager, and he let her in.

She busied herself with straightening up the place a bit, and then she fixed herself some iced tea and prepared scalloped potatoes while waiting for the pork chops to defrost. It was a little after six-thirty when she heard Dan's key in the lock.

He looked harried, and she sympathized. As Murphy had said, his was not a nine-to-five job. And then her heart went out to him, knowing that after days like this he had to come home to an empty apartment, a quiet one, where there was little to do, except for maybe watching a TV that would work only from one spot.

He deserved more than that, but they'd been over that enough already. He was just not prepared for a commitment right now.

Dan was carrying a grocery bag and a six-pack, but as soon as he closed the door behind him, he said, "Something smells good, and here I was ready to settle for frozen pizza." He glanced around at the organized and polished room. "You've been busy, or has Murphy been here?"

"That's funny, Dan," she told him, taking the bag from his arm. As he put the beer into the refrigerator, she asked him, "Everything settled at the Port of Tampa?"

He tossed his jacket over one of the chairs. "As far as I'm concerned, yes, but they're still unloading the stuff and labeling it all. With all they had on there, it's a wonder the ship floated. They also had enough firearms on board to start a minor revolution."

Marcy thought of the gun she had in her handbag, but decided not to mention that she had it. She was sure that if Dan knew she had one, he'd take it. He didn't have the greatest faith in her marksmanship.

He sniffed the aroma that filled the kitchen. "What've you stirred up?"

"How does pork chops, scalloped potatoes and broccoli sound?"

His face darkened. "Pork chops? You went out."

"Uh-huh, shopping and to the library." She said nothing about going to the house. "Your manager's a sweetheart; he let me back in. You may as well give me a key, Elliott."

Nodding painfully, he took his spare key from his wallet and tossed it on the table. "I'm going to shower."

"Go ahead. I'll have a cold beer ready for you when you come out."

He went to her and placed his palm along the side of her cheek. "You're something else, Marcy, real special, and it's nice to have someone here to come home to. I've missed that."

Marcy's heart fluttered, and she felt her cheek flush where his hand was. He slowly moved his fingertips across her lips, leaned down and gently kissed her.

SHE LISTENED to the sound of the shower and his off-key singing as she started the pork chops, and suddenly she felt like a young girl again, a young girl intent on making her man happy.

Her man. But was he? For now he was, and although the relationship was on his terms, she wouldn't have given up the happiness she felt at the moment for anything.

When Dan did return to the living room, his hair was damp and combed back, and as they drank their beer, Marcy told him about her trip to the library and her phone calls to New York and to Mark's office.

Dan said, "This guy Lasky is definitely the one you read about?"

"Dan, how many Victor Laskys from New York are visiting Clearwater right now?"

He nodded. "The whole thing fits in, doesn't it? Godette's running a front for another Lasky scam."

"Right here in our own backyard," Marcy added. "What do we do about it? Tell the FBI?"

Leaning forward on the chair, Dan rested his arms on his legs and clasped his hands. "We can alert them that something illegal *may* happen, but we don't have any evidence that it's going to. It would stop them here, but they'd just move on somewhere else.''

Marcy put her glass down. ''What if we could find some kind of evidence, some kind of proof? Wouldn't that put them both out of business?''

Dan had been thinking that all along. ''Unless *I* try to find something solid against them.''

Marcy didn't like that. ''Dan,'' she said firmly, ''I've done pretty well so far, haven't I? What makes you think I can't help any further? Why is it that a man always—''

''Marcy,'' he cut her off, ''I don't want you any more involved than you already are. These guys have connections, muscle behind them, and hired guns to do the dirty work.''

''I'm already involved. A bomb went off outside my door. A man shot at us in the middle of the night.'' She stood up. ''I'd call that being involved.''

Dan rose and took hold of her shoulders. His voice was soft, but his eyes were softer. ''Listen to me. We're talking big-league trouble now. I want you somewhere safe while I'm checking this thing out. I could wind up fertilizing an orange grove in central Florida, and I don't want you beside me.''

No man has a right to have such beautiful eyes, such sensual lips, she told herself, but to him, she said, ''I like the smell of orange blossoms.'' Then she put her arms around his waist and leaned against his comforting body. Resting her cheek on his shoulder, she said, ''Dan, they could already know you're a U.S.

marshal. That would put you pretty high on their mischief list.'' His arms tightened around her as she continued. ''Maybe it was you they were trying to kill with the explosion...and on the pier.'' She hugged him tighter. ''I'm frightened for you.''

Kissing her hair, he breathed in the clean, sweet smell of it. ''What's to worry about?''

She glanced up at him. ''Let someone else go after them.''

''On what evidence?'' he reminded her.

''Dan, you're one man. It's too dangerous.''

He'd already formulated a plan in his mind. ''It's too dangerous for you to be in on. Remember, I'm the trained marshal. I want you to promise me you'll stay right here. I mean it this time.''

''Tell me, bwana, can I breathe?''

''I'll get back to you on that,'' he said. He looked at her worried expression and smiled the smile that sent her spirits soaring. ''Please, Marcy. Just this once. Do what I say. If I have to worry about you, I'm not going to be able to do my best work. Promise me?''

''I promise,'' she said softly, hating the fact that she was lying to him.

''That's my sweet girl.''

Yes, I am your girl, Dan, she repeated silently as his lips touched hers quickly and gently.

They continued talking about the situation throughout dinner.

Dan said, "Mark's probably had a bug and eye surveillance on you for weeks."

"A what?"

"He—or someone—has been listening and watching your every move."

"*Our* every move, you mean."

"Yeah. They may have followed me to the Marshal Service office."

"And me to the county courthouse. We know they were at the Whitesands Hotel." She thought a second. "Do you think they followed us to Miami?"

"The way you drive?" He laughed. "They're killers, not kamikaze kooks."

She reminded him, "We got there safely, didn't we?"

"After you almost sideswiped that semi."

"You said not to dillydally."

He admitted, "I did, didn't I?"

After dinner, Dan helped with the dishes, and afterward, in the living room, he looked at his watch, thinking, *It's too early yet*.

When Marcy came out of the kitchen, he raised his hand and beckoned to her with his curled index finger.

"Don't do that," she told him. "You look like a scorpion."

"Come here... Please?"

"Why?"

"Because if you don't, I'm going to come over to you."

She noted the gleam in his eyes, saw the way his breathing had deepened. There was no way she was going to go running when he summoned her, she told herself. But her brain seemed reluctant to pass that message on to her feet. Standing in front of him, she asked, "What?"

"This."

His movement was swift. In the next moment, she felt his strong arms around her, felt his warm breath against her mouth, his moist lips covering hers with an urgency that took her by surprise. Her arms hung defenselessly at her sides as the taste of him sent shock waves rippling through her body. Slowly but surely, she moved her arms upward and slid her hands over his shoulders—such nice shoulders, so warm and strong. Her fingers cupped his firm neck and then slipped upward into his silky hair. When one of his hands eased down over the small of her back and then farther down, she felt her knees buckle. But his strong arms supported her.

Dan's lips were still on hers as he carried her into his bedroom, and then she became aware that her tingling body was being freed from the clothes that were suddenly suffocating. Dizzy with expectation, with languid eyes she saw him toss the bedcover aside, and she felt herself being gently lowered. She watched him undress, until he stood defiantly before her.

Her senses sharpened as she felt the bed give under his weight, felt the warmth emanate from his flesh and caress her own as his body slid next to hers.

Gazing at her, he said, "I could look at you the rest of my life. Maybe not just look, but I'd be content to be this close to you, to touch you." She quivered as his hand softly moved over her body, sliding, caressing, probing gently. She felt his eager fingers retrace pathways intimately known, as though he were trying to memorize her every curve. "Don't laugh if I tell you something," he whispered.

"I won't," she promised as his hand began that maddening caress at the most sensitive part of her body.

"When I'm with you like this, I feel like that kid again, the one locked in that big department store... the kid who could have anything he wanted. I thought I wanted lots of things then, but now I know this is all I've ever wanted, all I'll ever want." He leaned down, kissed one nipple and then slowly circled it with the tip of his tongue.

Marcy rested her hand on his curved back. His skin was smooth as velvet, warm and comforting. When Dan rested his face on her bosom and moved his leg across hers, she felt as if she were wrapped in love. Her fingertips dallied in the waves of his hair as his periodic kisses tormented her flesh. "The boy has become a wonderful man," she said softly.

"If you think I'm wonderful, it's only because I'm a reflection of the wonder in you."

As he spoke, she could feel his breath across her breasts, his fingers begin a soft exploration. She closed her eyes as she slipped her other hand across his broad shoulder to ease it down over his strong arm and move onto his abdomen. Her fingers searched and then caressed him.

For minutes they gave pleasure to each other, whispering endearments, sighing deep sighs. Then, Dan's whispers muted into kisses interrupted by taunting flicks of his tongue. His lips brushed across the alabaster sheen of her skin, lower and lower, his mouth spreading shivers of sweet solace over her as he neared his goal, all the while tormenting her. She tensed, felt the easy, rhythmic gestures he offered, and then she soared upward until millions of colorful stars exploded.

Bereft of a sense of time, her arms automatically opened to him, and she felt his weight upon her. Then came the joining of their bodies and souls, a unity that filled her with the assurance that she was a woman who was desired and loved.

Later Marcy lay quietly in Dan's arms, her cheek resting on his warm chest. She enjoyed the easy strokes of his moving palm across her back.

With closed eyes, he whispered, "I think you're just about the prettiest girl in the world."

Her eyes were closed, also. "I always wanted my father to tell me that. I wanted to hear him say I was the prettiest girl in the world, but I guess I wasn't that pretty."

Dan admitted, "I always wanted a father who'd come to the school football games to watch me play."

She asked, "Were you good?"

"Pretty good. But if a father had come, I think I would have been better."

Marcy kissed his chest, enjoying the manly taste of him. "I guess we both learned to live without illusions." Her hand eased up over his shoulder, and she felt the rounded scar made by the bullet. She asked, "Is your work always so dangerous?"

"It can be," he answered quietly, "but in my line, danger is an occupational hazard." He chuckled softly and said, "Your work has turned out to be pretty dangerous, too." He brushed his hand over her hair. "But you don't have to work. Why do you?"

She nuzzled closer. "If I were a man, you'd never ask that. Why do you work?"

Eerily he said, "To rid the world of evil."

Marcy didn't laugh. "Is it so important for you to rid the world of evil that you'd give up the chance of personal happiness?"

Stroking her shoulder, he said, "I have to believe in something."

Marcy rose up on her elbow and looked into his shining eyes. "Believe in me, Dan."

He returned her steadfast gaze and ran his fingers over her hair. "You want me to make you my whole world?"

Laying her head back down, she said, "I want you to say I am . . . whether it's true or not."

"There shouldn't be any lies between us, Marcy."

There was a terrible silence between them for a few moments, and then he finally said, "It just wouldn't work. Can you see yourself living on my salary minus my child support obligations?''

She was afraid to move. ''Why would we have to? I have money.''

''That money is yours, not ours.''

Her attempt to get up was thwarted by his powerful arm. ''You're living in the dark ages, Elliott. You and I are supposed to be equals. I even have the right to vote now. . . remember? Everything about us should be ours. . .not this is his, this is hers. Anyway, by some standards, I'm not that rich.''

''By mine you are, and I don't feel comfortable about it.''

''Are you going to feel more comfortable when it's time for us to say goodbye?''

He said, ''We'll cross that bridge when we come to it.'' Then he asked, ''What time is it?''

Marcy raised her head and checked the clock on the nightstand at her side of the bed. ''Almost ten. Why?''

Touching the tip of her nose with his index finger, he told her, ''Because tonight I'm going to break into Oceanview Villas.''

She raised the rest of her body. ''You're what?''

He smiled as he took in the beauty of her form, and then he said, ''So I'm bending the rules a little. You got a better idea?''

She nervously spread her fingers through her flowing hair. ''Can't you get a search warrant or something?''

Almost jestingly he told her, "The guys around the coffee machine at work are spreading the word that judges like a shred of evidence before stomping over anyone's constitutional rights nowadays. We'd need more than your having been fired."

"My house being bombed and our getting shot at aren't good reasons?"

"How would I convince a judge Mark or Lasky was responsible? I couldn't even show probable cause." He reached for her, pulled her back down and wrapped her in his arms.

Marcy's voice was filled with concern. "Can't you get some help?"

"Manpower is hard to come by unless you've got a solid case. We've just got suspicions."

She asked, "Why tonight?"

"I'm not going to chance that Mark and Lasky will clean house and run. I'm hoping they think the bombing and shooting were enough to scare you off. They'd have no way of knowing you were back in town trying to hassle them again."

Slipping her hand around his waist, she hugged him. "Well, at least you'll have me."

"What?"

"Me."

In a flash he was up, too. "Marcy, I'm not just dropping in for tea with that guy. I don't know what or who I'll find there. We're not dealing with fun people. There's no way you're tagging along on this one."

She poked her finger against his bare chest. "There's no way you're going without me."

As though talking to a child, he told her, "Marcy, Marcy, this is my work. Remember, I'm the trained—"

"Yeah, yeah, you're the trained marshal. You've branded that into my memory forever, but think about this, Elliott." She punctuated her next statements with more pokes. "I'm the one who knows his office. I've seen where he keeps things. Do you know where his safe is?"

"I'll find it," he told her, knowing he was losing ground.

"You'll find it a lot faster if I show you where it is."

"You could tell me."

"But I'm not going to," she said firmly, adding, "Besides, won't you need someone to hold things?"

"Like what?"

"How should I know? You're the trained marshal!"

The discussion went on as they donned their robes, and it continued on the way to the kitchen, where Marcy started to fix fresh coffee.

"Make it instant," he told her. "I don't have much time."

She adjusted the flame under the enamel kettle and then leaned back against the countertop. Her eyes started at his bare feet, went up those gorgeous legs that Murphy had said she'd die for, and then rose quickly over his short robe and up to his skeptical face.

"You know, Dan, you are quite a magnificent specimen." She smiled slowly. "People looking at you would see a confident man of power and intelligence, a dynamic and attractive man."

"They'd see all that?"

"Until they tried to reason with you. Then they'd recognize that you were lapsing into senility." She left him standing alone in the kitchen and sailed into the living room.

Dan's moan filled the apartment. In the living room, he saw her sitting on the love seat; she had a pout that would have done a child in her terrible twos proud. "Okay, you win, but once we get there, it's my party." He raised one finger. "I am *numero uno*."

His acquiescence transformed her pout into an excited smile. Sitting down next to her, he said, "Page one, right out of the manual . . . no noise."

"Really, Dan, I wasn't born—"

His palm covered her lips. "Put your mouth in neutral and listen. What we're going to do is not exactly legal. If we get caught, Mark could file charges, and we'd both probably only see the sky occasionally." She nodded her understanding, and he took his hand away. "Now, while I finish my coffee, you go put on something dark. Slacks if you have them. No jewelry."

Again she nodded.

"Now go." He watched as she bounded into the bedroom, then went into the kitchen and subsided into a chair. Listening to the racket she was making just getting dressed, he propped his elbows on his thighs, leaned forward and held his forehead in his hands....

CHAPTER FOURTEEN

IT WAS A LITTLE PAST MIDNIGHT when Marcy and Dan parked a block away from the building in which Mark's offices were located. The night was still, humid. Shadows cast by street lights spilled over the street. Once past the front of the building, Dan pulled her down an alleyway and around to the back. A quick slip of a credit card, and they were in the service entrance. Minutes later, they'd climbed the stairs to the fourth floor, and Dan was picking the lock on the carved hardwood door marked Oceanview Villas, Inc.

"What if someone saw us come in?" Marcy whispered.

"The only people up this time of night are vampires." He tried a different pick and jiggled it in the lock a bit to reposition the pins and tumblers.

"Dan, what if—"

"Be quiet!"

"Quiet? It's so quiet I can hear my hair growing."

The door opened. He glanced down the long hallway. "Okay. Let's do it."

She slipped inside the dark suite. He followed, silently closed the door behind him and took what Marcy thought was a pen from his jacket pocket. But it wasn't a pen: it was a little flashlight with the brightest light she would ever have imagined on such a small apparatus. He scanned the first room and then doused the light. Marcy stood frozen as she watched him go from window to window and close the drapes. Suddenly she wasn't feeling as brave as she had when Dan had agreed to let her come along.

"Come on," he whispered and started toward the inner office.

She followed right behind him. In a low voice, she asked, "What are we looking for?"

"We'll know when we find it."

Marcy tugged at his sleeve. "Dan, I'm worried."

His voice rose to an almost natural volume. "This is no time to be afraid."

"I didn't say I was afraid. I said I was worried."

"Shush!"

"Okay, okay, but listen *numero uno*, I thought the first rule of command was to inspire confidence."

"I'm gonna expire you if you don't keep your voice down."

Marcy's eyes followed the little spot of light as he checked out Mark's office. Quietly she said, "You really enjoy this excitement, don't you?"

"Beats sitting on a stakeout day after day. Where's that safe you were telling me about?"

She pointed to her right. "In back of that bar cart, there. The bottom of the wall paneling opens out."

"Good." He glanced over to the file cabinet near her. Silently he moved to it, pulled on a drawer handle and found that it was locked. Moments later his supply of lock picks were at work, and the drawer opened. "You check the files while I work on the safe."

"Dan," she asked quietly, "What if the police find us?"

"Don't dwell on negative thoughts," he ordered. "Get busy."

Still whispering, she said, "But shouldn't we have a story ready?"

"I have mine," he whispered back. "I just prove to them that I'm a marshal. I followed you up here and caught you first."

Full-voiced, she said, "Thanks a lot."

"Quiet! There's bound to be a night guard. While you're checking those files, try to come up with your own alibi."

"My hero," she mumbled.

Dan didn't hear her. Marcy started through the top drawer of the file cabinet, but she couldn't help but be intrigued with his expertise as a burglar. She heard the clack of the safe handle and saw him start to ease the door open. "How did you do that so quickly?"

"Piece of cake." He cocked his head and he said, "Freeze!"

Marcy froze, hoping that there was a private exit somewhere in Mark's suite. Then she heard it: someone was rattling the knob of the office door. She felt all the color drain from her face. Her mind began a tumble of alibi games. *I could say he forced me. I have amnesia . . . psychotic episodes.*

But the noise stopped, and they heard receding footsteps.

"Okay," Dan said and started checking the contents of the safe. "Well, well. Look what we have here." He stood up and put a leather-bound box on the desk near him.

"What is it?" Marcy looked in the opened box and saw two syringes and some paraphernalia that she couldn't identify.

"Your friend Mark is a regular stabber-in-the-arm." He held one syringe to his arm. "You know . . . a junkie." He shook his head and then asked, "Find anything?"

"No, but I don't know what I'm supposed to be looking for."

"Just keep looking. If anything is out of the ordinary, holler. No! don't do that, just tell me quietly." He returned to the safe, and Marcy started in on the second drawer.

She peered in the first folder. It had no label. All it held were two pieces of paper, a single long list of numbers on each. "Dan," she said quietly, but one look at the expression on his face told her he'd found something, also.

"My, my," he said, holding up several packets of certificates and bonds. "If these are bogus, we've got him on the illegal sale of unregistered securities, abusing the mail and a dozen other felonies."

"Dan, do these mean anything? These numbers?"

He scanned one page. "They're chronological. Could be bank account numbers...but where? There's something rotten going on here." His eyes settled on a piece of equipment on the table by the window. "He's even got a shredder." He turned his attention back to the list of numbers. "But how do we tie it all in with Lasky?"

She suggested, "Tell Mark we have these. Make him confess."

His expression went bland. "You don't happen to have any other brilliant ideas...ones that might work?"

"It was only a suggestion."

Dan noticed the computer setup along the far side of Mark's office. "Marcy, can you work this data control bank?"

She gave it a quick once-over. "I think so."

"Turn it on and punch up this first number."

She studied the keyboard for a moment and then typed the number.

He said, "Request the name and location of the account and get a printout on all this."

The printer clicked away. "Vernon Lowell, Southeast National Bank, Miami, Florida."

"Now this number," Dan said as he pointed to the second one on the list.

Marcy did so. "Vincent Lorry, First Federal Bank, Atlanta, Georgia."

Dan said, "Well, I'll be. They're probably all pseudonyms for Victor Lasky. The guy's got the ethics of a fungus."

"What does all this mean, Dan?"

"It means that when the money starts pouring in, it's sent to accounts all over the country in small amounts, all to Victor Lasky. With this list and a little footwork by the FBI, the IRS will hit him with a fine that will have him feeling it for life. And with the printouts you're going to get, Mark will talk like a well-schooled parrot." Then he told her, "Request a list of all account numbers, names and locations of accounts. We lucked out."

"A little bit of luck. A lot of Daniel Elliott," she told him.

"And Marcy Keaton. One more thing, hurry it up. We probably kicked off an alarm just by turning this thing on."

She looked up at him. "I didn't hear anything."

"You aren't supposed to."

While Marcy proceeded quickly, Dan replaced the folder she'd found in the file cabinet and locked it. After taking one bond certificate and one stock certificate, he returned the others and Mark's leather toy box back to the safe, closed it and put the bar cart back in position. Marcy gathered the printouts he'd requested and turned off the computer.

"Dan, should we—" The sound of a distant screaming siren filled her ears. "Oh, God, what're we going to do?"

"About one-to-five if they find us in here," he told her, grabbing her arm and pulling her toward the door to the suite.

He opened the door a crack, looked out and then rushed her to the staircase, just missing the guard who was scurrying down the hall toward Godette's office. In moments, they were back out in the alley, heading for the street. They both saw the flashing lights of a security car dart past the alleyway at the same moment. Next, they heard the screeching of rubber as the car pulled over to the curb.

Marcy quickly shoved the folded printouts behind the waistband of Dan's pants and pulled open the top buttons of her dark silk blouse. A bewildered Dan watched as she jerked it off her right shoulder, grabbed his arms and said, "Kiss me!" Then she thrust his body up against the wall of the adjacent building and pulled his head down to hers.

The next thing they knew, a blinding light was on both of them. Marcy put her hand up to shield her eyes, but kept her body pushed against Dan's for fear that the printouts would be spotted by the guards who had trained the light on them. "Oh, no," she moaned, showing the guards a little more shoulder. "I knew my husband would have us followed."

The guard nearest them said, "We're not interested in you or your husband, lady. Did you see anybody come out of the back of the building?"

"No," Dan said quickly, "but a man did go in about twenty minutes ago when we were back there." He winked at the man holding the flashlight on them.

The guard looked at Marcy's shoulder and smiled at Dan. Then he told his partner, who was still checking out Marcy's shoulder, "Roger, you take the front, and I'll take the back entrance. He's still up there." The two security men went about their duty.

Together, Dan and Marcy dashed for her car. They'd just gotten in when Dan saw a long black limousine pull up in front of the office building.

"Uh-oh," Dan said as he watched the man get out and rush toward the entrance of the building.

"It's Mark!" Marcy said.

"Damn! They must have notified him when the alarm went off. I was hoping the security people would check for a malfunction first."

Dan put the car in gear and drove off quickly. "Marcy, I'm going to have you drop me off at the Marshal Service office, but I don't know how long I'll be. I also don't want you to go back to my apartment alone. If Mark and his friends put two and two together, they may start looking for you, and my place may already be on their list. You need some sleep, though. Do you think Murphy would mind some middle-of-the-night company?"

"No, Dan, she's a good friend."

"Then I'll pick you up there when I'm finished." He looked over at her. He didn't want to tell her what he knew he had to. "Marcy, you're probably going to be called to testify when all this is brought to a head. Will you go through that again?''

The word "testify" shot through her like a sharp pain. *Not again,* she said silently, feeling her heart begin to race even more. Then she felt Dan's hand on hers, and she looked at him and nodded.

Dan said, "When I pick you up at Murphy's, I'll take you to a safe residence...probably in Tampa. I'm sorry to ask you to go through it all again."

Tiredly, she answered, "We have to do what we have to do, don't we, Dan?"

He pulled up in front of his office, kissed her, and Marcy took off for Murphy's.

When she got to the dark house, she sat in the car for a while and then decided not to intrude on her friend, after all. It was after midnight, and Murphy was a working woman. She'd just sit in the car and wait for Dan.

But a little after one o'clock, Marcy began to worry. It had seemed like much longer than an hour, but she knew there was no telling when Dan would finish up at the office.

After repositioning herself in the car, trying to get a little more comfortable, she decided that if she were going to be hauled off to some strange place across the bridge in Tampa, she'd want her handbag with her, and she didn't want Dan finding that gun in it. So she switched on the ignition and took off for Dan's apartment, pleased that she had thought to put his key in her pants pocket.

She wasn't gone very long when Dan pulled up at Murphy's. There was no Thunderbird there. He didn't like that one bit, and when Murphy told him Marcy had never arrived, he really began to worry. He'd told her definitely not to return to his apartment, but where else would she go?

Murphy suggested, "Maybe home to her house, Dan. Her home really is her castle."

He decided to give it a try since her place was closer than his, but when he saw that her car wasn't in the driveway, his worry turned to near panic. Not certain what he'd find, he decided to check the inside of the house, anyway.

He unlocked the door with the key she'd given him, went inside and switched the lights on. He was about to go upstairs when he heard her phone ring.

His lifting of the receiver automatically turned on the tape recorder.

"Yes," he said and waited.

"We have your Miss Keaton," Mark said. "If you ever want to see her again, you will do exactly as I tell you."

Dan bristled, felt his blood boil. "You hurt her... and you'll wish you'd never been born."

"You don't have time for threats, Mr. Elliott. I want what you took from Oceanview Villas."

It was Mark Godette, Dan assumed. "Word gets around pretty fast."

"Security phoned me the minute the alarm went off, according to my instructions," Mark told him.

Dan asked, "How do you know we took anything?"

"We already know what Miss Keaton *says* you took."

"If you've done anything to her—"

"Don't waste my time, Mr. Elliott. Just shut up and listen. If what you bring us agrees with what she has told us, she goes free."

Dan knew there was little chance they'd let Marcy go, but it was a chance he would have to take. "What do you want me to do?" he asked, his voice cold and sullen.

"Drive to the Clearwater Marina and park there. We'll take care of the rest. Be sure and bring what you took from my office."

Dan put the receiver down slowly. In his heart, he knew he and Marcy were as good as dead. They knew too much. But maybe by holding on to what they wanted, he'd have some bargaining power for Marcy's life.

"Damned if they're going to get away with this one," he said as he folded a few pieces of newspaper and shoved them into a manila envelope he found in the desk. Then he turned off the lights, locked the door, got into his car and drove off.

So preoccupied was he with desperate worry about Marcy that he failed to notice the black sedan pull away from the curb down the block behind him and begin to follow him.

In the back seat, Mark's fingers nervously tapped the phone he'd just used. "It worked. It was the two of them who broke in, and he thinks we have her. Where do you suppose she is? We need her, too," he told the dignified-looking man sitting next to him.

A smooth-sounding voice responded, "Don't worry about Miss Keaton. We'll take care of her later."

Dan parked near the entrance to the marina and waited. A few moments later, the black sedan pulled up next to his car. Dan got out, and the first thing he saw was a .38 staring him in the face. Mark was holding it. The driver of the sedan, a monster of a thug, frisked Dan and relieved him of his .45.

"Put on your gloves, Jo-Jo," Mark told the brute. "Drive his car back to the house and pick up the woman when she gets there. Bring her here and then get rid of his car."

Dan felt the blood rush to his head. "You don't have her!" He was almost relieved, but the thought of that ape getting hold of Marcy swept away his momentary peace of mind. But no, she wouldn't go back to the house. Where the hell was she? Car trouble, maybe? He hoped so.

He looked at the .38 the man was aiming straight at him. "Mark Godette, I presume," he said with a touch of sarcasm in his voice.

The man nodded.

Dan asked, "Why didn't you just take me at the house?"

"I detest noise pollution. Why disturb the neighbors when we could get you here nice and quietly?"

"We?" Dan asked.

"Yes. There's someone I'd like you to meet."

A well-dressed man got out of the car, and it occurred to Dan that he was the sort of man one would expect to see playing polo or sitting in a box at the opera. He had about five inches on Mark, was younger, had blond hair still untouched by gray, and his eyes were even bluer than Mark's. They looked sucked in, however, behind too narrow sockets. But he was elegant, all right, in an Yves Saint Laurent suit and a Pierre Cardin tie. Dan hated his guts instantly.

He chanced a guess. "Victor Lasky."

Lasky said, "You're well-informed. Mark tells me you're a United States marshal. Well, you and your FBI friends have been a thorn in my side for too long now."

Dan sized him up again and wished that Mark didn't have that .38 pointed at him. He was aching to wipe the smirk off Lasky's face. "One of these days, Lasky, my friends are going to put you out of business."

"You won't be around to see it," Lasky told him plainly. He turned to Mark. "Bring him along." Then he started down the dock.

Mark nudged Dan with his gun, and they followed Lasky onto a Ponderosa yacht moored in a slip at the end of one of the piers. Moonlight cast a blue-silver haze on the deck. Dan looked around in disgust at the plush furniture, the carpeted floor and well-stocked bar.

The elegant host leaned back against the boat's railing and eyed the manila envelope Dan held. "You brought what I want?"

Dan said, "You get it when I know Marcy's all right and is going to stay that way."

"I can be very persuasive."

"Why don't you give it a rest, Lasky?" Dan suggested.

Lasky nodded, and Mark whacked Dan on the side of the head with his gun and then stepped back as Dan fell to the floor, unconscious.

"Newspaper!" Lasky said furiously, holding the open envelope that had dropped to the floor with Dan.

"We know they took a bond and a stock certificate. They may have gotten something else," Mark said. "Keaton must have it."

Lasky said, "We'll know soon enough."

WITH HER HANDBAG ON THE SEAT beside her, Marcy drove back to Murphy's to wait for Dan. Seeing that his car still wasn't there, she decided to go by her house and pick up the Oceanview Villas file. If she were going to go into hiding again, at least she could make good use of her time. There was too good a firsthand story in all this, and she wanted to have it ready before the newspapers were filled with accounts of the uncovering of the land fraud operation.

She parked in her driveway and hurried into the house. Not bothering to turn the lights on, she went directly to her desk and retrieved the file from her desk drawer, but as she did, she noticed the light shining on the tape recorder that Dan had attached to the phone. That indicated that a conversation had taken place on the phone. The tape recorder wasn't like an answering service, Dan had told her. It only recorded two-way conversations. And the light hadn't been on when she had last seen it. Would Dan have been here and placed a call? she wondered.

Quickly she punched the rewind lever. In seconds the tape had stopped, and she pushed Play. As she listened to the tape, she began to feel sick to her stomach. Dan was walking into a trap, and it had all been her fault. If only she had stayed at Murphy's, as he had asked her to!

Then she heard the sound of the doorknob being rattled. She knew the front door automatically locked when she'd closed it. Maybe it was Dan, but maybe it wasn't. Quickly and quietly she went to the front window and peered out from behind the drapes.

A tall, ugly-looking man was trying to force the lock! And the gun was in her handbag on the seat of her car.

Adrenaline shot through her, and she rushed backward away from the door, bumping into one of the easy chairs as she did. She stifled a cry of fear when she heard the door start to give under the man's obvious strength.

With little time to think, she quickly slipped into the half closet that was built under the stairway to the second floor. The closet was used for storage; its door was not obvious because it was camouflaged by the same kind of wooden panels that were on either side of it. Marcy had just managed to close the door after her when she heard the front door crashing open. Footsteps thudded just outside the closet.

She trembled as she crouched—for lack of room—under the stairway. The footsteps stopped. It was quiet. And then they started again. They became more distant, but she couldn't tell where the man was. Then she thought she heard the sliding glass door to the Florida room being opened.

Should she run for it? she debated. No, she didn't dare. He'd be right on top of her before she even got to the car. Taking a deep breath, she decided to wait. And then she heard it: the sound of footsteps going up the stairway. She counted them: one, two, three, four. She continued listening until she thought he was at the top of the stairs. She forced herself to wait a few more seconds, hoping he'd start checking the rooms. Then she bolted out of the closet.

The front door was opened wide. She ran desperately. Thank God, she thought, that she'd been holding her keys in her hand all this time! She jumped in, started the car, slammed the door shut, then burned rubber as she backed out of the driveway, almost hitting the car that was parked across the driveway.

The back wheel of the right side went over the curb, causing her to bounce as she whipped out into the street, tires screeching.

Then she saw that the car in her driveway was Dan's, but she also saw the huge man come running out of the house toward her. She shifted gears and took off as though the devil himself was after her. Looking into her rearview mirror, she saw the man scamper into the car and take off behind her.

Ignoring a stop sign, she swerved around the corner and pressed down firmly on the gas pedal, trying to maintain good control on the wheel, although her hands were like ice. The car shot forward.

The neighborhood streets were deserted. She decided there was little hope of being stopped for speeding in this part of Clearwater, so she drove the car toward U.S. Route 19, hoping to attract some attention with the crazy way she was driving. *It's true,* she told herself as she checked the rearview mirror again and saw that the man was still almost right in back of her, *there's never a cop around when you want one.*

She turned another corner on two wheels, sideswiping a parked van. For a few seconds she lost control of her car. It swayed to the left and then to the right. She banged her head on the window, but then she was able to guide the vehicle back to her side of the street.

Then she felt it—her car was being banged from behind. Whoever was driving Dan's car was trying to force her off the road. She looked up ahead at the overpass construction going on. She knew the ramp was still incomplete. It was her last chance, she decided. "Here goes!"

She steered the car directly toward the ramp that rose up over the street, but when she was only a few feet away from it, she turned the wheel to the left. The rear of the car hit the cement railing at the foot of the ramp; again she was bounced around before the car careered toward the sidewalk and came to a sudden halt.

Jerking her head to the right, she shot a glance out of her car window in time to see Dan's car go shooting up the ramp. She gasped as it sailed out into space. Then, almost in slow motion, it went down, nose first, onto the street below. The sound of it crashing on the asphalt was deafening.

Marcy crossed her arms on the steering wheel and placed her head on them as she took in deep gasps of air. Then she reached into her handbag to get her handkerchief. She saw the gun and said aloud, "Dan!"

She tried to start the car, but it groaned and jerked and then stopped. "Dear God! Please!" She tried again. This time it chugged and then roared from the pressure she was putting on the gas pedal. She threw it into reverse, backed off the sidewalk and headed toward the marina.

It wasn't far, and when she reached it, she turned off her car lights and slowly drove into the parking lot.

Cautiously she looked around, stopped the car, got out and quietly closed the door.

Seeing no one in sight, she quickly made her way to the entrance and scanned the boats and yachts bobbing slightly in the water. It was quiet and it was dark—almost pitch-black, except for the small yellow lights along the main dock. She heard nothing but the sound of the water slapping against the boats as she walked down the dock and glanced at the yachts, one after another.

Then she saw a light on in one of the boats. Her heart beat faster as she quietly moved toward it.

She was two boats away when a huge fish jumped up out of the water and back in again, hitting the surface with a splash. She crouched down against a piling and listened. It was quiet again. Slowly she eased herself up and moved toward the prow of the yacht with the light on inside. Again she crouched down, trying to ignore the fishy smell in the humid air. She listened. Two men's voices were distinguishable, but she couldn't make out what they were saying. Stealthily she inched her way along the side of the white yacht. The voices became clearer, and immediately she knew to whom one voice belonged: Mark. Then she heard a low moan.

"Get on your feet, Elliott," she heard somebody else order. "This was a pretty dumb trick, but when Jo-Jo brings the woman, you'll tell us what we want to know."

On the yacht, Mark walked behind Dan as he raised himself and rubbed the side of his head. He looked at the blood on his fingers and stood up, unsure of his footing. Then he said, "You're a brave man, Lasky. I bet you even pull hair when you fight."

Lasky was too annoyed to even answer him. He crumpled the newspaper and turned to toss it over the side. Mark had his back to Marcy. In a flash she boarded the yacht by way of the ramp.

"One move from either of you, and you'll each have a third eye in your forehead." She amazed herself. She was even sounding like Dan!

Lasky jerked around and looked at the gun she was holding. Mark froze. For a moment everyone stood still, each wondering what to do, especially Marcy. Mark still had his gun aimed at Dan.

Her brain worked furiously, trying to remember what Dan had done that first day when he'd taken the gun from her to show her how it was used. She took a deep breath and flicked the safety to off. With her other hand she pulled back the sleek black slide cover, making the same god-awful noise that had frightened her that day. She said, "I mean it, Mark. Drop it!"

At that, Mark's hand started trembling.

Dan looked him in the eyes. "Do like she says."

He dropped the gun and Dan picked it up. Then he felt the side of his head again and looked at Mark. "Oh, what the hell." His fist flew into the man's face. Mark fell to the floor. Then he turned to face the other man.

"Look, Elliott, I'm a wealthy man," Lasky pleaded as he edged along the railing. "I can make both of you rich."

Dan turned to Marcy and winked. Then he gave Lasky the evil eye. "Get down on your belly, snake, and put your hands behind your back."

Marcy saw Mark's eyes flutter. "What about him?"

"If he comes to, I'll punch him out again."

Mark's eyes closed again. Dan knelt down and interlocked the prone men's fingers behind their backs and snapped thumbcuffs on each of them.

Satisfied that they were well secured, he rose and took the gun from Marcy. Moving her toward the other side of the deck, out of earshot, he removed the clip from her gun, eyed the bullets and quietly asked, "By any chance, did you get a permit to carry a concealed weapon?"

"Do I need one?"

His eyes rolled upward. "Bejesus!" He slapped the clip back into the handle and fixed his hazel eyes on hers. "I told you that you were dangerous."

CHAPTER FIFTEEN

IT WAS AFTER DAWN when Dan drove Marcy home. Lasky and Godette, along with what was left of Jo-Jo, had been taken into custody by the FBI, and a search warrant had been issued for Oceanview Villas. The information stored in the computer and the phony bonds and stock certificates were going to take care of Lasky's operation, so Dan no longer had any concern for Marcy's safety.

At FBI headquarters, Dan was kept busy with a plethora of paperwork while Marcy's statement was taken. The federal agents, the charges, the routine—all of it caused a renewed turmoil to tear at Marcy as memories of the pretrial period she'd gone through two years ago resurfaced.

When she and Dan finally got back to the house, sne was more than ready to relax, but Dan packed and left hurriedly, telling her that now his work was really starting. He was like a man possessed, and his abrupt departure left Marcy with a feeling of emptiness.

For the next two weeks Dan was busy on temporary duty with the FBI, mopping up the mess from Victor Lasky's well-oiled fraud machine. Dan was in

Atlanta, Miami, New York and Washington—and in Marcy's thoughts constantly.

His first night away from "home," he did phone from Atlanta, leaving her with a promise to call the next evening. Marcy waited, but the call never came. The first few nights when she didn't hear from him were painful; the next few were horrible. By the second week she still hadn't heard from him, and a defensive resignation set in, a game of pretense in which she told herself that he didn't matter at all. What she and Dan had experienced together was nothing but the exchange of momentary desires. It had been folly on her part to believe there was anything more, and the private hell she was going through would soon pass. It had to—it just had to.

At times she wondered if Dan ever even thought of her. Then she would smile ironically and tell herself that if he did think of her, it was probably as the dangerous woman he'd told her she was.

In moments of weakness, she'd recall his alluding to having loved her, and hope would well up in her breast, but then reason would confront her with the torturing fact of his silence. Over cold black coffee, she'd remember how often he'd told her marriage was not in the cards for him again. So what future would there be for her even if he had loved her.

Sitting by the phone waiting, Marcy would think of the men who had been important in her life. The sad thing was that she had not been important to even one of them. She thought of her father, of Robert, of Ed

Moray—and of Daniel Elliott. She would ask herself what good it was to have so much love in her when no one really wanted it.

Recklessly, Marcy threw herself into her work. She even tried to write that firsthand story on the Oceanview Villas fraud, but each time she typed the name Daniel Elliott, or even the pronoun "he," she would cry. That project was quickly postponed temporarily.

Instead she tried to busy herself with a fiftieth anniversary campaign for a local department store. She also took on a promotional assignment for a nearby dinner theater and began to do her research for a trade magazine article on the virtues of prestressed concrete.

Her overzealous approach to work assured her of falling asleep when her head hit the pillow each night, but it was of no help in permitting her continued sleep during the long, dark hours. Often she would awaken, and in a state of exhaustion, her hand would stroke the empty pillow next to hers. Her fingertips would search in vain....

IT WAS SUNDAY, a little after eleven in the morning. Marcy was working at her desk, or trying to, when her eyes drifted to the empty chair Dan always sat in. She wondered why her life seemed to be a series of painful losses and slow recoveries, why it seemed to be her destiny to love and then to lose. She started to get up, but then she looked at the tape recorder Dan had connected to her phone. Again she was reminded of him.

Memories, she mused as she rose from the desk. They were the source of much joy and pain for her. Gazing around the living room, her eyes landed on the ashtray on the table between the two easy chairs. She went and picked it up and held it in the palm of her hand. The crystal was cold to the touch. She took it into the kitchen and returned it to its place in the cupboard.

Back in the living room, she peered through the sheer panels under the drapes, picturing him walking toward her door as he'd done that first day. She smiled as she recalled his gruff manner, but her smile waned as the sun's rays warmed her face and she thought she felt the soothing gentleness of his palm brush across her cheek.

Her desire turned to despair as she slowly went upstairs to his room and stood in the doorway. If only he'd forgotten something, something she could hold on to, something he'd touched. But the dresser was clear.

She'd often been alone in her life, but never had she been as lonely or depressed as she was at this moment. A single tear formed at her eyelid, and then it slid slowly down across her cheek. "Dan," she whispered aloud and hurried from the room.

At the bottom of the stairway, she heard the door buzzer. With the safety chain in place—a habit with her now, even during the day—she opened the door a crack. In front of her face was a badge and an ID card bordered with brown leather.

A familiar voice said, "Daniel Elliott, United States marshal. I need to talk to you." They were the exact words he had said that first day.

Love and hurt clashed fiercely in Marcy's heart. For seconds she was motionless, steeling herself with a grim determination. Then she slowly closed the door and with trembling fingers she undid the brass chain. With a source of strength she didn't realize she possessed, she smiled and opened the door.

Her first thought when she glanced at his face was that he looked tired. His suit coat was slung over his shoulder, his tie was loosened, and the cuffs of his white dress shirt were rolled up over his forearms. Red and weary eyes met hers.

"How's it going, Marcy?" His voice sounded tired, too.

"Fine, Dan . . . just fine. Come on in." She opened the door and watched him all but drag himself to his chair and plop down on it. Biting her lower lip, she stood there at war with her feelings. A part of her wanted to rush to him, to comfort him, to welcome him. But another part of her was angry at him—how could he expect a warm welcome after not having contacted her for two weeks? Yet another part of her called up words such as self-protection and emotional survival.

But she couldn't be mean to him.

She closed the door and walked over to him. "You look like you've been through the wringer. Big celebration after netting the Victor Lasky gang? It's been all over the news."

He looked up at her with unsmiling eyes. "No, I haven't had time for that yet. I've been too busy driving."

"From where?"

"Atlanta... straight through."

She nervously clutched her hands behind her back. "You must have been driving half the night. Would you like some coffee?"

With an effort, he smiled. "That'd be nice."

Marcy went into the kitchen, wondering what to say to him, wondering what to think, how to feel. She had just come to grips with the fact that life without him was inevitable, and here he was again on her doorstep, flashing his badge at her, just as he'd done that first day. No, she told herself, she wouldn't retreat from the decision she'd made to forget him, to obliterate the desire for happiness with him that had become like an opiate, increasing her craving more and more.

Here he was again, wanting to pick up where they had left off. But she wasn't going to do that. Yes, she had told him that she would try to settle for the loving, but she knew now that that was impossible for her to do. Besides, he was probably here just to do his job, just to clean up unfinished business regarding James Moray or Victor Lasky.

"Instant is fine!"

His voice echoed into the kitchen and wrapped her in an unwanted warmth. She ignored the feeling and prepared the coffee.

After handing him his cup, she smiled and said, "If I had known you were coming, I'd have gotten some tacos for you."

He followed her movements as she sat down across from him, not liking thc lilting jocularity in her voice at all, the breezy way she was acting. He'd had a hard two weeks, and he had expected a warm welcome—not this casual aloofness. Suddenly she stood up again. She went to her desk, switched off her electric typewriter and yanked a piece of paper out of it.

He asked, "Working on Sunday?"

"I have a lot of catching up to do," she told him as she sat down again and sipped her coffee.

Sullenly he said, "You do."

Her smile was becoming more forced by the minute. "Really, Dan, you're not the only one who's been busy."

She saw him raise his hand to his head and plow his fingers through his dark hair. "It's been sweat city for the last two weeks, Marcy. I've been going on three or four hours' sleep a night, and most of that's been on planes. I didn't have time to call you."

If that was an apology, Marcy wondered why it hurt so much. "I understand perfectly," she said. "I even remember your saying once that you needed time, and now we both know just how much you need it." She looked down at her cup.

Trying to figure out what was going on, he said, "You've been through a lot lately. You must be pretty tired, too."

"*We've* been through a lot," she corrected, "and you're right, I am tired." To change the subject, she asked, "What will they do to James Moray?"

"He'll probably get probation. No priors. I'm sure he's learned his lesson." He wondered why she wouldn't look at him. "It was Mark who planted the bug. Lasky told him to find out just how much you knew, and when he heard us mention the FBI, he reported it to Lasky, who assumed we were after him. He got the muscle to plant the bomb and to shoot at us on the pier. They were after both of us. Seems that one without the other was no good."

"'One without the other,'" Marcy repeated without looking at him.

Dan had yet to touch his coffee; he was too preoccupied with trying to assess her strange mood. "You like to repeat things, don't you?"

"It's a flaw in my character."

"Don't kid a kidder," he said, still scrutinizing her nervous features. "Your only flaw is that you're perfect."

There was silence from Marcy.

He said, "I missed you."

Again she didn't respond, and then he thundered at her, "Talk to me, Marcy! I'm getting tired of doing a monologue, and don't sulk. It makes me crazy. I don't know how to handle sulking from a woman."

She jumped up, each and every nerve end sensitized. "What is it, Dan? Do I have a sign on my back that says 'Kick me'? I don't see or hear from you for two weeks, and then you walk in here and expect me to welcome you, to fall into your arms. Forget it!"

Watching her frenetic pacing, he said coolly, "Let's not blow it, Marcy. We get along, you and I."

She sent him a wistful glance. "Getting along is not enough for me, Dan, not any more."

"So I didn't phone you like I said I would. Listen, with some people, life is lived with little thought of the future."

Calmly she told him, "You aren't really like that. You've been made to think that's how you should be."

He slapped the arm of his chair and exclaimed, "Damn it, Marcy, I love you!"

She felt as though she were going down for the third time and someone had just thrown her a life preserver—but too late. She had to think clearly and quickly. She crossed her arms and dug her fingers into her flesh. She glanced at the man who was sitting in the chair and waiting for her to say something in response. Her glance darted to the front window and then back to him. "I don't know, Dan. I don't know if loving is enough to see us through. I think there's a demon pulling at you. I'm not sure you know what you want."

In a more rational tone, he said, "Marcy, I could get another job. Maybe it's time I got out...got something more normal."

"And do what? Sell insurance? Besides, it's not the danger in your work that really bothers me, although it doesn't thrill me, either. It's just that... I believe you're still afraid of commitment. I mean total commitment. And will you ever feel comfortable about this money business? Will it ever stop bugging you? And I'm not sure I could cope with your cynicism."

"I have to be cynical," he told her. "I have to have doubts, question things, people."

She asked, "Even me?"

"It's a habit."

"A nasty one."

He got up from the chair, took a few steps away from her, and then he shoved his hands into his pockets as he turned toward her. "We can get it back on course, Marcy. Once you said you loved me. Don't you love me anymore... even a little?"

Marcy wiped her eyes before she turned to face him. "I could never love you just a little, Dan, but I'm afraid we're both staring down a dead-end street." She went to her desk drawer where she picked up a little white box and she handed it to him. "You refused this once, but I really want you to have it... as a remembrance."

"Remembrance?"

She looked toward the front window. "Yes, I've decided to return to Europe... for a while, anyway."

Dan felt as if he'd just been kicked in the teeth. He stared down at the white box in his hands, and then he opened it and took out the gold chain he'd given back to her on the ship. His voice was hollow when he said, "Put it on for me."

Marcy opened the clasp, and then, standing in front of him, she reached around his neck to snap it shut. As she did, she touched his neck, and her fingers fumbled with the clasp. She brought it within view again to adjust it, and then she placed the chain around his neck properly. "There," she said in a whisper and watched him tuck it under his shirt.

"Twice received," he said quietly, "twice blessed."

Running her fingers through her hair, she said, "You must be starving—" she moved away "—or did you stop for breakfast?"

Feeling the little anchor through his shirt, he told her, "Haven't eaten since yesterday."

"Let's get out of here," she told him, afraid to be alone with him for another minute, knowing her dwindling resolve would collapse if he touched her. "It's my treat."

Taco Bell wasn't as crowded as it had been the last time they'd been there. Again they sat outside on the patio under an umbrella. Marcy looked over at Dan's tray, which held one taco and a cold drink. Then she glanced down at her own, loaded with a taco, a burrito, a tostada and a salad. Dan had gone before her in the line inside, and seeing that his appetite was under par, she'd hoped to lure him with her own selections, but he didn't seem at all interested in eating.

"Well," he said, "I guess this is the end of the line for us."

Now her appetite was gone, also. She cleared her throat. "Know who you'll be guarding next?"

He picked up his taco, looked at it and put it back down. Then he just shook his head.

Marcy picked up a small piece of shredded lettuce and began chewing it. Then, rather quietly, she told him, "If you get a Christmas card with a strange name on it, it'll probably be from me."

His glance darted up to meet hers. "You planning on changing it in Europe?"

"Just joking, Elliott...trying to make conversation."

"That wasn't funny." He lit a cigarette, took a few puffs, and then he said, "It really wasn't fair, you know."

"What wasn't?"

"I got all the credit for your bravery. Until you showed up on the yacht, I was a dead man."

"I was concerned about you."

Toying with the straw in his drink, he said, "Your motive is locked in my heart forever."

She said, "You're being cute again."

"I don't feel so goddamn cute right now." His voice was bitter, devoid of its usual sprightliness.

"Don't blaspheme," she warned him. "There's an afterlife, you know."

"Only if the U.S. Marshal Service says so."

Marcy pushed her salad around slowly with her plastic fork, realizing that their attempts at light banter were failing. She decided that lunch had not been one of her better ideas, but then, this was the last time she'd ever see Daniel Elliott. Soon—too soon—he'd drop her off at her house, and then he'd drive off...for good. The cola she sipped was cold, and it felt good going down her throat. She watched as he lethargically lit another cigarette. "You're good at your job, Dan. I gave you a hard time."

He took a long drag and blew a straight stream of smoke off to the side. "It wasn't all that bad. You've given me only good things to remember."

"You're a liar."

"I know."

Her fingers were almost crushing the moist plastic container holding her cold drink. She shook her head. "You're not really cut out to be a watchdog, though. You need more freedom. It's like the day on Esteban Island when we were parasailing. I looked over and saw you flying your heart out." She attempted a smile, but inside her heart was breaking. "I could have done without that experience, but I knew you needed whatever it was you were feeling as you soared like a bird under the clouds."

Dan's eyes brightened a little at the memory. He leaned his elbows on the table and said, "I knew you were close by, enjoying it with me." With renewed energy, he crushed his cigarette in the tin ashtray; his voice became more animated. "Marcy, we can't just go on pretending that—"

"Don't, Dan," she said quickly. "It just wouldn't work out between us." She wasn't so sure she believed that so strongly now.

"Marcy, you're the one who told me that my problem was that I was a family man without a family."

"I said a lot of things," she admitted.

Leaning back in his chair, he sensed a certain confusion going on in her mind. Watching her closely, he said, "I guess you're right. It probably wouldn't work out. I'd be away a lot, and a woman without her husband can get lonesome, and lonesome can lead to temptation…not to mention a lot of stress and strain, even anger. I know. I went through that with Hope."

Twirling her straw in her drink, she added, "And you'd always think of me as a dangerous woman in a mink coat." Suddenly she looked directly at him. "Dan, when you're away, just what is it you do for relaxation? Needlepoint?"

For the first time that day, she saw a sincere smile on his face. "I think about you, about how anxious I am to get back home to you. You know, Marcy Keaton, you're special. I sure could use your sense of balance in my life. I work with the worst of humankind, and you're everything that's good. You'd give me an equilibrium that would keep me sane."

She twirled her straw more and asked, "What would you give me in return? Ulcers?"

His smile waned as he shook his head slowly. "I'd try not to." He clasped his hands and then looked over at her. "I'd give you myself. My love. I don't have a lot more, Marcy."

She scratched at the cold plastic container with her thumbnail as she tried not to be influenced by Dan's words. She'd decided it was over, hadn't she?

Dan thought he saw something different in her expression as she sat there quietly—a kind of softness that settled on her features. Was it a weakening of her defences? He hoped it was. His head tilted slightly. Then, playing the devil's advocate, he said, "But I guess you're right. It wouldn't work. I'm a bad boy. I've got an untamed mouth. I yell a lot."

"You do," she agreed.

"You're gentle, rational."

"Usually."

"I'm tacos. You're caviar."

Her eyes narrowed. "You're strange."

"I'm suspicious. You're trusting."

"You're right."

Dan's eyes began to shine. He leaned forward, rested his forearms on the edge of the table, and entwined his fingers. "I suffer from deep-rooted hostility."

She said, "My problem is an identity crisis."

"I'm rigid. You're flexible."

"Sometimes."

"I'm selfish. I get too wrapped up in my job."

Defending him, her voice rose a little. "You're dedicated!"

His eyes were brilliant now, and he looked directly into hers. "I've got a short fuse, can get upset if someone even breathes too heavily on my badge. You're even-tempered."

Marcy wondered why she was whipping her cola so frantically with her straw. And why was her heartbeat starting to pick up speed? No matter. She had made her decision regarding Dan Elliott, and she silently affirmed that she would be adamant, as immovable as the Rock of Gibraltar!

Dan continued his observations. "I tend to be cynical and judgmental."

Avoiding the glow in his eyes, she looked aside and said, "With good reason," but his eyes were like a powerful magnet. They pulled hers toward them and succeeded in making contact. Looking into Dan's eyes, Marcy heard her own little sigh—or was it the sound of little chips of rock falling away? Softly she told him, "You can also be tender and loving."

His unruly dark eyebrows rose slightly as he asked, "I can be?"

Now Marcy leaned forward. In a weak voice, she said, "Trust me on that."

"No." He shook his head slowly. "You're the loving one, Marcy."

Her face was so close to his that she could smell the musky maleness of him, that wonderful natural scent that was made even more attractive by that lime lotion he used. The sounds of his words were still echoing in her ears. Quickly, as if just regaining consciousness, she pulled her face back from his and tried to get a hold of herself. With feigned nonchalance she told him, "Now you can go to Tahiti whenever you want." She felt him take her hand between his, but she refused to look down at it.

His low, musical voice said, "You're beautiful."

With a heartbeat that was jogging now, she tried desperately to maintain her air of insouciance. "I understand the beaches in Tahiti are very white and—"

"You're warm, caring and good-natured."

The fingers of her free hand moved nervously at the side of her neck as the stroking of his warm hands on hers sent erotic ripples charging up her arm. "And they say it's very peaceful there... very quiet. They may even have... parasailing. You'd be—"

"I love you, Marcy Keaton. Marry me, and we'll go to Tahiti together on our honeymoon."

A glorious burst of fireworks went off inside her. She wanted to cry, and at the same time she wanted to laugh, but most of all she wanted to scream "Yes! Yes!" but she couldn't say a word. Her entire body was tingling, and her throat seemed paralyzed. Then she felt herself being pulled up from the curved stone bench she'd been sitting on. Dan's hands were holding her arms, and his eyes were sparkling.

"Marcy," he told her quickly, "we've got something so special, we've just got to take care of it. Together we can work anything out. Say you'll give it a try!"

Marcy still couldn't speak; she could only gaze into his eyes. She was so filled with love and joy she could hardly think straight. And only a few moments ago she had thought life dark and dismal! Right now she saw only golden days ahead, and saw the reflection of her love for Dan in his eyes as he stood there holding her.

"Say yes, Marcy," he pleaded. "Say you'll marry me. If you don't I'll...I'll arrest you here and now...for something! You could be locked up for...for—" a sigh accompanied his glowing smile "—breaking my heart."

Oblivious to the people staring at them, Marcy felt her eyelids moisten. Her struggling voice repeated, "Locked up?"

Her tearful smile told Dan what he needed to know. He wrapped her in his arms, leaned down and kissed her passionately.

Neither of them heard the applause from the other customers. Dan's excitement was too intense. And Marcy heard only the echoes of Dan's words. As she returned his kiss with equal fervor, she knew she would never be alone again. She knew that she had found the right man to give her love to, and she knew that he returned her love totally.

She heard Dan's whisper in her ear. "Yes, Marcy, love...locked up. You'll be locked in my arms forever...."